Fairy Bear

by

H. M. E. Chambers

ISBN   148180667X
EAN   978-1481806671

All rights reserved. No part of this book may be reproduced or transmitted in any form or by any means, electronic or mechanical, including photocopying, recording, or by any information storage and retrieval system, without permission in writing from the copyright owner.

'Fairy Bear' is published by Taylor Street Publishing LLC, who can be contacted at:

http://www.taylorstreetbooks.com
http://ninwriters.ning.com

'Fairy Bear' is the copyright of the author, H.M.E. Chambers, 2012. All rights are reserved.

The cover is designed by Gina Dudjan, based on a photograph by Rob Lewis. All rights are reserved.

All characters are fictional, and any resemblance to anyone living or dead is accidental.

To David,
Love Hannah
((Chambers))

To Ross and Becka Jarvis, With Love.

And to Bob White of Missouri, who owes me five Euros, because Michael Crichton *did* write *Sphere*.

My life reads like a bad novel. I know because I have written bad novels about it. I don't like people to think my work is autobiographical. I like them to think I have a vivid imagination.

Take right now, for example. Right now I am lying on my back in a hospital bed. I'm lying on my back because it's the part of me that hurts least when lain upon. The reason I'm lying in hospital, you don't want to know. It has to do with Chinese guys and Taekwondo. A little too much of both.

These things are not my problem. My problem is the man who just left, and the armed guard who remains.

I have a suspicion that this is going to turn into a two act tale of woe, so I'll get on and recount the first part of it while my body is gluing itself back together ready for the second.

Chapter 1

I have what Science Fiction authors term a 'wild talent'. This means some sort of inexplicable ability to do something usually impossible. There are people who don't like their heroes and heroines to be imbued with attributes of this nature. Believe me, there are some heroes and heroines who don't like these talents either. Most of them are more trouble than they're worth. Take mine for example.

I was walking down a certain street in the sprawling stink they call the City of Angels, a street somewhere between the studio we were working in and my apartment. A load of industrial cardboard boxes, folded flat and tied together with string like a parcel, swung over one shoulder and my rucksack hung from the other. I was walking home after staying only one hour later to finish the set up for tomorrow, thinking about what I was going to have for dinner and what I was actually going to do with the cardboard, generally minding my own business, when I sensed something. I stopped in the middle of the pavement and poked my nose up, but it wasn't anything I could smell, not consciously. I've often wondered if I learned this talent of mine by osmosis from my dogs, but I don't think so. They had known what they were looking for, and they had known when they found it.

The dark alleyway gaped obviously to my right hand. I looked around, hoping for something else, but there were no other pedestrians to notice my odd behaviour or confirm my dark suspicions. Everyone else was driving home, jostling each other from the safety of their private metal boxes. Perhaps my wild talent was only the obstreperousness to insist on being the only habitual pedestrian in a city of drivers.

The alleyway at first glance seemed to be nothing but an oblong rubbish receptacle. I propped my cardboard load against the nearest genuine Dumpster wheelie-bin, and proceeded slowly between the ripped bin bags and spilled foodstuffs that advertised the restaurant beside me more clearly than its front signage. A pile of squashed cardboard boxes distracted my attention for a second, and in that second as I paused and the sound of my trainers on the tarmac faltered, I heard a wet, bubbling sound, like detergent going down a blocked drain.

Skirting the boxes, I spotted a slip-on dress shoe, slightly scuffed, and a bare white ankle protruding from it. The smartly creased chinos had been tweaked up slightly by an awkward movement, and above the shiny brown belt was a gooey crimson crater with white splinters protruding from it like the roots of a tree torn up by a gale. The bubbling sound was visibly emanating from the crater as well as the drooping mouth that hung to one side like a door off its hinge.

Dumping my rucksack on the ground well clear of the spot, I hurried to crouch over him, my fingers sliding through the slime on his neck for a pulse. I had to hold my breath to feel it, weak, irregular and fading. I dropped one knee into the mess at his side to extract my mobile phone as I leaned over and emptied my lungful of air into his mouth.

It almost wasn't worth asking for an ambulance as well as the police car, but I knew they would need one to cart the body away. Once they knew where to find me, I slipped the phone safely back into my trouser pocket, and pumped another breath into the top end of his pulmonary system. As it bubbled irrevocably out of the bottom end, I peeled his jacket out of the blood and felt for his wallet. He was still alive, he was somebody, and it might be useful to know who.

There was a business card in the front of his wallet. I slipped it out and read with interest:

Watts and Delphiki
Private Investigations
Spike Delphiki

A private detective found dying in an alleyway definitely made an interesting plot. I committed the telephone number to memory and shoved the card back into the wallet. His driving licence, however, told a different story. I gave him another mouthful of air, resisted again the reflex towards chest compressions - his chest had been thoroughly compressed already - and identified him as Wilson Peters. The face in the photograph was straight and naturally coloured, but definitely the man breathing his last beside me.

Bending again to deliver another lungful of air, I saw the ineffable change that signalled its irrelevance. Wilson Peters' last had now been breathed. I put his wallet back into his pocket and stood as the first blue lights strobed across the wall of the alleyway.

A young officer bounded eagerly out of the near side door as his partner brought the car to a halt. "Ms Gambetta? You called in a -"

"Yes. He's down here. He's dead."

The young officer paused for his partner to join us before he followed me into the alley. Standing over Peters' body, he glared hard at it before swinging away and leaning weakly on the nearest wheelie bin. The other policeman stooped to confirm what I had told them. The man was dead, and it was now his job to find out why.

So he began by asking me how I had come to find him. Which was inexplicable. Both of us were relieved when the second set of flashing lights alerted us to the arrival of the ambulance. We just had time to inform them that they were too late, we were all too late for Wilson Peters, and then the detective drew up in another police car.

It has been my experience that police force personnel go one of two ways. Either they are super-fit or too many stakeout-takeouts and too much drowning of sorrows take their respective tolls. Normally it's the detectives who feel the wear and tear most keenly and show it in their bodies, whereas the uniformed officers, who spend their days out on the streets, take more care of themselves. Detective Stocker, LAPD, was the opposite. He was not tall but looked like he spent every free minute in the gym. His hair was floppy and untidy, the last thing on his mind. He took one look at me and I felt as though my fate was already sealed in his eyes.

"You found the body?" Glancing around at the other cops, he picked off one of them with his eyes and the man started to lead him down the alley.

"No, sir. He was alive when I got here."

"And you are?" His sentences were crisp and direct.

"Hex Gambetta."

"Gambetta? Any relation of John Paul?"

"He's my brother."

Stocker glared at the unfortunate corpse as though my family were his fault. "Do we have an ID?" he demanded of the cop, who shook his head.

"His name was Wilson Peters," I offered. Both of them glared at me now. "As I said, he was alive when I got here, so I checked in his wallet."

The detective sighed heavily enough to fill Peters' lungs again. He drew latex gloves out of his pocket, and extracted the wallet himself. "Not a mugging, then," he mused. He turned so that I couldn't see what he was doing, but I saw the white of the business card, and when he pulled out his phone, I could guess what number he was dialling.

"Delphiki," he walked up the alley, back towards the car, taking his conversation out of ear shot, "I've got something I think you want to know about."

He returned a moment later. "The CSIs are here. Let's get you back to the station for a full statement and your finger prints."

Picking up my three foot square of flattened cardboard, I walked out to the car he had arrived in. As I approached, a uniformed officer hopped out of the driver's seat. "Hex! Not another one." It was Officer Pike, one of the cops who had come to the scene the first time I had found a corpse and the man saddled with arresting me for it. I opened the rear door of his car and he encouraged me gently. "Don't worry, Stocker's tough but fair. He won't lock you up for this one. Not unless you did it, of course."

"The forensics aren't going to help me this time. I touched him. He died under my hands."

Pike wriggled round in the seat to look at me as I dragged my cardboard into the back with me. He frowned but had more sense than to ask what it was for. "You tried to help him, right? He died but you didn't kill him. You don't need to worry. We only need your statement and your fingerprints so we can rule you out of the investigation. Then you're free to go. Now the CSIs are taking over the scene, Stocker will soon be back at the station, so it won't take all night. I'll get you a coffee while you wait."

"Yuck. My cardboard and I will just come quietly. We don't need any ditchwater, thank you."

Stocker's desk stood out perpendicular to the wall. In front of it, squeezed between the edge of the desk and a filing cabinet that was threatening to explode, was a single chair. I sat down and stretched my legs out into the room. My wide packet of cardboard was now propped against the filing cabinet, reminding me gently of its limitless potential. The clutter and bustle of the detectives' room is strangely reassuring. Most of the time everyone is far too busy with their own work to be concerned with what their colleagues have collected at their desks. This evening however, one of the frenetic figures paused at my feet.

Standing before me was a woman with tight, dark ringlets cascading to her shoulders. She had the pinched look of dieting and the wrong sort of exercise. Under her short tailored jacket she would be bony, with muscles like knots of string. Her eyes were as hard as her body and I looked up to meet her familiar glare.

"Hex Gambetta. Who haven't you killed this time?" She knew that I wasn't going to say anything; I hadn't said much when she had had me arrested. She rattled on. "No one believes for a moment that you're squeaky clean. Trouble doesn't waste its time on people who don't want it. Not like cops. And trouble does seem to follow you around, doesn't it? How many bodies have you found since you've been in town? You just walk down the street and people drop dead in your path. You even had the bomb squad down at the studios where you were working couple of months back. Some special effects guy blew himself up with an incendiary."

"That was my husband," I informed her.

"Oh my God." She deflated at once. "I'm so sorry. This attitude comes with the territory."

"Yeah, yeah," I cut her off before she could come out in an all over sympathy rash. "I know. I used to be a cop, remember."

She nodded, glad that I wasn't going shove her foot right down her throat. "Oh, yes, the British Bobby." Awkward now, she turned and strode purposefully towards the door, but paused at the coffee machine. Soon she returned. "Here, have a cup of coffee while you wait."

Curses! I couldn't really turn down a peace offering, so she left me sipping at the watery acid and bustled off, relieved.

The detective finally arrived with another man in tow. This man was tall, a little over six feet as far as I could estimate while sitting, and lean. His brown hair was cropped short in a military style cut. He was wearing a blue sport coat over a faded red t-shirt and jeans, and there were trainers on his feet. Focusing concentration on them, I picked up the conversation as they wended their way between the desks.

"That's the woman who found him," Stocker nodded at me. "She's a Gambetta, John Paul's sister. She's known as 'the world's only human cadaver dog' in the department. She's found four bodies now."

The other man made no reply.

"Ms Gambetta," said Stocker. I rose. "This is Spike Delphiki."

We shook hands. His knuckles were wide, his fingers long, but although his handshake was firm, he didn't feel it necessary to demonstrate physical superiority.

"Delphiki is a private detective. Peters was carrying his card when he died." Which I already knew this, but wasn't going to say so.

"It was a divorce case," Delphiki said in a quiet voice. "Peters thought his wife was cheating on him. He wanted me to follow her and find out. I don't take divorce cases."

"So why was he carrying your card?" Stocker asked.

Delphiki didn't answer straight away. He was looking at me and I wondered what he saw. I was wearing black, I always do, but he didn't know that. My sleeveless top revealed arms that were properly muscled. I was a stunt double but he didn't know that. My top also revealed tattoos on my deltoid muscles. I had a few others but he didn't know that either. I wondered what he was making of what he saw.

After a deliberate pause, he said, "Peters seemed threatened by something. He didn't mention it, only his wife, so when I turned down the job, I made sure he had my card so he could call me if anything else came up."

"Threatened by something?" Stocker turned that over in his mind. "How threatened? Did he mention the wife's lover, perhaps?"

Again, Delphiki didn't leap to answer. This time he was carefully recalling. "He was fidgeting, changing positions in his chair and checking his watch. He was very brief in his explanation of the job, and as soon as I told him I didn't take that kind of thing, he was hopping up to leave without protest. I had to stop him to give him the card, but he seemed pleased to take it, especially when I told him he could reach me twenty four seven." He paused again. "He didn't mention the wife's lover. He said, 'I think my wife's doing the dirty on me'. He asked me to tail her. He didn't actually mention an affair or use words like 'cheating' or 'lover', but when I did, he didn't pull me up."

Detective Stocker seemed more anxious to interview private detective Delphiki than the woman who had watched Peters die, but as Officer Pike had promised, he didn't keep either of us very long. "We'll know more once we get the forensics back," he said, shooing us out of his way. I picked up my cardboard with inky fingers, shouldered my rucksack, and planned my new walk home.

Then Delphiki offered me a lift.

It was getting late. Even brief police proceedings take hours and I decided that I needed sleep more than exercise. Dumping my belongings on his back seat, I climbed in beside him.

"How are you doing?" he asked, slipping the car into gear and extricating himself neatly from the parking space.

"Okay," I said, uncertain what he was getting at.

"It's a hard thing, finding someone dead."

"He was alive when I found him."

"That's worse."

I shrugged, wondering if he was speaking from experience.

"Is there anyone at home?"

"No." Why did he want to know? Getting into a car with a man I didn't really know was often more trouble for the man than it was for me, but I guessed that a private detective wearing a jacket was probably wearing a gun underneath. Still, that didn't bother me. I like guns."

"Is there someone you can call? A friend? Your brother?"

Understanding dawned. I'd watched a man die. I was supposed to be upset. "No. I'm good."

He turned from the road to look at me and I wondered again what he was seeing in this different light.

"What are the cartons for?" he asked, turning his attention back to the traffic.

"I don't know yet. I'd had an idea but then Peters put it out of my mind."

He smiled. "You really are a cool customer."

There were a thousand things I could say to that, so I said nothing, and the journey proceeded in silence. I managed to direct him successfully to my apartment, despite the fact that I rarely approached it from the road myself. My brother had lent me one of his fleet of vehicles often enough for me to avoid the usual directional errors of the non-driver, such as, 'Oh, you should have turned there'. As I thanked him and climbed from the car, he produced a now familiar piece of white card.

"If you're worried, or you think of anything you forgot to tell the police, or you just want to talk to someone, call me. This number will reach me anytime." He frowned when I didn't reach for the card, then smiled. "It's not the black spot. You won't be found dead in an alley with this in your pocket."

I recited his anytime number. "I found the card in Peters' wallet before Stocker did."

He was visibly impressed but only said, "Well, it'll still reach me. Seriously, if you need someone to talk to ... day or night."

"I get the gist. Thanks, Delphiki." I dragged my cardboard upstairs.

Chapter 2

"You're really happy to let Roly run you into a concrete wall without a helmet?" Tom 'Crash' Oliver enquired with great concern.

"Yes."

Two days had passed since I had found Wilson Peters expiring in an alley, and I had walked home twice that way without trouble. Of course, Tom didn't know about it. The whole incident had not infringed on work time, so I had felt no need to enlighten him.

Crash wasn't happy. "We could cut the shot so you could put a helmet on or change the camera angle, I guess. I'll talk to the director."

"It's fine."

He rubbed his spiky hair heavily, then wiped the gel off on his jeans. "How scared are you, on a scale of one to pants-wettingly terrified?"

"I don't feel fear."

He rubbed his hair again and repeated the whole manoeuvre by wiping his hands on his jeans.

"You should get some better gel."

He glanced at me. "Huh? Oh, Dezzie got me some styling wax, but I'm finishing up the old stuff. Seriously, Bobby, this thing is real. I mean, if it bombs, you guys could really get real hurt."

"Dude, if driving home bombs you could really get real hurt. Life's dangerous but you can only die once, right?"

"Unless you're a Buddhist." He grinned. "Okay. You know it's a damn sight cheaper to shoot it this way."

I nodded. The budget of Dangerous Visions, Stunt and Special Effects Outfit had been one of my primary concerns since the day Burns had told me how he had come to lose half his face. It was also one of Crash's, but the health of his people rated higher.

He keyed his radio. "Roly, I can't talk her out of it, so we're good to go."

As the radio crackled back, "Fuckin' A," Crash took the opportunity to hug me tight, as he had found an excuse to do every day since Burns ultimately blew himself up. "Let's be careful out there."

Laughing, I headed towards Roly and the pre-crumpled black and white car as people scurried back and forth with hands full of coffee and necks draped with wires. Shouts, orders, swear words, painted the air, and I walked through it all like a frozen installation. Wilson Peters stuck in my mind like a burr. He was just a cadaver, and let's face it, there are plenty of those. If you lift the roof off the doll's house that is this city, you'll find one corpse for every third fight, every other mugging, every couple of domestic beatings, every single contract hit. And there's a hell of a lot of all of those, just ask the medical examiners. If you ask me, however, I've found precious few, considering, but still, Peters stuck in my mind. The hole in his chest had been real brutal.

With the scene in the can, Roly offered me a couple of Tylenol to stave off the incipient headache that driving into a concrete wall engendered, but I refused, and strolling off, pulled out my mobile phone. The spotty teenager who had sold it to me assured me that it was the toughest cell on the market, and so far his words were proving true. The concrete wall had affected it less than me. If Peters had one of these in his breast pocket, his chest might not have resembled the police car Roly had just totalled.

I dialled Delphiki's number.

He picked up almost at once. "Delphiki."

"Hex Gambetta."

"Oh, hi. How are you doing?"

"Fine. Yourself?"

"Oh, I'm doing just fine." The banalities seemed to amuse him.

"You got anything on Peters?"

"It's not my case, Ms Gambetta."

There were no audible sounds in the background, and the number was not one for a mobile phone, so he must spend his time behind a desk. My mind's eye conjured up images of the flatfoot's office of the forties, or more accurately, of Roger Rabbit. I shoved the bar on the fire doors and wandered outside into the sunshine.

"Come on, don't tell me, a guy shows up dead because you didn't take his case, and you're not interested."

"Did he die because I didn't take his case? The job he presented me with had nothing to do with people trying to kill him. It may have been entirely unrelated." He had described me as cool, but he was talking as though he had a whole tray of ice cubes down his pants.

"You said he acted frightened .... as though someone was after him?"

"I also said that he didn't mention it to me. It wasn't part of the job I turned down."

Ignoring that, I went on, "And he wanted you to trail his wife because he thought she was up to something. He sounds paranoid to me."

"Just because he's paranoid, doesn't mean they're not out to get him." There was the hint of a smile in his voice.

"Well, quite. You're a detective, you pick up on this. And you don't drop it. Not when he winds up dead. Delphiki, I doubt you're a detective that a copper knows because you're no bloody good. Anyhow, you asked me to call if I thought of anything, so at the time you meant to stick with the case."

He chuckled. "Okay, you got me. What's your excuse? Have you remembered anything?" Cagey sod.

"No. I just wondered how you were getting on."

"Stocker told me you were a cop in England. I guess you don't drop things either. You want to discuss this in person?"

We arranged to meet for lunch and I headed back inside to shift cases of gear until hunger got the better of me.

The diner must have been a reject from the set of a high school movie. Delphiki was seated in one of the booths at the back, wearing what appeared at first glance to be exactly the same clothes he had come to the police station in three days ago. As I slipped on to the bench opposite, forced to sit with my back to the door, I realised that he had in fact changed his t-shirt. Today's was blue striped with narrow white bands. I, on the other hand, was wearing exactly what I had been three days ago, although I had been wearing different shades of black in between. We nodded at each other and ordered without exchanging a word.

Waiting for the food to arrive, he said, "Well, I've not got much on Peters."

My first thought was, 'Hello, a man who doesn't say things not worth saying'. My second was, 'Does this mean I'm paying for lunch?'. So I said, "What have you got?"

"His wife is an ER doctor who works long hours – shifts, of course. She said she'd have liked the time and energy to have an affair. The last time she had had time off was when she had their daughter. Then she took a career break until the kid started school. Doctoring is her life, she said, and despite grumbling, she loves it."

"She said that?"

He nodded. "I went to see them. The police had been there first, but when I explained who I was, she was happy to talk. She said her husband had seemed unhappy recently. Just a depression that had been building for a while. She hadn't even noticed until he got shifty, then in hindsight saw it coming."

"Saw what?"

Delphiki shrugged. "Some disaster ... but more likely the domestic variety. She wasn't entirely surprised that he suspected her of an affair, apart from the total illogic of it. She didn't expect him to die behind the trash cans, however."

"So what about Peters himself? What was his job?"

"Insurance. It was one of these jobs guys get when they find themselves suddenly needing to support a family. Dr Peters didn't know the ins and outs of it, but he had been steadily working his way up in the company, taking on more responsibility as Daisy grew up and didn't need so much of his time. He had been happy with his job, wasn't particularly ambitious. Didn't seem to have developed any of the neuroses men sometimes get when their wife has the more important job."

"So why the depression?"

He shrugged again. "Not enough sleep, not enough exercise, deadlines at work. Domestic, unremarkable. Nothing meriting a huge hole in the chest."

"You've seen it?"

"Detective Stocker showed me photographs." His voice betrayed no particular horror. He was giving the impression that all this was routine for him. But then, so was I.

"And the daughter? Daisy?"

"I didn't meet her. She was in her room working on an assignment, using school work to keep her mind off things. She's in high school. Seems to be doing well, but unremarkable."

"Nobody was up to anything shady?"

"Shady?" He smiled. "Not that they told me."

The food arrived and silence settled once more. I like to eat when I'm eating, and Delphiki was in no hurry to share the rest of his intelligence. I felt there must be more. He had admitted to speaking with Detective Stocker who must have said something when he showed Delphiki the crime scene photographs. I pushed my cleared plate away from me and settled back, stretching my legs. My work boot caught Delphiki on the shin. He raised an eyebrow and moved his own legs.

"What did Stocker tell you? Have they got the forensics back?"

He pushed his plate to the side and leaned forward so that he could tuck his battered shin safely under the bench. "They came back this morning. All the blood was Peters', but the way it splattered around him was strange."

"Strange how?"

"Well, there wasn't enough of it."

"There was plenty of it," I remembered, glad that black trousers didn't show blood stains like other colours.

"Not enough. He looked like he'd been hit with a wrecking ball. Picture that. Can you see the blood squirting in all directions like a kid chucking red paint?"

He was right. There had been nowhere near enough blood splattered across the alley. It had just pooled around the body. "That means he was done to death elsewhere and dumped to expire."

"Right."

I shook my head. "That man was a mess. He couldn't live more than a couple of minutes with wounds like that, and he must have stayed alive for at least thirty seconds while I found him. They'd have had to kill him incredibly close, even with a car to transport the body. My boss has a theory that it takes an hour to get anywhere in this city, even round the block sometimes. So he must have been attacked on the same block, I'd guess."

"Right," he said again. "Stocker and his people have had the block taped off, searching every inch. There'd be blood left somewhere, no matter how well they cleared up."

"But they didn't find it?"

"Nope."

"Did they find anything?"

He shook his head. "The only other thing forensics came up with was weirder. There were some white hairs on Peters' pants. Animal hairs. The lab guys managed to match them on the computer, which isn't as easy as they make it look on the TV shows."

"I know."

"Well, guess what? They were polar bear fur."

There goes the day, I thought. "Hmmm," was all I said.

"You're not surprised?" He leant further towards me, studying my face as he must have studied Dr Peters.

"Oh, I am, believe me." I was, really. I hadn't been expecting it to turn up like that.

"What do you know?" he growled suspiciously.

I took a deep breath. He wasn't a policeman. Maybe he could help me.

"The bearskin those hairs came from."

"Yes?"

"It's mine."

It had to be. How many polar bear furs were floating about in Los Angeles? Don't answer that. Probably more than I'll ever be aware of. But my fur had been stolen two weeks previously. I had come home one evening to see an apartment door that looked wrong. You get used to things that look wrong when you spend time hanging around with criminals. I checked the place over and found the television gone. Which was fine by me. Burns' stereo was also missing. No great loss. I just wish they'd had the decency to take his sofa as well. The only other thing they'd taken, the only other thing worth taking, was the polar bear skin I kept on the bedroom floor.

"Why didn't you report it to the police?" Delphiki asked, brows knotted tightly.

For a reply, I hauled my studio security pass out of my back pocket and showed it to him. It had my photo on it and the name read Bobby G. People tended to get upset if I displayed my whole name. He frowned further and handed it back. "The other reason is that it wasn't the most legal piece of kit I had, anyway."

"Guess not. Where did you get it?"

"Off the bear, of course. He wasn't terribly pleased about the deal. I shipped it to the States as a scientific specimen."

He digested this with his dinner and we ordered coffee. Well, he did.

"Is it a whole skin?"

I nodded slowly. "Head and claws, not a mark on it. If I find anyone's damaged it, he's going the same way as the bear."

Chapter 3

A few more black and white cars, pre-crumbled, de-crumbled, re-crumpled, totalled, and otherwise driven by Roly, completed the chase sequence Dangerous Visions had been working on for over a week. Tape still fluttered at the head of the alleyway, but all evidence of Peters and his untimely demise had been removed. There were no longer beat cops nodding me onwards as I made my way home. Stocker and his people couldn't have given up, but if they had no more to go on than Delphiki did, then they wouldn't be going very far. Probably, their best lead was my polar bear fur.

The question that bothered me most that evening, was whether Delphiki would feel it necessary to inform Stocker about the provenance of the white hairs. It seemed likely. Anyone who insisted on driving strange women home at night was the good citizen type. Beside which, it was the only lead either of them had. As I had said to Officer Pike, even before I knew about the hairs, it wasn't looking very good for me.

I'll come clean here and spoil the story slightly. It really wasn't me. At this stage in the game, I had no more idea than anyone else I have so far mentioned, except possibly Peters, who had killed the guy and why, how, or what that had to do with my missing fur. You may have gathered that I'm not a big discloser. It's pathological - nothing to do with my various jobs, upbringing or anything. I don't tell people the full story behind my possession of a genuine polar bear skin, I don't tell the police when it's stolen, and I don't tell Crash about finding dead people, provided I don't find them on the back lot first thing in the morning. Stuff like that only worries normal people. It's better all round if you just don't tell them.

Stopping at the head of the alleyway, I glanced down speculatively, thinking about how they got Peters here before he died of his wounds. It had to be more than one person. The mess that had been made of his chest had to have been caused by something sudden and fairly huge. Delphiki's description of a wrecking ball might not be far from the truth, and that would require one guy to hold him and one to swing the ball. Getting the dying man into the garbage without making a trail would have required two guys to carry him, and most likely a vehicle as well, and all that only moments before I had found him.

There had been no vehicle in sight at the curb as I had walked down the road that Tuesday evening. I may not have been concentrating as I had been thinking about the absorbing topic of my cardboard, but I would have noticed a van or whatever loitering at the mouth of an alley I was about to pass. Being the suspicious-minded so-and-so that I am, I would have looked down there without the prompting of my unwelcome sixth sense. There had been nothing out of the ordinary.

That was not the case now, though. Something was moving down there in the shadows. Being the sensible woman I am, I slipped the other strap of my rucksack onto my shoulder so that it was secure, and marched down there.

A man in shirt and tie was poking about in the rubbish bags beyond a pile of exploding boxes. He had brown hair that had been gelled back in the current style, but late in the day it was flopping forward as he bent and poked. The man's clothes billowed and sagged slightly, as though he had lost weight since buying them. A shoulder bag had been left with his jacket on top of the wheelie bin that the young cop had leaned on for support. As I drew level with them, with cat-like tread, he straightened up with an exasperated jerk, and saw me.

He made goldfish movements with his mouth, evidently struggling to come up with an excuse.

"Hey," I said. "You know a guy got killed down here the other day? He was found right there, where you're standing." I become more garrulous in situations like this.

He used his fingertips to tease his fringe back in to place, to compose himself. "Yeah, I heard it on the news. Did you actually see it? The body?"

"Sure did. I was the one who found it." My fist closed around a fat folding hunting knife I carry in my pocket. There was more to this man than a simple sick curiosity. He was no teen or geek hunting for grisly souvenirs. In fact, he looked oddly familiar. My talent for identifying bodies usually fails me when the person is alive and kicking. That was one of the many problems I had in the police force - I have no memory for a face.

The man paled, swallowed, and took a step backwards when I admitted that. He held his hands up as though trying to pacify me. "Okay, okay, listen. Look, I had a brother, okay, but he died. Chip died three years ago."

That made no sense to me. I released the knife and grabbed his jacket instead. He made no move to stop me as I rifled through its pockets, then threw it back and opened his bag. Pulling out his diary, I flipped it to the opening page and read his name. "Wilson Peters." Oh, right. This was the longpig's brother. Smashed up dying people don't much resemble themselves anyway. I forgave myself for not recognising him.

"If you're Wilson Peters, then the dead dude was Chip?"

He nodded emphatically.

"Why did he have your wallet? Where the hell have you been? And why the hell was he not already dead?"

"I don't know," he said weakly. As he approached me I shifted to a stronger stance, but he only picked up his things, swinging the still open bag to his shoulder. "God, I don't know. Christ, I don't know what's happening. Jesus ..." He went on mumbling as he followed me up the alley and back on to the sunlit pavement.

"Have you been to the police?"

He glared at me, startled.

"Have you spoken to your grieving widow?"

"Marie. Oh Christ, Marie. Oh, Jesus."

I glared back, hand on hip. "Enough of the blasphemy, Peters. Wake up. Everybody thinks you're dead." Still he didn't move. I suppose being dead is enough to startle most people. Making sure that he saw what I was doing, I pulled out my mobile and dialled the number Detective Stocker had given me in case I thought of anything pertinent.

Contrary to all the proper rules of cop stories, Stocker was actually available to speak to when I needed him. "Stocker," I said, "I've got something I think you want to know about."

Wilson Peters, the live version, had a car parked in a lot around the corner. We drove to the precinct where Peters was hustled into an interview room for an informal chat with Detective Stocker. I was asked to hang around, so I got my phone out again and called Delphiki.

It took him a few moments to pick up this time, and I could hear traffic in the background. Perhaps he had his office window open. "Delphiki."

"Hex Gambetta. I thought you'd be interested to know that I've just met Wilson Peters."

There was a pause while the private detective attempted to make sense of this statement. "They've let you see the body?"

"Nope. He's alive. He says the corpse is his brother."

"Nobody mentioned a brother," Delphiki replied. "Marie Peters identified the murdered man as her husband. They would have to be identical twins."

Now, that's a plot twist. "Maybe they were, maybe the wife didn't know. If she doesn't know there's someone else running around with the same face, she wouldn't look too hard to make sure it was him and not his brother. Wilson said Chip died three years ago. Obviously, he didn't, so they weren't in close contact."

"Marie and Daisy will be relieved," Delphiki said calmly. He wasn't getting excited about the possibilities. "Are you at the precinct with him? I'll be down in a minute."

Contrary to Crash's rules of transport in Los Angeles, Delphiki, although longer than a minute, took nowhere near an hour to appear in the detectives' room. His tall figure striding across the room was a comforting sight, as though he were turning up with the answers, until he said, "I guess now would be a good time to tell Stocker about the polar bear fur."

I shook my head emphatically. "Hey, we have no reason to suppose that the hairs came from my fur. This whole business has nothing to do with me."

"You found whichever Peters died," he reminded me.

"Chip," I said, "but that was sheer coincidence."

He sat abruptly on the chair before Stocker's desk, stuck his long legs out into the room, and rubbed his knuckle in the crease that had appeared between his eyebrows. "Was it, though?" he said, half to himself. "You were on your route home from work and Stocker said you have a reputation for finding bodies. You said there was only a tiny time window for you to find him alive, but perhaps that didn't really matter." He looked up at me.

"Perhaps they're trying to draw attention to the skin and it's actually got nothing to do with Peters. Either of them."

"Can you think of anyone who might want to get you in trouble?"

"No," I lied, so quickly that it was obviously untrue. "It would be a bit of a coincidence that the dead man just happens to have an identical brother, and has died once already."

Delphiki stood, took my shoulders gently, and bent over me a little. "Are you in some kind of trouble?" he asked in a low voice.

"Me?" I chuckled nervously. "No worse than usual." Which reminded me. I had places to be on a Friday night. I went to check my watch but he dropped his hand and grabbed my wrist. There is only so much physical contact of this sort I will take, so I broke his hold and stepped back fluidly.

He cocked his head to one side and watched me, but I was done, so I stood and waited to see what he would do now. After a few moments, he said, "Could you tell me somewhere else? We could go get a coffee, or a beer, I guess." Reflexively, he checked his own watch.

"No way, dude. When Stocker's done with me, I've got to go."

"How 'bout tomorrow?"

"Saturday? Do you work weekends?"

"Twenty-four seven," he repeated with a slight grin. "Somebody needs to know, Ms Gambetta. If you don't feel you can tell the cops, then please tell me."

I threw up my hands. "Okay, we can meet for coffee tomorrow, although I'm not promising anything."

Funeral Games

"He said once he wouldn't be seen dead in a suit, so I took him at his word." Nathan Bedford leaned over the open coffin. "I hope that's all right."

The body of John Mark Gambetta was laid out in a white shirt, grey jumper, jeans and trainers. Anybody who had seen him in life would recognise him in death. He had worn no other clothing for as long as I had known him, except on that interesting occasion in the Middle East, when he had appeared through the haze and the gun fire in boots, combat trousers and a sleeveless grey sweatshirt.

"That's great, Nathan, thanks. You've done a fantastic job with all the arrangements." I patted his hand that rested on the edge of the coffin.

"I suppose now isn't the time to ask the grieving widow where she's been for the last week?"

My guts ached in reply. I shuffled the plastic bag I was holding from one hand to the other and felt sweat trickle between the bandages as the weight shifted. "No. It isn't."

Ever tactful, Nathan didn't pursue it. "I'm going to say something and his brother wanted to say a few words. Do you?"

I shook my head. He was dead and there was nothing more to say about it. The ache in my guts was developing into a scream, so I stood back and straightened up.

"I thought you'd like to choose the piece of music they play when the coffin goes through the curtain. I don't know his musical tastes so I haven't chosen any other pieces to play."

This was a poser. John Mark had not been into music at all. All the other young executives we had ever dined with had owned shiny stereos and vast collections of things to play on them, but not John Mark. Our home had not contained a stereo, television, or even paintings. I thought back over all the tunes I had heard in my younger days when I had still been interested in such things, trying to remember some song that would appropriately sum up the man in the box. There was nothing that would come close without provoking the other mourners to ask about my choice, and I had less desire to explain myself today than usual.

The only option was the patently inappropriate. "Do they have 'Hotel California' by the Eagles?"

Nathan's eyes widened, but the pain of standing still was making my own eyes water, and thinking I was upset, he didn't comment.

"The crematorium uses MP3s now, so they can download the track if they don't already have it." The funeral director approached us, walking softly in carefully chosen dress shoes. He gestured towards the rear of the hall. "The guests are starting to arrive."

Nathan nodded respectfully to the corpse of his best friend and moved away. "Let's give Hex a moment alone," he murmured, and the funeral director turned away too.

I looked into the coffin again. The ineffable change had come over John Mark. All that lay in the box was a waxwork. He looked as though he had never even been alive. The morticians had done their job well, there was no longer any sign that a semi-automatic had filled his chest with more holes than a pair of fishnet tights, but my husband had drained away with his blood on the doorstep.

"It's okay," I said, straining my stitches to pull the lid closed.

The funeral director came over to fasten it down, his face a mask of non-judgement, and gestured his assistants to move the coffin to the conveyor belt where it would wait during the ceremony for its grand curtain call to the tune of 'Hotel California'. "Do you have some flowers for the top of the coffin?" he asked a patch of neutral air somewhere between Nathan and me.

I held up the plastic bag and the men watched me walk to the conveyor as normally as I could when I was secretly under doctor's orders to stay in bed. The bag rustled loudly in the sick silence as I removed a white cowboy hat and a pair of military style aviator sunglasses. Placing the hat on the widest part of the coffin, I spread the arms of the sunglasses, and balanced them on its rim.

"That's unusual," the funeral director could not help but mutter under his breath.

"Unusual, but right," Nathan whispered back. "I'm not sure about the hat, but the sunglasses ..."

I crunched the plastic bag loudly in my fist, realising that my dress didn't have a pocket to put it in. That was one of the many reasons that I almost never wore it. When John Mark and I had attended parties together, I had used his pockets ... but now? The funeral director felt obliged to take it from me.

I adjusted the black dyed cammo net I was using as a shawl to hide my tattoos as he gestured to the usher to let the mourning hoards in.

John Paul Gambetta marched in at the head, his dark curls bobbing on the tops of his ears. His appraising gaze swept from the coffin to Nathan and me, then back. He grunted and extended his hand.

"I'm sorry about your brother," Nathan said, taking it.

Ignored, I ignored back and wandered down the aisle towards my parents and elder brother. The Mallory family descended on me like a parliament of crows. Their sympathetic coos were almost as painful to receive as their hugs.

"Such a kind young man."

"So young."

"I'll look after you, little sis."

As I struggled out of their grasp, John Paul's strident tones cut through the other muted conversations. "They got the bastard, right, Nathan?"

"They got him, John Paul," I answered him without raising my voice in the ensuing silence. "I made sure of that."

He stared hard at me, a questing gaze that demanded to know if I had truly delivered on that boast. I had. The sweat beneath the layer of bandages made me uncomfortably aware of all they didn't know about that. The Gambettas, wife and brother, glared at each other. The Mallorys hurriedly stirred up conversation to fill the silence as they found their seats.

I'm with the Catholics on the subject of funerals. They are entirely for the living. The dead don't really need to be there at all. I didn't need to be there either, but that would have made it harder for everyone else, so I sat stiffly beside Nathan in the front row, and waited for it to be over. Finally, the last notes of 'Hotel California' died away. I evacuated my seat and hurried outside. Movement felt better for my mangled guts.

Nathan Bedford caught up with me. "I need to have a word with you. Can we walk?" I took his arm and we strolled into the garden of remembrance, past floral tributes and memorial stones. The cropped grass felt cool and damp under my bare feet. When we cleared the inner concentration, he began. "You know I was John Mark's lawyer? I was the legal consultant for G-Corp UK and I handled John Mark's personal business as well."

"You were a good friend to him," I mumbled.

"I wanted to talk with you before, but you just vanished after his death. You see, I organised his will," Nathan explained. "I know what's in it."

This was an issue of death I hadn't really considered. I had been far too busy in the last week to worry about the more permanent consequences of my husband's passing on. Actually, now that I did, I found that I wasn't really interested. Neither of us had much in the way of personal possessions. What would John Mark have considered important for me to keep? "The reading's tomorrow, isn't it?"

"I think you need to know now."

What was so important? "Do I get the house? The car, maybe?"

The lawyer smiled. "You get everything, Hex."

"What sort of everything?"

"Absolutely everything. The house, the car, and more importantly, the business. G-Corp UK is yours."

"Well, how does that work? Surely John Paul owns at least half of it. Surely people don't actually own business corporations outright."

"No, not exactly. Obviously I'll explain it all later. It'll be easier in the office, with the paperwork and whatnot. John Mark didn't want his evil elder brother to gain control of UK. He wanted you to have it."

I stopped walking and turned to face him. "Me? But that's daft. Look at me, Nathan. I'm a writer - I can't run whatever the hell G-Corp is." Quite frankly, I didn't want to. I didn't know what I wanted to do next, but running a business didn't make very interesting reading. I thought fast. "You were his right hand man. You know about as much as he did about how it all works."

"Yes. Of course, I'll be right there to help you."

"Oh no you don't. Think of it like a book. The publisher's the guy with the money, the deadlines, whatever, but the author is the one who actually produces the book. The book is the product, but how it's written has basically nothing to do with the publisher. See what I'm getting at? John Mark wants me to own G-Corp UK, so I'll own it. But he can't make me run the damn thing. It'll have a director, manager, whatever you want to call yourself."

"Me?"

"You're the obvious choice."

He nodded slightly in acquiescence.

"You'll have to award yourself the appropriate salary."

There wasn't much else he could say. Letting an adventurer run a huge organisation like the thing we called G-Corp UK, although it didn't have a registered name, or existence, was clearly asking for economic crisis. John Mark could not have intended that I run the thing. He must have known that Nathan and I would contract the solution that we had, although he trusted me enough to leave it in my hands. No one was better placed to take over the reins and hold the various companies together than Nathan, and if John Mark had trusted him, then so could I. Neither of us trusted easily.

We agreed to speak further back at the Fleet Street offices and headed back to the mourners to mingle. John Paul was ready to greet me with a glare.

"Plotting before his ashes are even cold?" At least his tone was jovial. Standing beside him was a man big enough and blond enough to be a Norse god. He too was wearing a beautifully tailored suit, and looked perfectly at ease in it and his mournful surroundings. There was a bald line through his left eyebrow, and another scar across the bridge of his nose, cheek, jaw and lip were similarly marked. He pulled his hand out of his pocket and offered it as John Paul introduced us. "Hex, this is Nicholas Nicholas Junior."

I smiled blankly and crushed back as Nicholas Nicholas Jr attempted to grind my knuckles to dust.

It was a stand-off, and Jr let my hand go. "I guess the lady hasn't heard of Hatch and Nicholas, John Paul." He spoke to me. "My father is Mr Nicholas, of one of the biggest law firms in LA. I'm also a partner. I handle the Gambetta account. John Mark was a good man. His loss affects us all."

That was twaddle. It had to be. Nathan Bedford handled John Mark Gambetta's work. Nicholas Jr must do shady deals for G-Corp US. As for the last two statements, they were true enough, but I had heard too much of this stuff expressed simply because people felt such things ought to be said at such times. John Mark could have been a mass murderer for all the difference it made now. All of that aside, what the hell was he doing here? Surely he hadn't flown all the way from LA for a couple of hours at a funeral of the brother of one of his clients? That didn't make good business sense.

I spotted the bald head of the only man in the crowd visible over Nicholas Jr, and making my excuses, hurried over to a more sensible conversation. "Awright, Yardie?"

Neal Yardell beamed down at me. "Awright, little girl. I'm really sorry about ..." He genuinely was. His dark eyes were damp, despite the smile that had faded at once. We stared at each other, each feeling we were more to blame for bringing the unstoppable force and the immovable object together than the other. Until Neal shrugged uncomfortably in against the restriction of his Marks and Spencer's suit. His muscles bulged, causing the seams to bulge dangerously. "Who are those clowns?"

"John Paul Gambetta and Nicholas Nicholas Jr, don't you know."

Clearly he hadn't heard of the internationally renowned Hatch and Nicholas either. But he was frowning intently at Nicholas Jr. "What?"

"Nothin'. I've heard of a Nicholson, but not a Nicholas Jr."

I had heard of Nicholson too, but before I could comment, my father appeared from Neal's hefty shadow. He took my arm. "How are you doing, love?" I'd heard more 'loves', 'dears' and 'darlings' from my parents' lips since I'd changed my name than I ever had before, but knowing they would rather use endearments than my chosen name didn't endear me to them.

"Fine, Dad. This is Neal. Neal runs a ... um ... recruitment agency."

Neal grinned widely at this description of his activities, and my father's small white hand was wholly enclosed in his enormous black one. My father winced.

"Bin proud to know your son-in-law, Mr Mallory. Best judge of character I ever worked with."

"Er, thanks, Neal." He extricated his hand and surreptitiously massaged it back to life.

"Proud knowing Hex, too. Only girl never let me down. Maybe we'll do some more business now, eh?"

"Maybe," I said. It sounded like more fun than the career Nathan had presented me with. Neal Yardell recruited mercenaries. He had used John Mark to vet candidates for sensitive jobs - the famous Gambetta test. I was the only woman who had ever passed and now my record would stand unbroken. "If you guys would excuse me..."

If I was writing this story, I realised, then Nicholson would be Nicholas' son, Nicholas Jr. It was so such an obvious a deception that it almost had to be true. He had one too many scars.

My mother had ambushed John Paul, whom she had only had the dubious pleasure of meeting once before at our wedding. Even now they were no longer family, she felt it her duty to be friendly. Did she not think that John Mark had kept John Paul at arm's length for a reason? Well, it was useful for the moment, and I was able to lever the Norse god away.

"Walk with me, Nicholas."

"Nick, please. My friends call me Nick Jr." We left the paved pathway and walked up across the garden again. "Are you okay going this way? You've got no shoes on."

"I'm good. I never found shoes to go with this dress." Not that I'd tried very hard. I leaned forward a little, ignoring the twinges from my gut, and tried to peer through the gaps between his shirt buttons. He was wearing no tie and his black silk shirt was open at the neck, revealing an inch or so of solid muscle, but not enough for me to catch a glimpse of what I imagined tattooed over his heart. "I think I knew a friend of yours, but he didn't call you Nick Jr. He called you Nicholson."

"Really?" He didn't sound taken.

"Yeah. He was called 'the Bombardier'."

We strolled in unconcerned silence around an evergreen. Then he grabbed the cammo shawl at my neck. Automatically, I bent my knees and slipped out of it. As I side-stepped and straightened up, guts forgotten, he stared at my bare shoulders.

"Hex Mallory. The Seventh Shadow. I was sure it must be you. Bomber tells me his friend Hex is the only woman to pass the Gambetta test, then John Paul Gambetta tells me that his little brother married a woman called Hex. It could only be one and the same. So, can I see the tattoo?" He could already see most of my others now and they convinced him that the black hell hound lurked beneath the bodice of my dress.

"You must be joking. I'm not stripping off for another man at my husband's funeral."

He could see the sense in that. "We have to make a deal here. The Bombardier called me Nicholson. Nothing else. John Paul calls me Nick Jr." He paused significantly.

I had already grasped all this. "Yeah, yeah. Clark Kent, Superman. The mercenaries know the mercenary boss and everyone else knows the lawyer. It's all pretty simple."

"Like John Mark. His brother knows the sappy businessman but it turns out the boy spends his holidays killing people. So, who doesn't know the murky details of your past? I gotta have something on you, for security." He may have been insulting my late husband, whom he clearly hardly knew, but apart from that he was making sense. His team, the Swooning Shadows, were the elite, and blowing their cover would blow a lot of important people open as well.

"Nick, I'm a writer. I've never been anything else."

"Sure, I get it."

There really was nothing to get. I had just told him nothing but the truth, but if it made him happy it made my life easier. He handed my shawl back, and I covered myself up as we rounded the other side of the evergreen and came back into view. Nick Jr had flown all the way from Los Angeles to see me.

Everyone was fidgeting now. It was time to break up the crowd and reconvene in the more manageable surroundings of whatever hall Nathan had booked and filled with small sandwiches and booze. My rotten family broke cover from their mingling to converge in a pincer movement, trapping me into sharing their car. They spoke in hushed tones about the nice things good old Nathan had said about their son-in-law, and I ignored them, imagining instead the sunglasses that I had placed on top of the coffin, buckling, twisting, slowly melting in the heat of the furnace.

Chapter 4

I wasn't limping as I entered the coffee shop, although my knee burnt with every step. There are a million good reasons not to limp, the best of which is that you'll just damage your other joints if you walk funny. Delphiki had not arrived, so I hopped onto the stool of one of those high circular tables that don't encourage you to linger. I had agreed to meet Crash later to go over our next sequence to figure out what we needed. He could basically do the job on his own - he had been doing it for years - but he needed someone else there to agree with him. And to trim all the frills off.

The private detective arrived at a smart clip, scanning everyone in the place. He was wearing the same outfit: jacket, jeans, t-shirt, trainers. All very comforting. He nodded to me, ordered his coffee, and swung himself on to the stool opposite.

"Okay," he said, "I've been checking on Chip Peters and I got bupkis."

"How many Yiddish beans?"

"Wilson Peters, born in Virginia, came out to California for college and settled out here. Chip Peters - nothing. I tried Charles ... Got nothing."

I sipped my hot chocolate. I don't order coffee. John Mark was never very complimentary about English coffee but I can't say that American coffee is any better. Only differently horrible. "So, the brother's name isn't Charles. It's Woodrow."

"Wilson told you that?"

I shook my head. "Stands to reason. Twin boys. One's called Wilson, what's the other one called? Oh, and the parents are American. Probably known as Woody as a child, so when he wants to get away from that, he might naturally move to Chip."

He cocked his head. "Yeah, okay, I could go with that. I'll run him again."

He probably Googled the names, then checked other databases and sources he had collected. That's the great thing about computers. If you're on the wrong track, they won't put you right.

"I also checked up on a Hex Gambetta. There's less on her than on Chip Peters. Bobby Gambetta gets a mention in relation to various films made in the last few years. John Paul turns up on every organised crime database in the fifty states, but he doesn't have a sister. So I tried cross-referencing 'Hex' with a polar bear, and guess what? I turned up a Hex Mallory, author of a volume of poetry called 'Fairy Bear'. It's about the arctic, I gather." He raised his eyebrows at me, searching for some sort of confirmation in my passivity.

"Fairy bear was the medieval name for Ursus Maritimus," I said blandly.

"Mallory has also written various travel articles, mostly about countries of the Middle East. But the earliest one seems to be about the Pilgrim Road to Santiago de Compostella, Spain." He released his coffee cup and flicked a long finger in the direction of my arm. "I guess that explains those arrow tattoos."

The two tattoos on my arms were red arrows in the form of lines radiating out from the forward point in a fan shape. It would take someone familiar with the signposting of the Pilgrim Road to realise that the stylised shapes were arrows. "I took the old Pilgrim watchword as my motto," I admitted.

"Ultreia," he said slowly, dredging it up from an ancient memory. "Enzo said it meant, 'keep on keeping on'."

"Or, as someone else once put it, 'No backing up'." I grinned to myself. That one was a private joke between myself and John Mark. "So, you've walked the Road?"

"When I was a kid. My mother had done it, and after she died, I went with my Godfather, Enzo. We had a deal: we'd spend quality time together doing the pilgrimage and then I had to start school. I was all for becoming a private detective straight away, at the great age of twelve, but Enzo had finally realised that there was more to being a parent than just hanging out. He and my father were the original Watts and Delphiki. But Jude, my father, died in a fight, and my mother got shot two years later, and I was given to Enzo, my godfather. We came back to LA, John Paul's uncle got Enzo his PI licence back, Enzo went back into practice and I went back into school." He dipped his hand into the neck of his t-shirt and drew out a bootlace, suspended from which was a shiny metal scallop shell, marked with the cross of St James. "Gil, my mother, Rose Gilchrist, got this when she made the pilgrimage, and I've worn it ever since she died."

I shrugged. What is one supposed to say to something like that? Sucks that your family died? Sometimes I wish mine would.

He returned from reminiscence to the present. "So, Bobby Gambetta is a stunt double, Hex Mallory is a writer. What is Hex Gambetta?"

"Hex Mallory married John Paul's younger brother, John Mark, in England. After John Mark's death, I came to California to visit John Paul and his family. I got picked up by a stunt outfit, but the Gambetta name bothered them. When I gave them my résumé and they saw that I'd been a cop, they were reassured. Someone remembered that English coppers were sometimes called 'bobbies' when they weren't being called 'pigs' or something worse, and it stuck. So, Hex Mallory is a writer, Bobby Gambetta is a stunt double, and Hex Gambetta carries the passport."

He seemed to like that, and chuckled, shaking his head. "No wonder you got the Woodrow Peters thing figured out. So you're really John Paul Gambetta's sister-in-law?"

"No. When I married again I think I voided that relationship. But John Paul and I are rather fond of each other, and we decided to drop the inaccurate in-law stuff and go with straight brother and sister. We're technically no longer related at all."

"You married again but you kept your surname?"

"Oh, yeah. Gambetta is a name to conjure with. Anyway, I always called Burns by his surname, and sharing it myself would have been weird."

"I did find out about Burns in my checking. I'm sorry about that."

"Yeah, well, them's the breaks." I slurped the rest of my hot chocolate, catching the foam with the last swish round the cup. "So, I guess you know now why I'm not so hot on bearing my soul to the police."

"No." He regarded me steadily, not braking eye contact to beckon the waitress. "I'll get you another and you can get slightly less opaque."

While we waited for our refills, I stared at him as hard as he was staring at me. If I was going to tell him anything else which wasn't a matter of public record, then I would have to be sure to know his face. He couldn't wear his uniform all the time, and if he had put on a shirt and tie, I might not have been able to pick him out of a crowd. His eyes were dark like his hair, and his skin was a Mediterranean hue, all of which fitted with his Greek surname. Around his mouth there were a few small scars, as though he had thought he could take up shaving as well as detecting at the age of twelve, but they were more likely to have been left by fighting. Unwilling to be too certain, I estimated his age somewhere in his thirties. His wasn't a face that stood out of a crowd at all but held its own curious handsomeness. I stood up and shook some of the stiffness out of my knee.

"You okay? I wasn't going to mention it, but you've got the best part of a black eye, as well as a welt the size of a small snake around your arm." Delphiki stood too, grasping my elbow as the table wobbled.

I glanced down at my arm where the raised, red swelling wrapped itself around the meat. The mark was as thick as his thumb that rested beside it. If the chain had caught me any nearer the wrist, the impact would probably have broken my arm. But I have more sense than to catch anything like that on the bone. "Don't you recognise it? It's the imprint of a Kawasaki bike chain. The make-up artists aren't going to like me for the rest of the week, I'd guess."

"Is this why you don't want to talk?" the detective asked quietly.

"One reason of many." I clambered back on to my stool to receive my refill, dislodging his hand.

"Was it John Paul?" His voice held a strange menace.

I laughed. "John Paul? You have to be kidding me. He fights like Roger Moore's Bond."

"Oh? What's your style?"

"Taekwondo. They've started teaching it in the police force but I took it up when I got back from Spain."

"And you're good?"

"Very. But I always fight dirty."

He laughed too, and sat down again, the sudden tension dispersed. "I guess I should see the other guy." He toyed with his hot coffee for a moment and I felt the atmosphere mount again. Back to business. "So you've had two husbands, both of whom have died and left you childless."

"Yeah, well, that wasn't their fault. To misquote Wilde, to lose one husband could be considered unfortunate, but to lose two is careless." I grinned, but he remained concerned.

"I understood that Burns' fate was an industrial accident. That's not anybody's fault. What happened to John Mark?"

And that's what you get for talking too much. Well, I suppose Delphiki could conceivably find it out himself, so I might as well save him from wasting time detecting me so he could get back to Peters, and more importantly, my bearskin.

"Okay. Listen very carefully, I shall say zis only once. I used to be engaged to a gangster called Johnny Mack. He drove passed one morning when John Mark was heading out to work and gunned him down on the doorstep. I knew where Johnny hung out, so I got my police buddies and went after him. When Johnny figured out I'd shopped him, he shot me. So, no husband ... and no kids... ever." To emphasise the point, I stood, raised the hem of my black vest and showed him the pucker I call my spare navel. Then I turned round and poked the squashed worms of flesh that clustered in the vicinity of a kidney. "This is the exit wound."

As I sat once more, Delphiki sipped at his coffee. "I'm sorry."

"What for?"

He shrugged.

"None of this has got anything to do with Peters, dead or alive, or my bearskin. Are you going help me find it, Delphiki, or what?" I discovered that I was annoyed now. Annoyed with myself for talking too much, and annoyed with him for seeing that scar and knowing what it was about. I just wanted to go out and hit people until they gave me my skin back.

The private detective was watching me, those dark eyes liquid and dangerous like a tar pit. "I'll help you," he said quietly.

He was about to say something else but I cut across his gentle words, demanding harshly, "How? We got bupkis."

"We'll get more. Stocker promised to keep me in the loop. He's a fair guy, the rare sort of cop who would rather have solved crimes than get the credit for it. If Peters - Wilson, that is - compiles a list of his enemies, and you do the same, we could check them against each other."

"You just want my enemies in LA, right? We could still be here all night."

He didn't smile at that, just shifted back in his seat. "You could start with whoever did that to you." He tilted his head at my face.

"Don't know." Which was true. It was one of a dozen people in the warehouse last night. I knew who was punching me at the time, obviously, but now I couldn't have picked any of them out of the crowd in Chinatown.

"You still haven't told me the whole story, have you?"

"Not even close." And I never will. I swung myself up, lowering the weight gently on to my injured knee. It was easing out. By the end of the day it would be workable again. "Look, Delphiki, I gotta go to work. Thanks for the chocolate." *You're paying, bub.*

"You're welcome." He rose too. "I've got your cell number, so I'll call you as soon as I get anything, okay?" What was that? An apology for using his initiative and saving my number when I rang him? "And if I'm buying you drinks and calling you, you'd better call me Spike." He extended his hand.

Oh, please. I shook it. Gambetta may be a name to conjure with, but in conversation I'd rather be called Hex anyway. "See you later, Spike." Shouldering my rucksack, I strode out of there as though I couldn't feel his eyes boring into me all the way onto the street.

Chapter 5

It was an interesting proposition, that someone wanted to kill Peters and fit me up at the same time. Interesting, but unlikely. I was an alien in LA. I knew who I knew, and Peters was not in any of the circles I travelled in.

Just in case, I phoned John Paul's house. His right hand man, Sidney, answered the phone as usual, and I asked him, but the names of Woodrow 'Chip' and Wilson Peters meant nothing to him. Sidney would have known if Peters was a name to John Paul.

Tom was hard at work when I reached the Dangerous Visions head office, a tiny rat hole on the third floor of an office block as ancient and crumbling as it is possible to find in a city as modern as LA. The outfit had once rented a suite of rooms with an integral bathroom in a hip and up-coming block surrounded by other movie outfits. Then Burns' first incendiary accident had lost them the job, insurance, and the office, as well as half his face. Still, if the cramped new quarters bothered Tom, he had never allowed it to show. His feasibility study was nearly completed, even if it wasn't very feasible.

"Do you think Martin can do it?" he asked breathlessly as I perused his scribbles and sketches. Most of the plan was on his state-of-the-art laptop, but I wanted to see his preliminary work first. Martin was the ex-military explosives expert we had hired to replace Burns. Nobody had the heart to give him a nickname yet, but it would come. You can't take things too seriously in this business or you start worrying about other things, like driving into concrete walls.

"If Martin can't do it safely, or he doesn't think that anybody can, it's up to him to say so," I pointed out, pretty certain that an army explosives man would have enough sense not to bite off more than he could chew.

"Tell him that, will you?" Tom pleaded, overanxious these days. "Oh, I'm sorry. I'll tell him."

"I'll do it," I said, knowing it would bother me less than him. Also, if I agreed to do it, he might stop whinging when I was trying to read. It was going to take me a while to get through and evaluate all his work.

Several hours later I had persuaded Crash that there was no way in hell that he'd get the insurance to run one of his sequences. Even if Martin could blow up the set without blowing up the entire studio, it would be impossible for a stunt double to survive it, were any of us willing to try. The fact that I was theoretically willing to try wasn't helping the argument. This was Tom's problem. On the ground he was as cautious as a vertigo sufferer on a glass floor, but on paper he had his lever under the corner of the earth and was just looking for a place to stand.

Common sense prevailed and the sequence was deleted from the laptop with the resulting deflation of mood. Defeating the resources of Dangerous Visions reminded us of other things we had lost.

Tom stretched his arms behind his head. "Why did it have to happen, Bobby?" he asked plaintively, knowing that I would switch tracks just as easily and follow his train of thought. "He was my best friend."

This was the sort of question that people often ask for years after other people have died. It was the sort of question I hated because what the questioner wanted to hear was platitudinous reassurance, not an answer. They simply wanted to know that those around them were as bewildered as they were. I hate questions like this because I've heard too many of them, and people still insist on asking me. Half the time I know the answer and I know they don't want to hear it. Not this time, though. "Maybe God hates you," I suggested. This idea was dreary enough for his mood.

"Maybe he's working up to smiting me because I'm not choosing to go forth and multiply."

He wasn't the only one who was never going to multiply. "We are what we are, and if anyone expects us to behave otherwise, wel, fuck 'em."

"Yeah, fuck 'em."

I gave him a hug because he needed one and decided that it must be lunch time, but even as I opened my mouth to suggest it, my trousers vibrated.

"Is that a cell phone in your pocket or are you just pleased to see me?" Tom giggled.

"Just pleased to see you, babe." I dug the phone out of my pocket and saw the number of an unknown mobile phone displayed on the screen. Stepping away from Crash, I answered it. "Hello?"

"Hex, it's Spike."

That was a relief. It's still harder to get hold of people's mobile phone numbers than their land lines, so it worries me when somebody I don't know is able to call me. "Hey, babe," I said automatically. I could have kicked myself. Glancing at Tom, I saw that he hadn't registered it because I nearly always answered the phone that way. But Spike Delphiki didn't know that. "What have you got?" I asked hurriedly.

"Not much," he admitted. "Woodrow was a good call. He was officially declared dead three years ago, though, so the coroner's having problems with our current stiff's death certificate. Both the guy you found and the living man have documentation proving that they are Wilson Peters, the one with the family, job, house, social security number, whatever. And Marie Peters can't make a positive identification."

"Doesn't she know which one she was married to?"

Crash's head turned like a radar scanner at this hint of gossip magazine scandal.

"As you suggested, Mrs Peters didn't know that her husband had an identical twin," Spike explained.

"How long were they married? Seventeen years or so, if they've got a kid in high school. She must know some distinguishing features."

"That's just it. She said that her husband had a mole at the back of his right knee and a scar from a childhood injury on his elbow." He paused. In the background, a coffee machine slurped and bubbled.

"And?"

Tom was watching my face intently, trying to guess who on earth I was talking to and what it could be about.

"The corpse has a scar on its elbow. The living man has a mole behind his knee."

That information took some digesting. "That's something, Spike." I glanced at Tom. "I'm still at work here, so could we chat about this later?"

"Sure. Shall we do dinner?"

Anything that would end this phone call before I had to tell Crash that I had found another corpse sounded good. We agreed that he would pick me up from my apartment and I rang off. "Come on, Tom. Time for lunch." Making dinner plans made me hungry.

An injection of blood sugar brought inspiration, and soon we were planning out the discarded sequence once more on deli napkins. Decamping to the office, we went back to the laptop before we were thrown out of Tom's favourite lunch spot for wasting trees. And then Dez, the Harry Potter reject, clomped in, declaring petulantly that it was six o'clock and Tom wasn't to work anymore as it was the weekend. I grabbed my rucksack and headed for my apartment, wondering if I would make it before Spike did. According to Crash's one hour theory, we should both set out and arrive at the same time, by foot or car, it made no difference.

Spike's dark blue sedan was sitting in the car park as I jumped the chain link at the back of the lot. He saw me before I reached him, and waved. Throwing my bag in the back seat, I slid in beside him. An hour is a good long time to play with the ideas he had given me at lunch time. Given what little information we had, the plot possibilities were almost endless.

I set off at a gallop. "Right, so Mrs Peters had no idea that Wilson had a twin brother. It never occurred to her that she was sharing her life with two men. Question is, did Wilson know? It's conceivable that Chip was slipping into the gaps in his brother's life. I mean, say Chip was the unsuccessful brother. Wilson's not exactly a hero, but it's all relative. So Chip had got into trouble, faked his own death, and went looking for Wilson. He found that he had the sort of life most people dream of, so he starts impersonating his brother. Maybe Wilson finds out, so he kills Chip, or Chip just decides he wants it all, so he kills Wilson."

The car was smoothly eating up the road, Spike silent at the wheel, hearing me out. "It is conceivable," he agreed when I had finished. "Wilson - the live brother, I mean - said that he had been out of town for a couple of days on business. Marie Peters says that her husband had said he was going away for the meeting but came back the same day saying it had been cancelled."

It sounded like a corroboration. "So, Wilson goes out of town, and Chip seizes the opportunity to muscle in. He turns up saying the meeting was cancelled. Wilson gets back from the meeting to find his life-stealer is dead. Paid hit, perhaps? Or he has no meeting, but it's a trap to lure Chip in, and Wilson kills him himself, with the cover of having been out of town. Or Chip knows Wilson is going out of town, so he grabs him and kills him, knowing he'll have a few days to get into the role permanently. Or the twins had arranged the whole thing between them. You know, taking it in turns to be Wilson, with the job and family, and Chip living in a bachelor pad somewhere, under the radar. Perhaps he makes a living from crime and just happened to burgle my apartment, hence the polar bear fur on his trousers. If we find his hiding hole, we'll find the skin."

Pausing to make sure I had covered all the permutations I had thought of, I realised that any of them could be possible, and we would never know which brother was which. No matter which story turned out to be true, if any of them could be proved, it would still be impossible to prove beyond reasonable doubt who had died in the alley. Forensics could not tell us which DNA was Wilson's and which was Chip's, unless a childhood friend could be found who remembered which twin broke his elbow falling from his skateboard.

Staring out of the window for inspiration, I suddenly jerked upright in my seat, registering the gaudy signs of Chinatown. "Where are we going?" I snapped.

"Nearly there," Spike answered calmly. "A little place I know just round the corner."

The car pulled up and I climbed out, my heart sinking as I recognised the street and knew which little place was around the corner. I cursed myself for getting carried away with the story and not concentrating on the present. I grabbed the door handle but Spike had already turned the key in the lock on the other side of the car. He stepped around the bonnet and took my arm.

"What's the matter? Do you need your bag?"

I shook my head. I was better off unhampered.

He steered me towards the corner, my elbow firm in his grip, his arm propelling me on as inevitably as an invading army.

"This little place of yours," I said slowly, hanging back as much as I could, "it isn't called the Laughing Duck, is it?"

"You know it?"

Curses! And we rounded the corner.

Two oriental men spilled out into the light on the pavement, arguing loudly but amicably between themselves. Their shirts were sharp, their trousers pressed, their shoes shiny. The taller man sported a ponytail of thick black hair pulled tightly back from shaved temples. The shirt sleeves of the shorter man were rolled up slightly, revealing the curling jungle green of comprehensive tattooing. They paused, gestured, turned, and froze.

"Gambetta!"

Spike stopped, frowning, uncomprehending. His free arm moved slightly, loosening the hang of his jacket.

The pair seemed to swell as they moved side by side into an impenetrable barrier like a scrum line. "You're dead, Gambetta!" the shorter one called, his voice low and teasing. He tucked his rolled sleeves more firmly as he moved. The taller one raised his chin and rolled his shoulders as he stepped beside him.

"I don't think so," I replied, scanning their clothing for the possibility of weaponry.

Then their movement was arrested. They turned again to catch the words of someone speaking inside the establishment. The nearest one called something in reply, but I didn't understand what he said, then both stepped back as a higher authority came out to see what was going on.

The man made up in presence what he lacked in stature, making his own space on the pavement simply by being there. I didn't have to know his name to know who he was.

"We don't want trouble," he said.

"We're not here to make trouble," Spike replied. Then he looked at me.

I detached myself from his arm and took a step forward. "We're just looking for some food. We'll go somewhere else. No trouble."

The old man looked Delphiki up and down, which required considerable movement of his head. Then he stared hard at me. "No trouble?" he said, "Just food? Come in," he beckoned us.

The other men growled and grumbled, protesting, but the older one made a gesture to silence them. "Be my guest," he said.

I dropped my hands to my legs and made a small Taekwondo bow to him. He smiled and returned it. Spike took my arm once more and we entered the Laughing Duck unmolested. The three men melted into the shadows, leaving one of the hostesses to seat us and bring menus.

"What was that?" Spike asked.

I was still scanning the joint, trying to fix every detail in my mind. I'd never seen the inside of the place before and wasn't likely to again. Unless it was the last thing I ever saw. "Don't ask."

The food came with remarkable speed and I enjoyed every mouthful. In just the same way that Italian food in America is quite a different experience to eating it in England, 'a Chinese' bears little resemblance to the meal of the same name on the other side of the pond. The names of the dishes are different and they are categorised obscurely too. Americans insist that their way is more authentic but I'm no connoisseur. It was put before me in a Chinese restaurant, so I assumed it was Chinese, and shoved it down my gullet with chopsticks.

Spike went out to find the toilets and returned grinning. "Do you know what I saw on my trip to the men's room?"

The images that filled my head don't bear repeating. "Do I want to know?"

"I walked past the kitchen. Welts like yours must be in fashion this season, 'cos there were a lot of the guys in there wearing them. And there was one guy sitting on a chair near the door who was in a plaster cast."

"Odd that," I agreed. I had heard it snap as I pressed the arm lock home.

He shook his head and beckoned the waitress for the bill, only to be informed that we were guests of the house. As we left, I saw the tiny old man standing back at the end of the counter, watching us. I made the small bow again, and again he smiled and returned it. I love the men who are big enough not to take it all too seriously.

Returning to the car, Spike said, "Okay, let's forget the Peters for a second. Why don't you tell me about what I just lived through?"

Well, he was bound to ask. Here we go again. The car pulled away from ground zero and I drew breath for a tale as short as I could make it. "John Paul managed to contrive a bit of business that annoyed one of these - what do you call 'em - tongs, or families. One of their outfits anyway."

"Triads? Yakuza? Chinese Mafia?"

"I don't think it's all that clear cut. Anyway, I came down here to see about it and found myself a new Taekwondo teacher. He's Korean. Turned out his lot were against the Laughing Duck lot who were the guys John Paul had pissed off, so we banded together and went down there. It all went down pretty hard, but for some reason it became a regular thing. John Paul's still pissing them off, and they still want him dead, and my dojang still hate the Chuckling Ducklings, so ..." I shrugged.

"Haven't the police done something?" Spike asked. He seemed slightly shocked by the idea of weekly tribal punch-ups.

"They try to have a lot of oriental cops patrol this area, and they're related to people who ask them to overlook the blood on the streets on Saturday mornings. God knows where they get to on Friday nights."

He laughed then. "What you're saying is that these guys tried to kill you last night and you let me take you right into the lion's den tonight without even flinching."

"Well, their boss made us his personal guests."

"The kitchen was full of cooks with cleavers. If I'd known what was going on, I wouldn't have been so cool."

"You had a gun and a car. You don't have to fight my battles. Saving the bearskin, of course."

He said nothing for a time and I stared out of the window at the thick lurid sky. "Where are we going now?" This was not the way back to my apartment.

"What makes you think I'm carrying a gun?" he asked abruptly.

"You a private investigator in LA, you're wearing a jacket, and you're not stupid."

He considered this for a moment. "I think I'll take that as a compliment."

"I think I'll mean it as one."

He pulled the car to the curb and stopped, both hands resting on the wheel. His brow creased as though he were thinking hard. "Where did all that stuff about Peters come from?"

"What, those stories I made up? Just thinking. It's not like we've got much to go on."

"A writer and a fighter." He rubbed his knuckle between his eyebrows. "Accepting that you have no prior connection with Peters, has what happened tonight got anything to do with the bearskin?"

"No. All that goes down in Chinatown or with John Paul. They've got no reason to know about the bearskin. They weren't there when I won it and they weren't there when I shipped it into the country. I don't talk about it. The robbery was more likely to have been opportunistic. The thief took the TV and stereo as well."

"Who knows you've got it?"

I was about to declare a shortlist of John Paul and the Dangerous Visionaries, but I remembered that John Paul may own the apartment, but he had never been into the bedroom since I had taken up residence. Out of my work mates, only Burns had been in the bedroom, he never discussed it, and he was dead. That was Los Angeles taken care of. Beyond the city limits, John Mark had shared a room with it, but he too was dead. The survey team had been there when I got it, had helped me have it declared a scientific specimen, but now they were scattered. I was not in touch with any of them. None of them knew the skin was now in the States. That left Johnny Mack as the only one who knew what it meant to me, but he was safely in jail in England. "No one," I concluded.

"What if the hairs were transferred from your clothes to Peters' when you tried to help him? We might be on a wild goose chase," Spike suggested.

"Unlikely. Those clothes were clean on that morning and the skin had gone a fortnight before. The transfer might have been from Peters' assailants."

"Perhaps they had the skin and used it to move the body," he mused.

Every muscle in my body turned to rock. "If they've got blood on it ... if they've damaged it ... if they've harmed a single hair ... I'll kill every one of them," I growled.

He regarded at me quizzically. "Hey, calm down."

My fists clenched, my short nails unable to break the skin. I curled my toes inside my trainers until they cramped, choking down the reflex to leap from the car and kick something until it broke. The leather of the car seat creaked beneath me. I had managed to stay so calm for so long, but now, with the clues on Peters' trousers, my skin ought to be close enough to jump up and grab. But it wasn't, and I was losing patience. For a moment, I couldn't even shake myself. "I can't. That's my fairy bear skin."

Spike leaned over me, looming into my unfocussed vision. "This might help." He kissed me, then started the car up and pulled back onto the road.

I stared, still unfocussed, out through the windscreen, startled out of my rage, and trying to decide what I thought of that. On the whole, I wasn't going to object. I dragged myself back. "Where are we going now?"

He was smiling to himself. "We're going for drinks. Somewhere safe."

"How do you know? You don't know who else I've pissed off."

"True. But I do know of one person who is definitely not trying to kill you. Me. We're going to my place."

It didn't matter where he lived. It would still take me an hour to get home. I settled back in the seat, feeling the stressed leather relax, and enjoyed the ride up into the hills.

His house wasn't big, not by Hollywood standards. It was a hefty wooden thing, built like a barn and cut into the hillside. The garage was underneath the front of the house, with the basement on the same level at the back, firmly underground.

He drove passed the driveway and reversed onto the bottom of it, parking there as though he anticipated a hurried getaway. "This was Enzo's house," he told me.

"When we came back to the States, we lived here together. It's where I grew up, I guess." He took my hand and we wandered up to the porch. He stopped and frowned at the door. "Someone's been here."

Pulling out the gun I knew he was carrying, he tried the handle, but the door was locked.

"Do you have an alarm system?"

"No. Enzo always said that anyone coming all the way up here to break in wouldn't be put off by an alarm system, so there was no point putting one in. The cleverer the alarm system, the cleverer the criminals you attract." He unlocked the door and opened it silently. No sound came from the house. Preceded by his gun barrel, he leant in, and flicked the light switch. The hallway was bathed with light. Nothing moved. "Stay behind me," he warned in a low voice, and stepped slowly down the hall.

He slammed open the sitting room door furiously, covering the room with his weapon. Still nobody. No sound. Spike was about to step into the room when I grabbed his arm. There was something horribly familiar about that room. It was nothing that could be made to stand up in a court of law, but if a photograph of it was sent to any of the police stations around the city of Portsmouth, England, it would come back with the caption, 'Crime Scene of Johnny Mack'. This wild talent wasn't mine alone. Anyone who had experienced the one-man crime wave that was my former fiancé would have recognised it. We couldn't tell you how we knew, but we knew.

"Spike," I said grimly, "go out to the car. And stay there."

He turned a questioning gaze on me, but our visit to the Laughing Duck had taught him that I was in earnest. He complied. His gun still in his hand, he left the house.

I moved cautiously into the sitting room, stepping low in a strong position. The walls were lined with bookshelves and I ached to know what a man like Delphiki might be reading, but I told myself firmly that I could find out later and moved on. The kitchen was modern and spotlessly clean. It looked like Mack had been there too, but there was nothing for me to pick up on.

A faint scratching caught my ear as I set foot on the first stair. I cocked my head. Something was scraping at a door upstairs. Stepping on the edge of the treads, I made my way up as noiselessly as possible. The scratching came again, more urgently. Whatever it was could hear me approaching, but it wasn't a human sound. Spike hadn't mentioned a pet, but why would he?

All three doors on the landing were closed, two to the right, and one on the left. I listened. The scraping redoubled as the creature sensed me nearing. It was behind the left hand door. Grasping the handle, I turned it cautiously. And felt a click.

An electronic voice filled the house, seeming to resonate through the floor. *This house will self-destruct in five seconds.*

Theatrical sod! I thought, looking wildly around. If I had doubted my recollections of Johnny Mack, I was reassured in the worst possible way. Where was the device? He must have been all over the house and the thing didn't have to be big. I had no chance of finding it.

This house will self-destruct in four seconds.

I threw the door open. A bundle of brown fur leaped back as I charged into the room. To my right was a bed, its covers boot camp tight apart from a round dent below the pillow where the animal had been sleeping. Beyond it stood a chest of drawers with nothing on the top. Facing me was a window. The rest of the room was empty.

This house will self-destruct in three seconds, vibrated through the floor.

Whirling round, I saw the creature. I leapt for it and it leapt for the open door.

This house will self-destruct in two seconds.

Lashing out, I grabbed the thing by the scruff of its neck and hauled it back. I jumped to my feet, clutching it firmly against my chest.

The stairs led straight up from front to back, towards the hillside. The window to the left would look out over the slope. There was a good chance I wouldn't have to fall very far.

This house will self-destruct in one second. I charged across the room, twisted and jumped.

The glass shattered under the impact of my shoulder. As Spike's pet and I sailed out into the angelic night, the roof of Enzo Watts' house blasted upwards, punched out by a fist of flame.

Instinctively I curled around the bundle of fur squirming in my grasp. My feet hit angled ground and I relaxed my legs, dropping my shoulder to send the impact into a roll. I plummeted sideways down the steep incline, barrel-rolling and crashing down again on to my knee. Dirt scattered around me as my knee cap broke the fall. Scratching and biting, the creature fought free of my embrace and stumbled onto the grass. It was a slightly flattened racoon.

Running footsteps heralded Spike's arrival. I wobbled to my feet, trying to catch my breath. My ears rang with the roar of the inferno behind me. His hand on my shoulder alerted me to the fact that he was speaking.

"Are you okay? Are you hurt? What the hell happened?"

I waved him away, struggling to fill my lungs with the acid vapours pouring from the house behind me. The racoon was trying to run towards him, one hind leg splayed out at an awkward angle. Spike caught it up in one stride, lifting it against his chest.

"Come on," he said, pulling at my arm with his free hand.

I followed him down to the car, saved by its paranoid distance from the house. I was limping freely now, and knocking a few pieces of glass from my shoulder as I went.

Still clutching the racoon, Spike slid his jacket off and wrapped it around the creature. "Here." He handed it to me and unlocked the car. Specks of ash floated down around us, scorching the paintwork. "Let's get out of here." I got in, the racoon held in place on my lap, and the blue sedan roared away from the scene of destruction.

"What in the hell just happened?" Spike demanded after five minutes of stunned silence.

"So much for somewhere safe," I said. "I don't know what just happened." Johnny Mack was in prison. I had put him there. He was not in California. He was in England, behind bars. Wasn't he? "I think I squashed your racoon." I stoked the creature's head with one finger. It didn't seem very impressed.

"His name is Cadaver," Spike told me. "I think you saved his life."

Pinning Cadaver inside Spike's jacket with one hand, I pushed myself up and wrestled my phone out of my trouser pocket with the other. I asked for a fire engine, the only emergency appliance I hadn't used yet this week. Good thing I pay my taxes.

Spike drove us down to an emergency vet. While I struggled out of the passenger side door with the wrapped racoon, Spike wriggled out of his shoulder holster and locked it and the gun in the glove box. Inside the palely lit waiting room, fat soggy people sat listlessly clinging to chains on the ends of which slobbering dogs tried to drag an extra inch to reach the dog beside them so that fur could fly. Spike spoke to the receptionist and we took our seats. I handed the straight-jacketed racoon back to his owner and stretched my abused knee.

My trousers were irreparably shredded. My knee cap felt like it might be too. Nothing remained of the bruise inflicted the night before. Now the halfway bend of my leg was a miniature replica of Chip Peters' chest - a ragged and bloody crater, coloured by braking patterns of dirt.

"Is it bad?" Spike asked, seeing what I was looking at.

"Nah. Worse things happen at sea," I told him, thinking that a dose of salt water might be just the thing for that mess.

When he took his abused racoon in to see the vet, I checked my watch, made a quick mental calculation, pulled my phone out again, and dialled a number I hadn't used for a while. It was an English phone number. I didn't recognise the voice that answered, or the name he said. "Can I speak to Sergeant Steven Strong, please?"

"Sergeant? You mean Detective Sergeant Strong? This isn't his extension," the man grunted helpfully.

"Sounds like he's been promoted since I last called him. Moved into CID, has he?" I asked patiently.

"Yep."

"Okay. Could you put me through to him or give me his new number, please?"

"And who are you?" he asked.

"Hex Mallory. An old friend of his. If you look at the desk opposite where you're sitting, you'll find my name carved on the end."

There was a thump on the line as he dropped the handset. A moment later, it clunked and he came back on the line. "You used to work here?"

Now I was fed up. "Yes. Now, can I have your name and badge number, and Steven Strong's phone number? This is urgent."

"Alright, alright, keep your wig on." He grudgingly looked up Strong's new extension number and gave it to me.

I disconnected the call and tried again.

"Strong," mumbled a sleepy voice.

"Hey, babe. It's Hex."

"Hex!" He was instantly alert. "How are you?"

"Slightly singed but I can't complain. Yourself?"

"Singed?" I could almost hear him shaking his head. "I'm alright. Got into CID. That's thanks to you, that is. So, what trouble are you in now?"

"Do you think you could find out if Johnny Mack is still in jail?"

"Of course he's still in jail. He won't be up for parole anytime this century."

"I'm not thinking parole. He might have escaped."

"What? What have you heard?" His voice was taut.

"Nothing," I said, soothing. There was no point panicking him unnecessarily. If it was unnecessarily. "Call it paranoia, but please just check."

"Okay," he said at once. He knew enough about Johnny Mack not to need to be asked twice. "Give me your number. I'll call you back."

The private detective returned without his racoon or his jacket. "His leg's dislocated. They've sedated him, prior to popping it back. I can pick him up tomorrow. The veterinarian said he'll be sore for a week or so, but there's probably no permanent damage." The relief in his voice was palpable.

"I'm glad," I told him. We headed out to the car and I started wondering where Spike was going to go now. "What's Enzo going to say about his house?"

"Nothing. He's dead."

"Oh. Well, that's one less thing to worry about." What I was worrying about was what Steven Strong might be finding out in England. Then I realised Spike was driving me to destinations unknown, yet again. "Where are we going?"

"My place," he replied.

"We just blew up your place."

"No. That was Enzo's house, where I lived while I was at school. When I finished my tour with the army, I got myself a condo down in Culver City to give us both what Enzo called 'man space'. I moved back into the hills for Cadaver's sake. So we're going to the condo now. Are you still up for drinks? Coffee, at least. And I want to take a look at your knee."

Coffee? Oh, well, if, after all that Spike still wanted to offer me coffee, I would drink it without a murmur. "Are you sure? You might have figured out by now that I'm not in trouble so much as I *am* trouble."

"I think I can handle it. Or do you have anything else planned for tonight?"

"Hey, none of that was my fault. It's just that your venues are biased against me." Then my pocket vibrated. I yanked out the phone. The number displayed was Strong's new extension. "Hey, babe. What have you got?"

The detective sergeant was taking quick, panicked breaths. "He's out, Hex. Johnny Mack escaped yesterday. But we've got on to Customs. He won't get out of the country."

I said, "Too late, Steven. He's in California."

"Oh, fuck. He moves quickly. Has he contacted you?"

"No. Not unless you count blowing up a house as contacting me."

"How do you know it was him?"

"What would the message, 'this house will self-destruct in five seconds' suggest to you?"

"Shit."

"Quite."

"You'd better get on to the Los Angeles police."

"Actually, could you do it? I'm not flavour of the month at the LAPD. And it would sound more official coming from you. You know, get a rocket under them."

"Okay," Strong sighed. "I won't ask what you've done to upset your local bobbies. I don't want that trauma in my head. Please be careful. No. You don't know how. Just don't get killed, alright? Mack isn't your responsibility any more. Let the professionals deal with him."

"I will if I can," I promised. I returned the phone to my pocket and shoved my skull back into the head rest with both hands. Why would Johnny want to blow up Delphiki's house, especially the very day after he had escaped from a multiple life sentence stretch at her Majesty's pleasure? The fact that he had managed to get from London to Los Angeles, find Delphiki's house and rig it in such a ridiculous fashion in just two days didn't surprise me. Johnny's success had lain in his unpredictable behaviour, backed up by an organisational network that could put rockets on the moon at a moment's notice. Knowing that I was in LA, it wouldn't have cost him much trouble to find me.

But why destroy Spike's house? Had he anticipated that I would spot his handiwork and be the one inside when it went up? If he was trying to kill me, why had he set up his bomb with an audio countdown? The only explanation was that he was not trying to kill me.

Then what was he up to?

"Bad news?" Spike's voice penetrated through my hands.

I released my head. "Do you remember the guy I mentioned who killed John Mark? Johnny Mack."

"The guy who shot you?" he growled. "I remember."

"I'm afraid he just blew up your house."

He didn't reply to this piece of information. So I sat back and attempted to eff the ineffable: the inner workings of the mind of Johnny Mack.

My musings were interrupted by our arrival at the condo, and gladly so. Much to no one's surprise, I was getting nowhere in my head. The last time I had seen Johnny was at Christmas, when Burns and I had been in England spending the holiday with my family. As usual, I had been up to visit Johnny, and as usual, he had been cheerful and pleased to see me. We talked on the phone as frequently as either of us needed something from the other, and were generally as friendly as ex-lovers can be once they have shopped and shot each other.

Spike retrieved his gun from the glove box and put the shoulder holster back on while I fetched my rucksack from the back seat. He carried the weapon at the ready as we entered his condo. He need not have worried. All was peaceful and there was no sign of Mack. The door opened onto a front room that was sparsely but comfortably furnished. Instead of bookshelves, the walls were lined with gun cases. I let go of my rucksack as I dropped onto the sofa and surveyed the arsenal with an exhausted bewilderment. Spike moved into the kitchen area and returned with a green box that held a first aid kit and a bowl of hot water.

"Roll up your pants' leg," he instructed cheerfully, ignoring the fact that he had just introduced a strange woman to a room full of weaponry. But then it was me. And I was loving it.

I rolled up the remains of my trousers and gazed around the room as he gently cleaned the Hollywood hills out of my knee. It was like the best catalogues of my days as a rich man's wife. Every big name was represented: Heckler and Koch, Glock, Smith and Wesson ... Western pieces, European makes, they were all there, gleaming and ready for action behind the obligatory glass.

Spike broke into my reverie. "Does that hurt?"

"No."

"No? There must be some nerve damage. We should get a doctor to look at this." He dropped the stained piece of cotton wool and dipped another into the bowl of already muddy red water.

I dragged my eyes away from playing 'name that gun'. "What? No, it's fine."

"Fine?" He sat back on his heels and looked at me. "Okay, I guess someone ought to explain this to you. Bleeding is not the normal human condition. If you are bleeding, bruised, or otherwise battered, you are not 'fine'."

I laughed at him. "Yes, it hurts. Not enough to mention, but the nerves are fine - I mean, working." I leaned over to survey the clean wound for myself. It was just a deep and ragged graze. These things are never usually as bad as they feel. "That doesn't need a doctor," I told him in a tone laden with years of experience.

"If you're sure ..." He folded gauze and padding over the wound, taping it securely into place. "How's that?"

"Good as new. Thanks."

It took a few more minutes of glassy-eyed gun gazing before I realised that he hadn't let go of my leg. He was watching my face with his curiously intense expression. I leaned down and kissed him. He responded enthusiastically and in a few moments coffee had been entirely forgotten.

There was another case of guns in his bedroom but I didn't care. I freed him from his gun and holster, which he laid carefully on the bedside table, before I could peel off his t-shirt to reveal evidence that he did not spend all his time at a desk. He skinned me out of my vest and set to work on my underwear. I closed my eyes and explored his contoured muscles by touch.

Then I realised that his activities had halted. I looked down and saw that he was staring at my chest. And not in a good way. Following his gaze, I saw it rested on the black curling lines of the hell hound drawn over my heart. Was he really the kind of man that objected to women having tattoos on their chest?

"Spike?"

"You're one of them," he whispered huskily.

Then I understood. "No, I'm not. It's a long story but I promise you I'm not."

His smile was slow but broad. "Tell me later," he said, and got on with the task at hand.

Training

The departures board finally revealed the platform of my train and I got gingerly to my feet. The material of my clothes pulled across my chest as I swung my rucksack to my shoulder in a way I had never paid heed to before when it did not rub like sandpaper across the pain underneath. I hunched my shoulders forward to provide a little relief and pushed on, threading my way through the people on the station.

As I walked, I called to mind once again Neal Yardell's instructions: catch the 9:36 from Victoria, there will be a few others on the train.

At first, I had anticipated being able to spot them. We would look at each other and know we both belonged to some secret club. Through carefully chosen words and signs, we would converse about the task before us as the train carried all the normal people northwards with us. Soon enough, I had realised that they would look like normal people. There was no way of knowing who did what: who was a spy and who a suicide bomber; who was a childminder and who a paedophile; whose journey was routine and whose a beginning or an end. What was mine?

The train was packed, even though Yardie had deliberately chosen the first train after rush hour. It seemed that everyone else had had the same idea. I pushed through those who had taken up residence between the doors, already plugging in headphones and struggling to unfold their newspapers, and started to make my way up the train between the seats. Even though there was a distinct chill in the outside air, the train *was stuffy. Too many bodies packed in and too few seats. Struggling up the aisle, I stumbled from suitcase corner to pushchair, my clothing dragging more and more at the sore patch. I wouldn't normally mind the pain but it was reminding me about other pain that lay underneath, and it made me determined to get a seat and relieve the pressure.*

The train started to slide slowly out of the station. I paused and watched London gathering speed. It felt as though I was bidding my home goodbye at last. I had in fact done that a couple of weeks ago, but those weeks had been a blur of new faces and ideas, as I bounced from pillar to post around the city, making ready. There had been no time for farewells for my life, and I had wanted none.

The aisle kinked to the outside of the carriage and I knew I had come too far. Now I was in the first class section, and beyond that was only the driver's cab. I almost turned back, then remembered that there was sometimes a compartment at the beginning of the first class section that contained second class seats. Indeed, there was one. In it were five men. On the left, three men with short hair sat with their luggage on the rack above them. They were dressed like business men headed for a group fell walking expedition, kitted out with expensive waterproofs, self-drying trousers, and solid boots. On the right, a thin, slightly older man stared glumly out of the window, distanced from the compartment as though he were on the outside of the glass. Beside him sat a huge hairy monster of a man, his thick brown locks pulled back into a ponytail that spilled over the shoulder of an enormous winter overcoat. A duffel bag bulged across the rack above him, but beneath it one empty spot remained.

The member of the expeditionary force nearest the door saw me pause and stared icily through the glass at me, challenging me to walk on. I grasped the door handle and slid the door back.

"Is this seat taken?" I asked the big man quietly, pulling the door back into place as I did so.

"Doesn't look like it," he drawled in a slightly Southern American accent.

I sat thankfully, wrapping my arms around my rucksack on my knee, feeling the rough cloth drop forward from the painful spot. I let out a silent breath of relief and met the glare of the man opposite.

He was leaning towards me, unwelcoming to the point of menace. "We are going to discuss the war in the Middle East," he said in tones clear and cold. "Because we are going out there."

No fell walking? Shame. Was it that these men, all five of them, were the other mercenaries Yardie had put on this train, then? Even were this not so, I could do with learning everything I could about the war. I knew little about it, having been rather insular in Portsmouth recently. All I knew was I wanted to fight. "Suits me," I said, settling back coolly and trying not to wince as my top made contact again.

The man leaned further forward, resting his thick forearms solidly on his knees. "Perhaps you didn't understand me," he said. "Get out."

I glared at him, trying to think of some witty retort that would show them that not only was I not intimidated, but that I was one of them. I could slip Neal's name into a casual sentence to let them know who I was. I wished I had a horrific scar I could display to let them know that I was as hard as any of them. But I didn't. I didn't have any retort, so I just glared.

"Out," commanded the man.

"Ah, shut up, Worthing," said the bear of a man beside me, calmly. "It ain't like you're gonna start screwing your rifle together right here." He turned his head towards me and I saw that his front teeth were missing. "Just ignore the walking steroids. They get uppity 'cause they know they'll be takin' the orders tomorrow."

The man opposite me, Worthing, transferred his glare to the bear. "I don't think you ought to be saying things like that," he admonished in a low tone.

"Aw, get the stick out your be-hind. The kid don't know what I'm talkin' about."

I couldn't hide my smile. "I do, actually. I'm shipping out too."

Even the thin man at the window turned his head to look at me now. "No way," he said, shaking his head.

"No one cares for your opinion, Temple," said Worthing curtly, without even turning to look at him.

"Who are you?" was directed at me.

"Hex Mallory," I told him, knowing the name would mean no more to him than his did to me.

"You're a mercenary?" His face was as disbelieving as Temple's. Temple himself had gone back to staring listlessly out of the window.

"I am now," I replied, trying to keep the pride out of my voice, "I passed the Gambetta test."

"The what?" said Worthing, bursting my bubble.

But the bear man said, "Shit. Did yer? You shore as hell ain't no kid. Who did you serve with? Previous, I mean?" He waved his left hand explanatorily.

I skipped back an occupation, back to things anyone could be proud of, back to the time the new tattoo was to remind me of. Back then, at least one person thought I was worth saving, even if that person wasn't me. Walking the beat and handling dogs were the closest I had been to a military life. "The police."

Worthing sat back and laughed. His two companions beside him laughed too. "You've got no combat experience?" one of them asked.

"Not as such," I admitted.

"No matter," said the bear man imperiously, "she passed the Gambetta test. I shore as hell never did."

That shut them up. Even if they hadn't heard of the test, they knew when to respect the American's word. I wondered if he were the one they would be taking orders from tomorrow.

The silence lengthened and became more comfortable. After some time, and without opening comment, one of the expeditionary force produced a pack of cards. Ignoring Temple, they dealt me in. Chat developed, and I listened quietly, trying to pick up places and names, weaponry makes - learning templates for the sort of tales I would soon be telling myself.

The game ended, winning and losing of equal unimportance, probably, compared to the war ahead. As the cards went out again, somebody - I don't even think it was me - mooted dealing in the outcast at the window. After all, he was still in the compartment with us.

"Don't," growled Worthing, "Judas'll only try to cheat us."

"Use his right name," the bear man, whom the other called the Bombardier, admonished quietly. "We don't wanna confuse the kid."

Temple made no sign that he had heard any of this, and Worthing looked at me. "I call him Judas because he's a traitor," he said, the clear, cold tone resurfacing in his voice. "Nothing to do with Iscariot who never betrayed anyone."

"Who's Iscariot?" I asked, trying to turn the conversation away from the subject of Temple for whom I felt a little pity, probably because I didn't know why he was a pariah.

"Not who, what," said the Bombardier, standing up, filling entirely what little air space was left in the compartment. "Arms dealers. Crack the window, Temple, it's getting mighty hot in here." Temple obeyed and the Bombardier pushed the coat off his right shoulder. "Give me a hand, kid."

I tugged at his left coat sleeve, and as it slid down his thick, hairy arm, he caught the garment with a twist of his wrist, folded it, and shoved it up on to the rack with his duffel bag. Turned now so that his right side was towards me, I saw that his right arm was smooth, hairless and not quite matching his skin tone. It was prosthetic. He was going out to war with a prosthetic arm!

A trickle of sweat ran uncomfortably down my back, and although I had been wearing less to start with, being a native of these chilly shores, I decided to shed a layer too. I peeled off my close-fitting, black sweatshirt, rolled it, and stuffed it into the top of my rucksack. The instant cooling effect was a great relief to my chest scabs but I sat back to find all the men staring at me. I glanced down at myself, just to make sure that I hadn't accidentally skinned myself out of my vest as well, but I hadn't, and if there was blood soaking through it, it wasn't visible on the black cloth.

Temple was half out of his seat, barely containing a lunge across the compartment. "Where did you get that tattoo?" he demanded. For once no one shut him up.

"She's got both," Worthing reported, bobbing his head to check my left shoulder.

For a moment I had believed that they could see through my clothing to the latest addition to my body art, but then I realised what they were referring to. I touched my right deltoid, indicating the stylised red arrow. "These? It's from the pilgrimage. I walked the Pilgrim Road to Santiago de Compostella."

"When? Who with?" Temple barked, a crimson flush spreading ominously up his neck.

"On my own, about four or five years ago." I found myself getting annoyed. "My tattoos are my business." So I reckoned, if I could get into the police force with them.

"Your business!" gasped Temple, as though I had just set fire to a crucifix in a Catholic church. His tether broke and he burst across the tiny space, his hand closing around my throat.

I kicked out, cracking him in the groin with the shiny toe of my police boot. He stumbled back into Worthing's lap, who propelled him unceremoniously, head first, into his own seat. He wriggled round, puce, his hands clutching between his legs, and glared at us all.

Swallowing hard, I asked him angrily, "What did I do?"

He made no reply. I turned to the Bombardier, who had been the most friendly and forthcoming, but he was looking at Temple with a strange mixture of sympathy and disgust. It was left to Worthing to fill me in. "There was a group of them who did that walk years ago. They all got tattoos just like yours, but not in red. Temple's the only one left, now." He paused, then added, "And he betrayed them."

"It was a mistake!" came an agonised hiss from Temple.

"A mistake?" Worthing yelled at him. "You were a spy! You turn your CO over to the authorities in a trap you set for him, and call it a mistake?"

"I thought he'd done it," Temple groaned weakly, reading through the tattered script of an ancient argument. "I thought he'd ordered the massacre. All the available evidence pointed to war crimes. I made a mistake." He turned his face into the grimy material of the seat cover.

"Is that what made England great?" piped up one of the other Millets models, "I'm tho thorry, I made a mithtake!"

He was quoting John Cleese in an episode of 'Fawlty Towers', and I joined in the laughter. The atmosphere cleared as the temperature dropped, and soon all of us, barring Temple, who appeared to be sleeping now, were playing cards again.

Chapter 6

Despite sleeping in an unfamiliar bed, I woke bright and early as usual, raring to get outside. I lay still for a few minutes, watching the reflection of the gently billowing curtains in the glass of the gun cabinet, and listening to the small sounds of Spike's sleeping. It's against the rules to leave a man asleep unless he has a good reason to know you're coming back, like a ring. I leaned over him and his eyes opened at once.

"Good morning." He smiled sleepily.

I sat up and stretched.

"Are you okay?"

"I'm going for a run," I told him, extracting myself from the sheets. When he started to sit up, I added, "Don't get up."

He watched me locate my underwear. "I'll make us some breakfast."

Out in the living room, I found my rucksack and got out shorts and t-shirt. When you're me, which I usually am, it's useful to carry various items with you. My rucksack also contained: my work boots, toothbrush and paste, a pocket first aid kit, a roll of cash, a book and a miniature tool kit.

Peeling the bandage off my knee, I found that it was starting to heal well, so I left it bare to get some fresh air. I let myself out of Spike's condo and measured out a mile square, which I proceeded to run several directions at several speeds. The knee was working fine. When I was done with that, I ran through my usual Taekwondo exercises. All this takes a while, and by the time I was knocking on Spike's door, he opened it fully showered and dressed, releasing the aroma of fresh waffles. I took a much needed shower and joined him to eat.

He mopped up the last of his maple syrup. "So," he said, without further ado, "if you're not a Swooning Shadow, why do you have the black dog tattooed over your heart?"

The story was not so much long as slightly stupid. The rule is that you must always run to, never from, and one morning in the concourse of Victoria station, I had felt like I was running away. All the previous chapters of my adult life had their triumphs and corresponding tattoos, except my stretch in the police force. That had ended with the stabbing of my second dog, the perpetrator's hurried departure for casualty, and the gentle suggestion that I might be more suited to a career outside the force. Sergeant Strong's worst fears were confirmed as I slid straight into the employ of my fiancé, Johnny.

Now, although I wore his tattoo on my right thigh, I had left him too. In a few short hours, I would be quitting the country of my birth, with no guarantee of a safe return. I had taken my last moments of freedom to sprint into the first tattoo parlour I saw and ask for a dog. The resident artist had the black dog picture, which he had been given by someone else some years earlier, and that was how it happened.

"It wasn't all that long before I saw Bear without his shirt and realised that I was in the soup," I concluded. It was all right to talk about Bear, because that wasn't his real name, or even the name anyone else used for him. When he died, another man had emerged out of the underbrush to cut the tattooed skin off his chest because a shadow isn't mortal. I could talk about Bear, Orson, the Bombardier, because he wasn't a shadow.

He was dead.

Spike didn't say anything about it. He finished stacking the washing-up and changed the subject. "I was thinking, if this Mack guy is out to get you, you should stay here till we get it - him - cleared up. Okay? We'll go by your place and you can get some things together."

If Johnny could bomb Enzo's old house, then it seemed to me that he could just as easily bomb Spike's condo, but I didn't feel like arguing about it. The private detective collected his gun and an identical, clean jacket, and we drove across the city.

The door to my apartment swung open, revealing an interior just as I had left it, but I saw it now with new eyes, wondering what my private detective was seeing. These walls were not lined with bookshelves, but cardboard and pulp. Stacks of books were divided and supported by strips of cardboard stretched between floor and ceiling. The system works, provided you own nothing but pulp fiction. Only a couple of items of furniture were not made of cardboard - Burn's stereo unit, which stood empty and accusing, his TV table, which now supported a fish tank, and his sofa.

Delphiki perused my makeshift, vertical pulp shelving as I went in to the bedroom, dug out a holdall and shoved black garments into it. There was a lot of empty floor between the door and the bed.

Spike was running his finger down the soft and bent spines of my detective stories when I returned to the living room. "Hey, Enzo had a lot of these books. Gil had filled the front office of the English detective agency with detective novels, and Enzo had them all shipped over when we moved back here. I spent most of my high school years reading them. I guess they're all charcoal now."

That statement, calm and not accusatory, left me feeling slightly sick. "Have these ones," I told him. "They won't be good editions like yours but at least you'll still have the stories." I took one of the flat cardboard cartons resting behind the door and folded it up into a box.

"You sure?"

"Sure. I've got more books than are good for anyone." I started yanking books out of the stacks.

"You've got two sets of these," he suggested.

He was pointing at the Robert Crais novels which enjoyed pride of place on the one real shelf the apartment had come supplied with, floating above the sofa. I swallowed. "You can have the paperbacks. The hardbacks were John Mark's."

As I filled the box with the books he had been looking at, he drifted over to the murky fish tank. "Where are the fish?"

A pile of books slipped and tumbled to the ground around my feet. "You're a private detective. Surely you know that fish tanks aren't for keeping fish in."

Intrigued, he removed his jacket, and plunged a bare arm into the water. I gathered the books up, putting some into the box and shoving others back between the cardboard. By the time I had finished, he had dipped out two rings and my spare keys. "I thought you said the thieves had taken everything worth stealing."

"My wedding band from John Mark is brass, the other is Burns' frat ring. If they're already in, my spare keys do them no good and my laptop's too old to have much resale value."

"Laptop!" He stared at the fish tank, alarmed.

"Oh, no, that's in the bin. I'd better bring it too." I went into the kitchen area and pulled the plastic swing top bin out from under the counter. Removing the lid, I pulled out the liner bag and reached in underneath. Here was my laptop, quite safe, wrapped in another bin bag. "I wish you could hide and enjoy a bearskin, but I just couldn't figure out how."

Delphiki carried the box of books out to the car. As I threw my rucksack and holdall into the boot with it, I caught sight my watch. I was just going to make it to the gym on time if I sprinted.

"The gym?" exclaimed Spike. "You've already been running this morning. I know you're fit, but that's ridiculous."

Randy's Boxing Gym was not the sort of place Spike envisaged. It had remained one of the old-fashioned American gyms, equipped with punch bags and a ring, rather than machinery and personal trainers. Some progress had been made, however. It now offered kickboxing and Thai boxing to keep up with modern demands. Also, the punch bags were flanked by tattered notices reading: 'In the interests of hygiene, patrons are requested to wear gloves while using this equipment. If you must work bare knuckled, please rub the bag down afterward with the disinfectant wipes provided. The management take no responsibility for any nasty diseases caught by patrons trying to be macho.'

Some of John Paul's boys had brought me down and introduced me to Randy when it became apparent that I would be staying in LA for more than just a holiday. He had welcomed me, welcomed improving female patronage of the right kind, and now he needed me on Sundays for ladies' kickboxing heats. Taekwondo is strong on kicks, so it stood me in good stead, and I was doing quite well, almost making up in Randy's eyes for the occasions when I forgot myself and got disqualified for fighting dirty.

Spike dropped me and my rucksack off at Randy's and headed on to pick up Cadaver from the vet's. I made out quite well, then went on to the Juice Bar with some of the boys. The Juice Bar wasn't the sort of place that sold juice, not if it attracted boys from places like Randy's. It was a bar for juicers.

I pressed my battered knuckles against a cold beer and thought about Peters. Both of them. I thought back over all the stories I had made up to try to explain what was happening. I had missed something. I must have. There had to be something else to go on. No one could tie up all their loose ends so tidily. There had to be a lead, or at least somewhere to look for one. But my brain revved in neutral, not getting beyond the Chip-Wilson-Marie triangle. My gaze wandered around the bar, from boxing poster to protein shake advert. Suddenly, remembering Spike up to his elbow in my fish tank, I was seized by the urge to go fishing.

Getting to my feet, I spoke to the bartender and jumped up on to the bar. "Okay, meatheads, listen up! Chip Peters! Chip Peters, anyone?" My voice cut through the conversations around the room and everyone stopped talking to think for a moment. Most of the guys in the bar were vaguely familiar to me by sight. They worked out at Randy's, or similar establishments. John Paul's boys would be able to dig most of them up.

Conversations resumed. Chip Peters' name meant nothing to anyone in that room. It had been worth a try, I decided, twisting to drop off the bar. As I did so, I noticed a skinny man wearing a fading muscle shirt and tattoos. He was sitting in the corner by the window, drinking with two other men, watching me and sniggering.

I jumped down and strode over to him.

"What's so funny?"

The skinny man waved his beer around. "Nothin'. Just your asking about Chip Peters in here. This ain't his kind of place."

Pay dirt! "No? What is his kind of place?"

"Dunno. Just I've never seen him round here." He turned back to his two friends and laughed as though he had said something comical. I saw flecks of grey in his short hair and wondered what he was doing here.

"Where can I find Chip Peters?" I asked, putting aside for the moment that I could probably find him in the morgue's fridge.

The man turned back to me, his thin rat face sucking inwards sourly. "Didn't you hear? I don't know."

I shook myself and became patient. "Do you know where I can find someone who would know where to find Peters?"

He ignored me.

"Hey!"

"Okay. Jeez. I guess you might find some guys … Oh, I dunno." He sniggered again.

Shaking myself wasn't enough. I grabbed double fists of his shirt and swung him off his chair. His beer skittered across the table and smashed damply on the floor. At once several sweaty, muscled arms pulled me back. It's impossible to pick a fight in a room full of pumped up pacifists.

"Whoa! I didn't know it was so important to you," the man said, picking himself up without offers of help from anyone else.

I freed myself from the grip of three men and told him, "I think he has something that belongs to me."

The self-made bouncers watched me warily as they returned to their seats. Again, interrupted conversations picked up. None of these proceedings were particularly unusual. My antagonist rubbed his stubbled chin meditatively. I leaned forward, attempting to menace him into speech, which is hard when you're shorter and lighter than everyone else in the room. Eventually, under cover of everyone else's chatters, he spoke quietly. "There's a dealer operates out by Jaywalker's. He'll know how to get hold of him."

"Thank you," I said curtly. As I walked away, the bartender decided it was safe to nip in and clean up the broken glass. I beckoned to him. "Get this guy another beer, please." I handed him a few bucks.

He took them and shook his head at me. "If you have to pick fights like a guy, at least you settle them like a gentleman."

I took my leave and caught a bus back into Hollywood. Jaywalker's was a night club popular with movie industry types. Mostly the rich ones. The Gambetta name had been efficacious there on crowded nights past, when the Dangerous Visions gang wanted to go clubbing in style for a change. During the day, however, the place was deader than Chip Peters. I dumped my rucksack down on the pavement and strolled up and down the darkened facade. This was a scene out of one of the detective novels I had given Delphiki, the hero going down to meet a criminal source on a street corner, and it was stupid. I had no idea who I was looking for, and how I was going to tackle them.

A black Mercedes slowed and drew up to the curb near me. The tinted window slid silently down to reveal a dark shaven head, balanced by designer stubble. A hand bearing a heavy gold ring beckoned, reflecting the sun from his gold chain. "You walkin' or workin', baby?"

I glanced around and caught sight of myself in the blacked-out window of the night club behind me. The barely bruised eye that Spike had blown out of proportion yesterday had faded entirely, and as Randy insisted on full padding, nothing else had taken its place. My usual black outfit wasn't revealing and I was surely too buff to look desperate in any sort of way. However, there was no one else on the pavement. The man was talking to me. "It's a bit early in the day, isn't it?" I went over to the car, staying a door's width away. "I'm looking for someone."

"You want someone at Jaywalker's, you better come back when they're open," the man said, settling back into his seat and reaching for the stick.

"I was told I could find a dealer here," I told him desultorily, turning back to my bag.

"Who told you that?" he barked after me.

"Some guy in a bar."

He jerked his head at the car's interior. "Get in."

Grabbing my rucksack, I hopped into the back seat. The black Mercedes roared away from the closed night club, turned off the main drag, and blocked round before my driver deigned to speak to me.

"I wanna see some money before you see any gear. What you wantin'?"

I dug into my pocket and slipped some notes off the roll there. "I'm actually wanting information."

"Ah, that's a valuable commodity these days." He turned right and began to block round again.

I flipped the notes on to the passenger seat beside him. "The guy in the bar told me that you could help me find Chip Peters."

"Some people talk too much." He poked his fingers into his shirt at the stomach, scratching in an obvious manner, which plucked the material of the shirt upward to display the black butt of a gun.

"Ain't that the truth. But Peters has something that belongs to me, and I want it back."

He craned his head round to look at the woman who didn't care about his gun, and leered, revealing a tooth that matched his chain. "I ain't seen Chip in days."

I was getting somewhere. "Where would you see him, if you did?"

The car pulled back on to the main road. "I see him all sorts of places. His place is up this-a ways."

"Where?"

"You stick with me, baby. I'll take you all the way."

Chapter 7

My phone vibrated silently in my pocket as I stood on the pavement of a residential street in north Hollywood. The black Mercedes had roared away in a cloud of fumes as soon as my foot had touched the road, the driver clutching a wad of notes. The number on the phone's display was Spike's mobile.

"Hey, babe. Where are you?" I said cheerfully, looking around at the quiet houses as I spoke.

"In the parking lot outside Randy's Boxing Gym, where I've just been informed that you left hours ago. Where on God's green earth are you?"

"I'm outside Chip Peters' house."

"Where?" I gave him the address. "Now stay there. I'll be over ASAP. Don't do anything stupid. Just don't do anything." He was beginning to sound like Steven Strong.

"Bring some food with you," I said quickly before he could hang up. "It's only the beer that's keeping me from starvation. Something meaty, with plenty of calories."

Yet again, Spike Delphiki broke the one hour rule and parked up by the curb. "Here you go, Hex," he said, clambering out, hampered by a fast food bag, stained with grease. "Something meaty, with plenty of calories, in a sesame bun."

We sat side by side on the curb, munching on burgers with everything the chain provided squeezed between the buns, and huge portions of chips. Remembering my penchant for hot chocolate, he had brought me a chocolate milkshake big enough to swim in. However, it didn't take me very long to polish it all off, and, feeling much better, I preceded to explain how I came to be sitting on that particular curb.

"So, some dealer who was cruising for a hooker and carrying a gun tells you to get in his car, and you do?"

That was how it had happened. "Yeah."

He didn't make further comment.

"So, are we going to call Stocker?"

He chewed his last chip thoughtfully. "We will," he said slowly. "When we've finished."

We mopped our greasy fingers, dumped all the wrappings back in the car, and made our way up the garden path. "How's Cadaver?" I asked as Spike rang the bell.

"He's okay. A bit stiff and sore. Didn't think much of spending the night at the veterinary hospital, but he'll be quite recovered in week. I've shut him in the office for the moment." Spike thumped impatiently on the door with his fist.

"We know the guy's not in, Spike."

He flashed a grin at me and reached into his jacket. From a slim leather case, he produced a shiny lock pick, and set to work. Within moments, we were inside.

Two doors opened off the hall before it kinked at a right angle, the left into a kitchen and the right into a sitting room. Spike went left and I went right. There was no white bear skin laid before the hearth or spread over the back of the old and tattered sofa. I plunged into the kitchen. Spike had yanked on a pair of latex gloves and was sorting through papers that lay on a side cabinet. There was no fur, but another doorway beyond the dining table. The far room was a small study, furnished with a desk supporting a computer, a filing cabinet, and an armchair, but no polar bear fur. I cut back through to the hallway, following it round to find three bedrooms, two bathrooms, and no fur.

I stood in the final bathroom and saw my anguished face in the mirror. "It's not here!" I howled.

"Hex!" Spike called from the kitchen, not seeming to have noticed my frantic search, "Bring your devious little brain in here."

Shaking myself, I gave up on the bearskin in this house and went back to the kitchen. "At last, a man who wants me for my mind!"

The detective produced another pair of latex gloves from his jacket pocket and handed them to me. "Look everywhere that you would hide something. Anything you find might be the thing we're looking for." He didn't insult my intelligence by telling me how to conduct the search - to replace everything exactly as I found it. I had been a copper and a criminal. At the same time.

The next couple of hours were spent flipping through books in the shelves, shifting every piece of furniture out and back, yanking up the carpets, hauling clothes out of the closet to check the pockets, and so on. Delphiki was systematically working through the rooms, checking likely things that weren't hidden, and searching the obvious places where people normally hide things: inside the attic, in air vents, in the bottom or on the top shelf of closets. We needed to find out who Chip Peters was and why someone might want to kill him.

One of the books I shook out was a yearbook from Charlottesville High. A page displayed what appeared to be the same photograph twice, side by side. Holding the book up to the light, it became clear that one of the boys pictured was wearing a blue shirt and the other was dressed in green. The caption of the left hand photo read: 'Chip/Billy Peters'. The caption of the right hand photo read: 'Billy/Chip Peters'. We weren't the only ones to have problems telling the Peters twins apart.

I worked the place like a sniffer dog and turned up nothing. It was Spike who found the drugs. They were in the filing cabinet in the study. "What do you reckon?" Spike asked, holding up a small bag of white powder. I shrugged. Dogs might be able to identify powders by smell but they had never taught me how. He put the packet back. "That explains why your dealer knew him."

"You didn't say that the tox screen came back with anything," I remembered.

"It didn't." He frowned. "Guess he hadn't taken a hit for a while."

"Or he wasn't the one using it. If both Peters were working together, then both of them made use of this house. Maybe the living brother is the one with the habit. Both have been living as Wilson, so both could have been living as Chip."

Spike rubbed the crease between his eyebrows with a latexed knuckle. "This is all just speculation. It's all very well finding more clues, but we just don't know which brother they apply to. We need to know who's who to figure out what's going on here."

"Great, but how?"

He smiled and started peeling off his gloves. "Thank God for reunion websites."

We left the other Peters' place just as we had found it, and climbed into the car for the drive to Watts and Delphiki's office. The time I had spent idling on the pavement outside the house had not been entirely wasted and I filled Spike in on what I had been thinking. "It's not me they're trying to fit up. It's you. You know those scenarios I was making up? Guess what I forgot?"

"What?"

"Your business card. There are a couple of possible reasons for them visiting you, okay. One, Wilson doesn't know about Chip, but suspects something's odd, so everything he told you is true. Eliminated, because both men saw Marie often enough for her to think that one man had two marks, and Wilson doesn't go on business trips every other day, so he had know about it. So, two, they're working together and they want you involved. They spin something about an affair to give you a job but you turn it down."

"Why would they want me involved?" Spike asked.

"Not sure. Two possible reasons I thought of. What's your reputation like?"

He smiled deprecatingly. "I don't exactly make headlines."

"Okay, so they're not waving bait under your nose in the hope that you'd put all the non-existent pieces together and solve whatever they're messed up in before it catches up with them, Sherlock Holmes style."

"Which I didn't."

"No, it wasn't possible. So, two, they want you tangled up in their mess. Maybe you should be writing out a list of enemies."

"Just the ones in L.A.?"

The great detectives' think tank was just another suite in an anonymous office building. It was sandwiched between a recruitment agency on the first floor and a psychiatrist on the third. The outer office was clean and business-like, but struck me as odd, even as I entered. The walls were decorated for the most part with framed prints of stills from Manga films. A coffee machine stood dormant on top of a locked metal cupboard. A large desk stood opposite the door so that its occupant would face visitors, but it wasn't a receptionist's workspace. The surface of the desk was entirely bare, but it was pitted and chipped, and no amount of polishing had removed the brown stain that spread from the middle of the far edge. There was no chair, just a few more holes in the plaster beyond where it would have stood. It didn't take much imagination to realise that I was looking at the scene of Enzo Watts' death. He had been ripped to shreds by a gunman in the doorway as he sat at his desk.

Above his desk, where every visitor would see it, hung a framed and faded printout, embellished around the edge with hand drawn swirls.

It read:

House Rules

1. *Don't ask about Delphiki.*
2. *If you're going to do it, do it right.*
3. *If you're going to do it, don't get caught.*

"I guess asking why I shouldn't ask about Delphiki is asking about Delphiki," I observed.

"It's okay," Spike said. "The Delphiki in question was Jude, my father. I've been thinking about updating Enzo's rules, but he distilled them over thirty years of experience and I don't think I could better them. Now people often think Delphiki was the victim of this." He nodded at the desk. "When they think at all."

"You told me Enzo was dead."

"They shot him while I was out. But we always left comprehensive paper trails when we were working on separate cases, so it didn't take me long to track the men down." His jaw clamped, his eyes telescoping into the pain of the past.

"How old were you?" I asked quietly.

"Twenty-four. It was a long time ago."

A thought struck me. "Your father, mother and godfather died violently? You and I are right up there with Miss Marple,

Hercule Poirot and Jessica Fletcher - everywhere we go, people drop dead."

Spike tried not to find that funny, and failed. "Hey, it's a living."

To change the morbid subject, he took another key from his ring and opened the inner door. A limping racoon hurled itself out, swerving around Spike's leg. Spotting me, Cadaver veered sharply and leapt up on to the cabinets to sit, curled and angry, alongside the coffee machine.

"Guess chucking a 'coon out of a window doesn't make me his favourite person."

"He'll get over it," Spike said, unconcerned. "He's not one to hold a grudge."

The inner office was in use. A keyboard, mouse, and flat screen monitor trailed wires down to a CPU tower under the desk which was angled so that, when the inner door was open, the outer one could be seen without standing up. A telephone was the only other item given permanent desk space. Filing cabinets lined the opposite wall, apart from the last unit, which was an industrial, fireproof safe.

The far wall held a bookcase stacked with books of law and procedure. Spike walked over to it and removed a copy of Yellow Pages. He riffled through the pages and laid the book open on the desk. "Look at these."

I cast my eye over the entries for private investigators, until I saw the listing for Watts and Delphiki. 'Watts and Delphiki. Private Investigations', it read, exactly like the card I had found in dead Peters' wallet. Instead of Spike's name, it gave the office address but the same phone number. That was all.

"Compare that to the other listings. If you were picking a detective to bate with an unfaithful partner job, who would you chose?"

The other listings, those that were adverts rather than single names and addresses, contained phrases like, 'matrimonial matters' and 'infidelity investigations'. They didn't make Watts and Delphiki look especially attractive. "So you're buying the idea that they're fitting you up?"

"Somebody is out to involve me in some way," Spike said. "Perhaps they chose an agency who did not advertise matrimonial issues in the hope that I would turn the job down. I'd better call Stocker now." He seated himself at his desk and fired up the computer. Then he produced yet another key, a small one, and unlocked the top desk drawer. He brought out a card index and found Stocker's card, but when he dialled the number, he obviously didn't get Stocker. Even Delphiki's favourite homicide detective took time off.

"Could you give him a message, please? Tell him I have an address for a residence of Chip Peters, and if he wants it, to give me a call. Delphiki." He spelled it out, then rang off. "I thought it best not to involve you at this stage, although you'll get the credit for the find if there's any going." Not that I cared. He pulled the computer's keyboard towards him and connected to the Internet. "See?" he said, clicking through links so quickly that I couldn't follow his navigation. "I wasn't wasting time this morning either. Our men attended Charlottesville High, and several old students from their year have signed up to this website." Click. A welter of information downloaded itself and flowed down the screen. He got up and turned the screen towards me so that I could see Virginia addresses and phone numbers. While I squinted at it, not seeing how this was going to help, he closed the Yellow Pages and returned it to its place on the shelf.

The private detective settled himself on the edge of his desk. "I could call them up, but basically there's no point. If I want results, I'll have to go down there, sit in their front rooms, drink lemonade and keep them talking till they say, 'Yeah, I still remember the time old Chip fell off his skateboard and broke his arm'."

Okay, I thought. *Makes sense.*

"I don't want to go to Virginia," said Spike flatly.

There might be a million reasons why not. I ran through some of them. Perhaps he had driving violations in the state. Perhaps he had left last time being told that if he ever set foot over state lines again, bad things would happen. Maybe he believed that aliens had promised to end the world if a Delphiki ever returned to Virginia. Maybe the water there made him sick. Perhaps he had an irrational hatred of Virginians. Possibly he was afraid of flying. I gave up. "Why not?"

He looked up at me, those tar pit eyes threatening to suck me in and never let me go. "I love you."

Steady on!

He continued, "I've known you less than a week. It's too soon to go away and leave you."

"You're not leaving me permanently. You'd only be gone a couple of days," I said lamely.

"In the short time I have known you, I have seen more convoluted and concentrated trouble than ever before. If I go away for a few days, I'd probably return to find you involved in a plot to assassinate the president."

I laughed. "I've never assassinated a president before."

"For Pete's sake, don't start now!" He reached out, pinched a wrinkle of trouser leg and pulled me close to him. "Seriously. It took Jude, my father, five years to admit to himself and Gil that he loved her. If he had realised how little time they were going to have together, he wouldn't have wasted so much of it. I always told Enzo that when I met the right woman, I wouldn't waste any time."

I put my arm around his shoulder and stroked his neck, wondering what to say. I'm not into wasting time either, but surely finding out about Peters wasn't exactly wasting it.

"But I guess I'm not going to find your bearskin sitting here." His arm squeezed my waist as he voiced my own thoughts. "I'll get a plane out tomorrow morning and get back here ASAP. And you'll go to work and keep your head down. I've got a good idea."

"What?"

"Let's go home."

Chapter 8

"Turn here," Spike nodded to the right.

The click of the indicator told me that I'd found the right control for the first time that morning. I had been expecting the wipers to start. An unfamiliar car seems to have ten thousand wiper controls and no lights. I'd been checking the mirrors constantly, so I hardly needed to look again as the car began to change lanes, but suspicion is a great teacher. A symbol of a plane emblazoned a sign ahead of us. "Er, Spike. Airport's that way."

"I want to get you a gift before I go."

We turned off the highway and followed the slip road down towards a shopping centre. Spike pointed over to the right again and we entered the car park of a long, low building of metal and glass. Despite looking naked and glaring in the California sunlight, it was strangely impossible to peer inside and see the merchandise, which I could attempt even while reversing, because LA parking lots are so much bigger than any car park in London. Climbing out, I read the drippingly hand-painted sign, hung jauntily over the entrance way, as though the new building had taken the place of a Mom and Pop shack, and felt unwieldy and embarrassed, lurking like a goon in the space.

"MacHone's Military Machines. Western Weaponry and Contemporary Collections for the Discerning Warrior."

Spike was watching my face for signs of approval. Satisfied that he had taken me to the right place, he offered his arm, and we promenaded into the mother of all weapons shops.

From the first foot beyond the security gates, racks of gleaming metal were loaded in every direction. "It's a wet dream," I muttered, awed by the sight of more potential violence than I had ever seen in one space.

"It's the best stocked gun store in LA," Spike informed me proudly. "Right MacHone?"

Off to our right was a long white counter, behind which one skinny man leaned, resting plaid-shirted elbows on the counter top. The grey-haired man winked at him.

"Choose yourself something you like," Spike instructed expansively.

He had to be checking in for his flight in less than an hour. I turned on the spot, bewildered by the sheer variety of goodies. Then, through a glass door at the back, I spotted it. Breaking from Spike, I charged out into a back lot containing not one, not two, but three (count 'em) Sherman tanks.

"Sorry, but we don't have the parking space for one of those," Spike said from the doorway. "Perhaps you should choose something that will fit in the trunk of the car."

Reluctantly, I returned inside, only to see half of the shop that had been out of sight from the entrance. It was jammed with guns from the Old West. Moments later, I was playing with guns made by the hands of men who were now only brand names.

"How about something a little smaller for the feminine hand?" suggested MacHone, approaching quietly in worn cowboy boots, something black and microscopic on his palm. "This would easily fit in a purse."

"Do you see a purse?" I demanded, swinging a Colt revolver around my finger as though I could slot it back into a holster strapped somewhere down my thigh. "There's small and then there's ridiculous." MacHone was not offended but I realised that I'd better hurry up if Spike was going to catch his plane. "I'll take a SIG Sauer P238 with an ankle holster," I said decisively, knowing I could do much worse than have one of those handy. And I like the SIG aesthetic.

"A woman who knows her own mind about weaponry," said MacHone to Spike as he collected the gun and went behind the counter to wrap it up. "She's a keeper, Delphiki."

"I know it," Spike said proudly, reaching for the bag as though he could read my mind and knew exactly what I was going to do the second I got my hands on it. He had a plane to catch.

He turned me towards the door. "Don't I have to fill a form in or something? I haven't actually owned a gun in California before." I glanced over my shoulder and saw MacHone studiously straightening magazines in a rack behind the counter.

"Who paid for this gun?" Spike asked. "Who's carrying it?"

Before I could worry that he was going to withhold the gift, we stepped out through the automatic doors and added, "If you want to go the whole legal hog, you'll never get to use it. MacHone's covered because I'm licensed, but you're a foreigner, so it might get complicated. I'll see about getting it worked out when I get back, but I want you to have it for now." He was thinking of Johnny Mack.

That killed it slightly for me, so I just sat and drove while he outlined what I needed to feed Cadaver while he was away. Surely he didn't think that a handgun was an adequate substitute for himself? When I felt I needed a gun, I had simply borrowed one from John Paul, as I had cars. Now I was driving Spike's car, with a gun he had bought for me. Even as I tried to feel annoyed, I found that I wasn't. He didn't want to go off and leave me at this juncture, so he was trying to cover me in every way he could, handing over all of his life for and to my protection. He was my insurance, giving me a home, transport and a weapon, and I was his, looking after his pet and his house. Spike was making us a part of each other even as we were parted. Which, as he had only known me for six fun-filled days, was remarkably stupid. No, not stupid - trusting. A shiver ran down my spine as I realised that I was sitting next to a man strong enough to trust a woman like me. I kissed him goodbye with gusto.

"Oh, look at the poor boy. He hates it!"

"Shove off, Roly." I vocalised Martin's feelings as Roly sat on the floor, holding his ribs, howling at our new man's attempts at breakdancing. It was the Dangerous Visions crew's morning 'Jump Start', an invention of Tom and Burns designed to break the ice and get everybody warmed up at the beginning of the day. It was a much better idea than meetings and pep talks, and I had rather enjoyed learning to dance, even if military man Martin found it more than a little humiliating. "I remember the first time you tried a head spin," I reminded the stunt driver.

"I don't," Roly laughed, pushing his fringe back to reveal a whiter patch at his hairline where a minor concussion had left a permanent scar.

Crash narrowly avoided Martin's whirling legs as the big man spun out of control and skidded on to his reddening face. He stood beside me, evaluating his performance critically, even though Martin would not be doing anything dangerous on film. "I came by for breakfast this morning," he said quietly, "but you weren't there."

"No." For a moment I estimated what time Crash would have been knocking on my empty apartment's door, wondering exactly where I had been at that point. On the freeway? In MacHone's Military Machines, drooling over tanks? He knew that I ran often in the mornings and would have waited in case I was out late. He would know that I hadn't been there at all and would want to know more than just my specific location. He would want to know why. To avoid a drawn out discussion, I said simply, "I was in Culver City. Getting laid."

Conflicting emotions wrinkled his brow as he tried to accept that I had to move on eventually. Eventually, perhaps, but not yet. I turned away to avoid the disappointment that won out, and went to check on Cadaver. I had decided that I couldn't leave the racoon shut up in the condo all day, so I had found a climbing rope in the bottom of one of the gun cases and lashed Cadaver up in a makeshift harness. Now he was secured to a suitably sturdy strut supporting the scenery.

The next time Crash spoke to me, an hour or so later, he was obliged to do so by the policemen who were looking for me. Detective Stocker, flanked by Officer Pike, approached carefully thorough the tangle of wires and equipment. Tom called my attention to them and stalked off.

"Morning, gentlemen." I straightened myself up from where I had been crouching beside a Gordian knot of wires that Martin was convinced would become attached to a computer. I couldn't see it myself, but it was something to do while the star I was doubling for fluffed her lines and giggled hysterically.

"Ms Gambetta." Stocker didn't seemed terribly pleased to see me, even though he was the one looking me up. "Your name came up this morning. In another context, apparently, but nothing is ever as it seems, is it?"

"Johnny Mack?"

"I want you to tell me that this has absolutely nothing to do with the murder of Peters. And I want you to tell me the truth."

"As far as I know, it does have nothing to do with it. Mack only escaped on Friday."

"Yet again, apparently, he has already announced his presence by doing a demolition job on a certain private detective's house." Stocker was not convinced of some part of the tale.

"Who did you speak to in England?" I asked. "Have they sent you his file? I helped put him in jail and I think he's after me now he's out. That it coincides with my discovery of Peters in his death throws is unfortunate."

"For whom?" Stocker asked darkly, ignoring my questions. "Me, I think. And perhaps Delphiki. He's not answering his phone."

I understood his bewilderment. Delphiki had often reiterated that he could be reached at any time, and if they had done much work together, then Stocker would have experienced the truth of that. "He's probably still in the air," I replied.

"In the air?"

"Yes. He's on his way to Virginia in an attempt to sort out which Peters is which."

Stocker nodded calmly. "We've notified the state police who have been asking questions but making no headway. If anyone can get the information out of those people, it's Delphiki. We can leave the identity of the victim in his hands, Pike, and concentrate on figuring out who killed him and how." Then he spoke to me again. "If you have your finger on Delphiki's whereabouts, then maybe you can tell me the address of Chip Peters' house. He left a message for me yesterday." He grinned apologetically, not expecting me to answer.

I told him the address.

Pike wrote it down while Stocker stared at me. "Should I ask how you know that?"

"No. What do you mean, how Peters was killed?'."

"Dying men don't just appear in alleyways," Stocker said heavily, hitching the knees of his trousers and lowering himself towards a box. "Can I sit here? Somebody attacked him somehow, somewhere close by, and dumped him there.

But we've had crime scene investigators crawling all over the whole block and they've come up with nothing. Not even a good theory. We don't know what Peters was attacked with, or where, or how he was dumped before he died. We don't know how you found him either, but we'll ignore that phenomenon for the time-being."

Pike smiled at me. "The science people tried reconstructing it on the computer. You know, one of those 3D things. But it's got them stumped."

"Why?"

"Well, there are no tracks. The body wasn't dragged in, so it must have been two guys carrying him, but they've left no footprints, even though the guy must have been bleeding all over the place. And they can't have moved him far or he would have died before you found him." Pike was getting very enthusiastic. My rudimentary knowledge of crime scene forensics, gleaned from the Scene of Crime Officers of my home force, had saved me from wrongful imprisonment after finding my first corpse. Since then, Pike had taken a close interest in such things. This had naturally brought him into contact with Stocker who championed the more modern, cerebral approach to policing that some detectives still regarded with a certain amount of suspicion, believing that there would never be a real substitute for spadework.

But Stocker was frowning. I wondered what information they intended to withhold. Did they have something that they hadn't told Delphiki?

"And the murder weapon was a blunt object, about this size," Pike motioned the diameter of a football with his hands, "but I guess you know that. They reckon it was a sledgehammer or something like that, and that would have made a huge amount of blood spatter, but like Stocker said, we found nothing."

"There had been cars, maybe trucks down that alley," Stocker said. "The CSIs can't be sure but suspect that he was dumped out of the back of a van. You didn't see it?"

"There was no van," I told him, certain of that.

"Maybe you just didn't notice it?" suggested Stocker.

"I'm a pedestrian. If a vehicle had crossed my path, I would have noticed it. I would have remembered too, once I found the long pig."

Both detective and officer cringed at my language, but I wasn't worried about offending these professionals, I was thinking about the alley. If he had not walked, was not carried, and was not driven into that alley, how did Peters come to die in there? Until we knew that, it didn't matter if Delphiki came home with definitive proof of who was still alive and guilty. We needed a method to make a case that would stand up in court. Eyeing the area of the studio we stood in, I paced out the length of the alley, turning and looking at bins and rubbish and the end wall in my mind's eye. The far end of the alleyway was blank, boxed in by the corner of the left-hand building that jutted out. The alley remained as a side entrance for deliveries to the restaurant.

Then I had a thought. "Do we know what live Peters was doing down the alley when I found him?"

"*We?*" Stocker repeated sceptically.

"Do you know? Because I don't. And are there fire escapes and stuff down the alley? I was preoccupied when I was down there."

Pike moved along my imaginary alley, squinting at the picture in his own brain. "Here, the fire escape came down, above the dumpster there. There were windows overlooking on this side." He pointed at gaps in the air.

"This is dumb," said Stocker. "You want to see the graphics the lab boys have done."

I didn't want to see graphics, I wanted to see cardboard. Gathering a box knife and some gaffer tape, we set to work, constructing a cardboard scale model of the alley. The three of us knelt there on the studio floor, cutting and sticking like school kids. We even attracted the interest of Edwin Harris, DV's set designer. We called him 'Headwind' because, tall and lanky, he always leaned a little forwards, his hair swept back, high stepping. His loose clothing flapped behind him as though he were pushing his way through a private gale. He stood over us for a few minutes, watching Pike reconstruct the crime scene with a tiny cardboard cadaver. When it was completed to the satisfaction of Stocker, who had collected all the dimensions in his head, we three sat back on our heels and contemplated our diorama.

"So," said Stocker, pointing with a pencil, "we've got blood here, some tyre marks here, and nothing else. Ms Gambetta says no vehicle, so how the hell did the corpse," he jabbed the cardboard cut-out viciously, "get there?"

Headwind's shadow moved across the light as he walked round us and viewed the miniature alley from the other side.

"This doesn't look like our sort of job, Bobby," he said. "Nothing on that blows up. And the storyline isn't our problem."

"It won't be our job if we can't sort the kinks out," I replied, deciding not to enlighten him as to the model's true purpose.

"We could drop him, I guess." Headwind crouched and peered over the cardboard wall, making a line of sight. "That'd make a good squelch."

"He didn't squelch," snapped Stocker, moving closer again to consider Headwind's idea.

The designer raised his eyebrows at me over the detective's head. He didn't want to work for Stocker, which was fine, because he was never going to. "Okay," he said slowly. "Don't drop him from so high and he won't squelch."

"That window." Stocker punched the side of the hole in the cardboard decisively. "He wouldn't squelch if you dropped him from there."

"What's the scale?" Headwind stood up, walking away as he asked the question.

We all stood. "That would be about eight feet," Stocker said after him.

He returned in a moment with one of the extendible A-frame ladders the lampies used for adjusting lights on the gantries. He set it up in the space that had been my imaginary alleyway. "That rung's eight feet, Bobby." He pointed, following our usual working protocols.

Although I was still wearing my work boots and not the trainers I always changed into for stunt work, unless my feet had to be in costume, I climbed the ladder. Headwind and Pike steadied it and I leaned back to fall from close to the horizontal, as a body posted out of a window would have. I dropped. Falling backwards onto bare floor is not the greatest of ideas, but I had done it before and knew how to avoid smacking my head and pulverising my brain. Actually, falling floppily, like an unconscious person, I caused myself very little damage. I did not squelch.

Chapter 9

As I've said already, when you hang around criminals, you get to know when something looks wrong. However, even an idiot would have noticed that my apartment door stood open. John Paul had a key, he owned the apartment, but no one else had access. There were scratches around the keyhole.

The rest of Monday had gone quietly, if you ignore the odd racoon-occasioned hiatus, and indeed, mess. He was behind the scenes, so the only thing that prevented the filming from going smoothly was our leading lady's inability to recall her lines and deliver them with a straight face. Every actor has this problem now and again, but that day only stern words from the director were enough to sober her. Still, we got through the day's work eventually, and Cadaver was given permission to return the following morning.

Spike rang in the evening, and actually indulged in some small talk, just to make sure that I hadn't got into any more messes since he flew out. Then he got down to business. "It was Chip with the damaged elbow. An elderly neighbour recalled the boys attempting to recreate the bicycle scene from ET, using her cat as the eponymous alien. The bike nose-dived, throwing Chip over the handle bars, breaking his elbow. The cat leapt clear and landed safely."

"So Chip's our dead dude. And Wilson is indeed the man to survive."

"Right, which begs the question, who died three years ago? There must have been a corpse for the coroner to sign off as Chip - Woodrow Peters. I've got on to the coroner's office and spoken to one of the medical examiners. I'm going to go in and look at their paperwork tomorrow. Hopefully I can get a plane home tomorrow night."

"What did Stocker say?" I wanted to know.

"I haven't spoken to him yet," Spike said. He had called me first. Well, Stocker could tell him about the method by which the body was dumped.

Pretty certain that he would veto the idea, I wanted to check my apartment before Spike got home on Tuesday. So I went over before work, only to find that someone had got there before me.

Silently, I entered. Somebody was talking in the hallway. It was a voice I recognised.

"So, Mr Scientist," came Stocker's voice mockingly from the vicinity of my bedroom, "tell me who lives in a house like this?"

Creeping closer, I could see another man with him. This man was a little taller than Stocker, and dressed in jeans and a sweatshirt. If he was a scientist, he was having time off. The man turned slowly, and I saw the side of his face, green eyes with a curiously inward expression, like a medium attempting to contact the recalcitrant dead. He was moving his head like a small section radar, viewing my bedroom from the doorway. He didn't swing round far enough to spot me.

"Obviously I can't make many definite statements at this stage," he said in official tones that clashed with his clothing, "but this is the home of your basic paranoid obsessive, and probably, judging by the interesting selection of books in this room and in those stacks in the living room, I wouldn't be overstepping my bounds to say that we're dealing with a psychotic personality here."

Fat head, I thought. Then decided to scare the pair of trespassing gits. Moving back into the kitchen, I could hear the psychologist man waffling on.

"A home this obsessively neat indicates someone who needs to keep their external world under tight control, which is a good indication of inner turmoil, of fear of life spinning out of control. This man is dangerous, and he knows it."

A home this obsessively neat indicates someone with very little clobber who has lived with John Mark. John Mark was the obsessive one, not me. He washed his Jeep every week, even if it had remained in the garage. He called it Self-Respect.

"Man?" Stocker queried. His voice was louder. They were heading back towards me, but I was ready.

Before the scientist could reply, I rattled the tea mugs loudly. "Milk and sugar, boys?"

"Jesus Christ!" the scientist yelled, jumping backwards.

Stocker stepped back nervously too, one hand on his gun, apologies pouring from his lips. "Sorry, Ms Gambetta. This is Dr Neil Clayton, a professor in criminal psychology from UCLA. We were just conducting an experiment in profiling. I mean, you must have realised that you're a suspect ..." His voice trailed off. His position, in my home without a warrant, was indefensible. He must be hoping that a Gambetta wasn't going to report him.

"Sit down," I told them, nodding at Burns' sofa, surprised to find at last that it was good for something. I carried the tray of tea things to the cardboard coffee table.

They sat side by side, awkwardly bolt upright, terrified to find themselves at the mercy of someone about whom they had just drawn such conclusions.

"How long have you been here?" Stocker asked, shamefaced, as he took his cup of tea, stirring sugar into it.

Long enough to make a pot of tea, but how long did that take?

"What I said," Dr Clayton began, "I didn't really have enough information. I was making sweeping generalisations based on what is open to view." He was trying to backpedal. "We didn't touch anything. But the continuation of the black and white colour scheme, coupled with the cleanliness, suggests a ..." he struggled for another word meaning 'obsessive', "focused personality."

I wondered what he would make of Spike's home. "You know nothing," I informed him calmly.

"No," he grabbed at the straw gratefully, almost babbling, "nothing. Nothing, at all." He was terrified by whatever he saw in this place. Had I accidentally left my collection of shrunken heads out again?

"I guess I'm a suspect because of my unfortunate habit of finding bodies," I suggested.

"Unfortunate," Stocker echoed, remembering my use of the word the day before.

Dr Clayton helped him out. "That and your reaction to what would be normally be a traumatic experience: watching a man die. And your ob- ... focused ... following of the case. A murderer will sometimes insert himself into the investigation of a case, often reporting the crime himself. As you say, you have found bodies before, which might help to explain your lack of reaction, but you haven't previously attempted to investigate the murder personally. Even the one you were arrested in connection with, you had a police officer do the work."

"Pike," I said. "And Mack turning up isn't going to help my case, especially as you only have my word for the fact that it was him who blew up Delphiki's place." Put this way, it wasn't looking good for me, again, despite the help that I had offered Stocker yesterday. I had made it worse for myself. I wished that Spike was back to put in a good word for me. The thought suddenly crossed my mind that this could all be some elaborate scheme of Johnny Mack's, designed to put me in jail as securely as I once put him in it. "I spent the whole evening before Delphiki's place blew up with Delphiki. He could alibi me. And the afternoon I'm covered for as well. I was working. I don't have an alibi for the time of the attack on Peters, because I was there, but I didn't have time to change. I wasn't blood spattered. Smeared, but not spattered."

Stocker nodded, thinking this over. "What about the sudden interest in this case?"

Time to come clean, I thought. It would come out eventually and it would look better if it came from me. "The white hairs on dead Peters' pants. Your computer thingy said they were polar bear fur."

Stocker nodded again, his brows knitting, attempting to pre-empt my admission.

"I had a polar bear fur but it was stolen two weeks ago. I want it back."

Before Stocker could respond, my mobile phone buzzed twice to indicate a text message. I pulled it out and saw Crash's call to work: "T - 1". I had one hour before I was needed for filming.

"Why didn't you report it?" Stocker asked.

"The skin was shipped into the country as a scientific specimen belonging to the British Arctic Survey."

"By John Paul?" Stocker said.

"No, by me. It really is authorised by the British Arctic Survey but it's more of a trophy than a scientific specimen. I figured that when the authorities found out what the taxidermy was really for, it might be confiscated."

Stocker sat back and drank his tea, calmer now that he was back on the familiar territory of being the one in the right. He put my possession of the fur to one side for the moment. "So you murdered Peters because he had stolen your polar bear."

"No. I didn't know he'd been anywhere near it. Not until Delphiki told me about the forensic report."

"You knew the address of Peters' house because you had a prior acquaintance," he continued, as though I hadn't spoken.

"No, I got that from a dealer I met outside Jaywalker's."

Stocker raised an eyebrow sceptically. "How do you know this dealer?"

"Some guy in a bar?" I knew how this was going to sound. I was beginning to think that I would not be spending this evening with Spike but in a police cell. He was not going to like coming home to this. "Think of the racoon," I pleaded.

The detective and the psychologist exchanged significant looks.

"Forget the racoon. I need to get to work." They couldn't arrest me there and then, in my home without a warrant. It would surely be inadmissible.

"Go ahead," Stocker directed. "We'll fix the door. But don't leave town."

It appeared that Tom was willing to speak to me again. He came over as I picked my way across the set, only five minutes late. Then he said, "I came by for breakfast this morning." He had only just missed Stocker and his tame psychologist. If he had been a little later, I might still be a step back from suspect.

I held up the end of Cadaver's rope leash. "I was racoon sitting."

"In Culver City?"

"Yes."

He handed over the bundle of clothes he was holding and I swapped them for Cadaver's lead. I stripped off my black and put the costume on over my sports underwear. I pulled the shirt down over my head to see Crash crouching beside the racoon, rubbing him behind the ears. Man and beast were connecting.

"Can you hold him while I get painted up?" Maybe Cadaver could bridge the rift caused by my opinion that death did us part.

Crash and Cadaver bonded happily for hours while I was made up and beaten up. The terrible trend for carrying the spoilt guinea pigs they called lap dogs, one of the entourage of our leading actress was carrying hers, was now being trumped by a wild animal, and Tom was feeling rather pleased with himself, striding around the studio with the racoon trotting happily in tow. He was amusing himself by chewing on cables whenever Tom had to stop and talk. I caught up with the pair of them at the catering van, eating sandwiches.

"Headwind tells me you were tendering for another job yesterday," Crash said, through a mouthful of ham salad. Cadaver had removed the bread from his and taken the mayonnaise-coated lettuce out.

"We won't get it," I lied readily. "The guy doesn't like my ideas."

Tom swallowed the gob of ham. "You should pass him on to me."

"I don't think he was really looking for our sort of thing anyway. Do you want a coffee?" The catering team had learnt my foibles, and I returned with a polystyrene cup of coffee and another of hot chocolate. Cadaver was licking mayonnaise off the ground rather than his lettuce. "Here," I told him, balancing my hot chocolate in the crook of my elbow to fish a cereal bar out of my pocket. He snagged it enthusiastically.

Tom crushed his sandwich wrapper. "Something about a body. A cop show, I guess." He took his coffee. He was still talking about Stocker's visit.

"Yeah, a cop show. But it's not going to work out. Headwind said himself that it wasn't our kind of job. Nothing goes bang, and thanks to Headwind, nothing goes squelch either."

"Damn the pair of you," Tom said cheerfully. "Come on, little 'coon, we've got a director to redirect."

"His name's Cadaver," I called after them.

"I don't want to know!" Crash chirped back.

Another peaceful day of car chases and being shot at, and I was done by mid-afternoon. Finding myself free to go reminded me of another occasion, about two years previously, when I had made Burns take me out for a drink instead of scurrying home to hide in his studio flat and watch sport on television. That day I had told him that I didn't fancy him, but if I did his face would only add to his mystique. It took another six months or so before I had realised I was lying. A week later, I had taken him to London (we were in England at that time), and introduced him to the bearskin. Burns was in the cold Californian ground now, but somebody other than God had to know where my polar bear fur was.

I extracted Cadaver from Tom and decided to take him to the beach so that I could have a swim. I didn't know whether racoons swam, but I wanted to get out of city for an hour or so, out of the place of John Mark's birth and Burns' death. Perhaps I could go fishing again.

Tuesday afternoon is not the busiest time on the beach. I didn't meet anyone to ask about Chip or Wilson Peters. Cadaver ran about on the sand, digging for shellfish, or something, and I swam lengths parallel to the beach. The Californian coastline is a statistically good spot for being eaten by sharks, but I had never yet seen one while swimming, although I did my best to look seal-like. Soon after my arrival in the States, John Paul and his family, wife and small son, John Luke, had taken me out in a glass-bottomed boat. We had been shown various sharks and other exotic sea life then, but it's not the same as encountering them with nothing between you apart from a swimsuit.

A habitual pedestrian, as I have said, I didn't feel like driving home. Dumping my wet swim things in the boot of Spike's car, I tied Cadaver back up in climbing rope knots and we hit the pavements. I could come back for Spike's car after we had had something to eat. We found a rundown diner whose staff didn't shriek at the sight of a racoon, which is technically worrying, and made a reasonable meal. Cadaver's leg was beginning to bother him, so I picked him up and tucked him under my arm when we left. Delphiki had been right: the racoon had forgiven me for jumping out of the window with him.

We were on the outskirts of Culver City, passing a post box, when it happened.

A black SUV with illegally tinted windows squealed into the road and slowed as it headed down towards us. As it got closer, it increased speed again and crossed the central reservation, making other drivers swerve. Horns blared and I was watching a scene like those we had just been filming. Cadaver's claws digging nervously into my arm as he hugged close to me, reminded me that this was real and not a movie. Swinging sideways, the black vehicle slowed again and the tinted windows started to slide silently downwards. I was going to see a drive-by shooting.

Time had slowed with the vehicle. The muzzles of guns appeared at the front and rear windows but that was all that I could see. I wasn't looking because I was held in fascination by the hypnotic eyes of the gun barrels levelled at me. I stood and looked death in the eyes, waiting for the blows I would feel even before I saw the flash at the muzzle and the ground that would hit me before I heard the reports. I could smell the metal and scorching, and if I had moved at all, I would have run straight for it. Out in the Middle East, we had run the guns, time and time again. One day, I would feel the kick of lead in my guts again. Or maybe I wouldn't even feel it.

The blow came at my legs like a rugby tackle. I was thrown to my back on the pavement. Cadaver was knocked from my grasp. We crashed to the ground behind the cover of the post box. The world cracked and ruptured, glass smashing in a deadly hail all around us. There was no pain, just noise.

Rubber squealed as the SUV powered across the road again. The last pieces of glass dropped from the shop windows and there was a moment's shock before people started screaming. My legs felt like a herd of elephants had taken up residence on them. I focused on the sky and took a deep breath before looking down to avoid fainting.

It was not a herd of elephants but one man lying across me. He had short, dark hair and was wearing a blue sport coat. He looked up.

"Miss me?" asked Spike Delphiki.

Cadaver jumped joyfully at his master's shoulder. I lay back in the glass, finally allowing myself to consider missing Spike. He picked himself up so I could follow suit, and we brushed the pieces of glass off each other.

"I got an early flight," said Spike, his fingers curling tightly around my belt as though it was the racoon's lead. "I thought you'd still be at work, so I got a taxi home. I see you walking down the road, so I get out, and the next thing I know somebody's trying to kill you. Again." He shook little bits of glass out of my hair. "Did you get the licence plate? I was too busy running. Which brings me to 'Lessons in Life, number two'. If someone is trying to shoot you, move out of the way."

I could sense it like the sulphurous wafts of the cracks of doom, that non-smell that highlighted a corpse like a neon sign. It hadn't been there when Enzo's house blew up - Johnny hadn't been trying to kill me - but now I had stared down the barrel of guns shooting to kill. If it had been Johnny Mack, then the house bomb must have been a warning shot, and now he wasn't working alone.

Soon after I had married Burns, someone had threatened me with a gun. It's another story entirely. (In fact, it's published by the same people.) But I still recalled the resentment I had felt when I first realised that being married again meant that I was no longer free to get myself killed.

Apparently I had got myself saddled with the same responsibility once more. My life was no longer my own but I didn't find myself resenting it. Instead I felt a profound sense of relief. Relief that he had returned.

"I missed you," I said, taking a deep breath, "like an amputated limb."

Spike bit his lip and swallowed a laugh. "That's not the most romantic sentiment I've ever heard, but from you, it's really quite sweet. You missed me, didn't you, boy?" Despite not having anyone holding the end of his leash, the racoon had been frightened by the shooting, as had everyone else on the street, and so had remained pressed against Spike's ankle. The tall man bent down and picked up the rodent with the hand not hanging on to me.

Two-tone sirens filled the air as completely as gun fire had a few minutes before. Those who didn't want to be questioned hurried on their way. The issue of whether it was Johnny or someone else a Gambetta had annoyed, which was possible, was soon answered. I had seen the licence plate and one of the patrol men called it in to the station. It was run through the computer while details were taken from witnesses. Johnny Mack had bought the SUV that very morning.

Spike Delphiki, Cadaver and I sat side by side in the detectives' room, being glared at by Stocker and an FBI agent in a trim black suit. She introduced herself as Sandra Bandidas and explained that big time bastards like Mack were federal cases as she flicked chestnut hair over her shoulder. Stocker was not impressed. He resented the feds as much as any other policeman, afraid that his toes were going to be trodden flat. No one was buying my assurances that the Peters case had nothing to do with Mack apart from timing. Stocker wanted to discuss whatever Delphiki had found out in Virginia, but Bandidas insisted on taking precedence, despite the fact that no one had been killed in her case, yet.

"Ms Gambetta," she said, "are you sure that you are the target? It was Delphiki's house that was bombed and you were not shot at until Delphiki had joined you on the sidewalk."

I wanted to slap her. How dare she raise a complication that made me feel so sick that I was glad I was already sitting down? Johnny had gunned down John Mark in a drive by. He could guess what I might do but he had learnt all those years ago that he could never be certain of how I would react. He could not be sure to plan what I would do when I saw that he had been in Enzo's house, if I was even there. The way that evening had been going, Spike could well have given up and taken me home, so I might not have been at the house at all. Believing that Mack was in jail on the other side of the Atlantic, I might not have spotted his handiwork. I might tie my brain up in knots trying to work out what Johnny was thinking. Why had he murdered John Mark? Was it because of me and was that a reason for him to attempt to kill Spike now?

Then I decided that Cadaver might as well be the target as he had been shut up in the house with the bomb and he had been in my arms on the pavement. I started laughing.

Bandidas glowered all the more and I could almost see Stocker filing this reaction away in his mind to tell his psychologist.

"Have you got the fax?" Delphiki asked Stocker.

"Fax?" Stocker hurried off to find out.

"It's the coroner's paperwork on the corpse formerly known as Chip Peters," Spike told me.

"And?"

Bandidas saw that she had been trumped for the moment, so pinched another chair from a desk that was currently unoccupied and settled herself down to find out a bit more about her case by observing Stocker's.

The detective returned, clutching a sheaf of fax sheets. "What have I got, Delphiki?"

"Chip Woodrow Peters died in a car crash three years ago," Spike said. "The medical examiner's report is the most interesting part. He had a distinguishing scar by which he was identified."

"On his elbow?" I interrupted.

"Yes, the one he got reconstructing ET."

Stocker nodded sagely. Spike must have filled him in after phoning me.

The private detective went on. "Further on in the notes, however, the doctor describes the body as part of the autopsy examination."

"Autopsy?" put in Stocker. "The car crash was suspicious?"

"It seems so," Spike replied. "You'll have to get the file from your counterparts in Virginia. They wouldn't give me the time of day. Which isl why I got back so soon." Stocker made a note in his book and Spike continued. "Behind the right knee of the victim was a mole."

"Shit!" I exclaimed. "That was Wilson! Marie Peters said Wilson had a scar and a mole, and she was right! So Wilson Peters died three years ago, Chip died last week, so who the hell is still alive?"

The Question

"Go ahead," said Sergeant Strong, "we'll not get anything useful out of him, so you might as well give that interview technique of yours a bit of practice." He handed the man over to me at the door of Interview Room Three. "I'll get us all some coffee." He winked at the man as I opened the door.

"No, I -" But he was gone.

The man winked at me, so I dragged him inside and settled down to the interview. Starting the tape and giving all the right information was simple, but figuring out what to ask next was another matter entirely. I hoped something would come to me before Strong joined us so that he could be confirmed in his opinion that there was a chance for me.

"Interview started at ten thirty-two. WPC Mallory presiding ..." awaiting the return of Sergeant Strong. "Could you state your name for the tape, please."

"Johnny Mack," he said obligingly.

We were pretty certain that 'Mack' was an alias, but his true name was still unknown and unfathomable. More able minds than mine had not wheedled it out of him, so I dismissed that as a possible line of questioning. The next request should be, "Where were you at ...?" but I already knew that he would have an answer. It didn't matter that everyone who had seen the mess on the river bank knew that Mack was responsible, he would have a watertight alibi ready to be investigated. If I asked him for details of his work or personal life, he could spin me a yarn as strong as a spider's web. He was a seething mass of answers just waiting to tumble out on any question I might ask.

Even coffee would come as a welcome relief to this dilemma. I glanced at the counter on the interview room's recorder, watching the seconds tick by. Johnny shifted in his seat, bright hazel gaze hovering over me like a hawk waiting to pounce. A small teasing smile played across his mobile mouth. He leaned back casually in his chair, knowing that he was armed and ready for any question I might have. The minutes slipped by and he flicked back chestnut hair from his forehead. The heavy, gold watch rattled on his wrist as he moved.

I coughed and tucked my feet under the chair, waiting for inspiration to strike. It did not. Chunks of silent time were preserved on the tape for the investigating team. Where the hell was Strong? Then I realised that the gentlemanly git was giving me a chance: a chance to shine, a chance to get something no one else had got before - anything useful out of Mack. Oh, pants.

I shuffled round again, stretching my legs out towards the door, desperation setting in. Mack mirrored my movements, stretching his long, chino-clad legs out, mimicking mine. I looked up at him and found his eyes waiting to catch mine, the teasing smile ready. Anything I could do, he could answer.

Time was lying as heavy as dust in the small room. Minutes lengthened, and the pressure got bored and wandered off. I could sit there forever, provided I wasn't expected to sit perfectly still. Waiting is not wasting.

Mack laced his fingers together and leaned forward across the table, prompting me towards starting the questioning. But if I didn't ask, what good would his ready replies be then? His wit could devastate mine but not if I didn't give him the opportunity. He rippled his eyebrows at me, the smile beginning to falter. He would be wondering what my game plan was, whether I was trying to trick him into showing his hand. That he had one, a strong one, I was certain.

He sat back again, running his fingertips into his immaculate hair. The smile had faded and a confused expression was directed at the ceiling. I began to realise that he was desperate to talk, desperate to show us, yet again, just how clever he was. He could anticipate everything the police might want to know, he could run rings around us before we even started walking. He had built a labyrinth for us lab rat bobbies and was just waiting for us to start exploring.

Half an hour or more passed in silence. The only sounds on the tape would be shuffling and coughing. Mack's were becoming more frequent. Now that I had a strategy, or non-strategy, I was perfectly calm. I could sit and watch him sweat for hours. He was pretty easy on the eye.

Then he sat upright. If I wasn't going to ask a question, he would. He could push me into talking. "Will you marry me?" He smiled.

"Yes," I said. "Interview terminated at eleven seventeen." I stood, clicking the recorder off. "You're free to go." I left the room before he could gather a reply.

"What is this, Mallory?"

I faced an irate DCI across the desk. "It's an interview tape. I'd guess it's the recording of my interview with Mack yesterday."

"Interview? Do you call that an interview?" He didn't want an answer. He wanted a rant. He had one, the upshot of which was that Strong and I were despatched to pick Mack up again and do it properly. Thanks to his attempt to give me my moment in the sun, Sergeant Strong was in as much trouble as I was.

We cruised round Mack's usual haunts until we caught up with him. We anticipated that he would not be best pleased to be dragged into the police station again and we were going to have a rough ride, but when we pulled up at the curb, I suggested that Strong let me do the talking. Perhaps deciding that I couldn't make things much worse just then, he let me.

I wound the window down. "Hey, Johnny. Remember me?"

He turned away from the men with him who laughed at us as Mack stooped to the car window. "Remember you? I asked you to marry me only yesterday, WPC Mallory. Good morning, Sergeant Strong."

Strong grunted, a little taken aback by Mack's reply as he had not heard the whole tape, if anybody had bothered listening to the complete forty-five minute silence.

"Listen," I went on, "I'm in some trouble over that interview. The guv's heartily dischuffed with me and I was wondering if you'd mind coming back with us for another chat. Turn the gas down under the hot water I'm in." I smiled *as ingratiatingly as I knew how, breathing gusts of a cologne I could guess was expensive.*

"I'm all yours, Mallory," he said, and dismissing the other men, he got into the back seat of the car entirely of his own free will. Without arrest, caution, or any other method of persuasion, we brought Mack in for a chat and got more information out him than ever before. It wasn't perfect by any means, but Johnny Mack was almost co-operating.

Chapter 10

It was left to Detective Stocker to answer that question. He got on the telephone and stayed there until the Charlottesville police force had sent all the relevant information to LA. Meanwhile, Federal Agent Sandra Bandidas got on my case and stayed there until she had rung all the relevant information about Johnny Mack out of me. It was hard work remembering exactly what I had, and had not, told the Hampshire Constabulary about Johnny and my involvement with him.

That the engagement had started as a joke was common knowledge. Quite how it had become serious, neither Johnny nor I could have told her. I had never been able to trust him, having to attach my warrant card to my thigh with surgical tape whenever I spent time with him to make sure he couldn't steal it. Things became easier when I left the force. By that time I was receiving money from him anyway and providing alibis for him on frequent occasions. He was also providing them for me but I wasn't about to tell Bandidas that.

For a long time I had really believed that I would marry him, but that trust never materialised, and eventually I knew we would have to call it quits. And we had. Johnny understood what my problem was and he accepted it with good grace, setting me up with Neal Yardell in London. Travelling abroad for over a year, that had been the last I had seen of Johnny until a rattle of gunfire had called me outside in time to see him drive away.

The Portsmouth police had been delighted to follow my lead into Johnny's world, not even hinting about pressing charges, in return for information that would lock Mack up and throw away the key. With him inside, they could give the whole city's force a fortnight's holiday. I sold him out, took him down, and when he saw the tactical unit creeping out of the shadows, he shot me.

If Bandidas saw the gaps in my story, she didn't call me on them. I had been no passive gangster's moll, all spit and no substance. As Johnny used to sing, misquoting the Pet Shop Boys who provided much of the soundtrack to his life, "I've got the brains, you've got the moves, let's make lots of trouble." And we did. That was what Johnny was interested in - not money, but trouble.

And now he was causing it in Los Angeles. This time, however, I did not have the inside track. I didn't know where he was and what he was doing, and I didn't know how to find out.

"Can we go home now?" Delphiki demanded.

They released us eventually, pinning us down to Delphiki's condo, but obliging us with a lift back to his car on the sea front. Perhaps they had hoped we would chat in the rear seat of the car but they didn't know us very well.

Spike, Cadaver and I climbed wearily into the blue sedan and watched Pike drive away in the black and white.

"Another routine day with Hex Gambetta," Spike sighed happily as he slipped behind the wheel.

I was relieved to strap myself in to the passenger seat. "I never thanked you for saving my life." One always feels obliged for such a service, but right now, released from the cop shop, the crime only inches away from being solved, I was genuinely thankful.

He managed to keep a straight face as he replied, "You'll have plenty of opportunity to thank me later."

"So Woodrow and Wilson Peters are both dead, but someone who looks exactly like them is still running around calling himself Wilson."

"What is that rather artistic rodent tattooed on your thigh?"

"Spike, will you please concentrate." I pulled the sheets back into place and tried to focus my mind.

"I was concentrating," he grumbled, sitting up.

"On the case. We've still got a bearskin to find." My stomach growled. "I need something to eat now. I bet you do too. This has been a very long day." I climbed out of bed and skinned into the kitchen to raid the fridge. "Do you fancy omelette?"

Spike had followed me out and leaned against the counter watching me blearily. "How do you switch off like that? I've had a traumatic day. We both nearly died this afternoon. Not to mention that fact that we spent several hours with the FBI, an experience I never intend to repeat. I should have stayed in Charlottesville with the extremely helpful and rather beautiful Dr Lacey Belcher."

He was trying to tease but I nearly dropped the omelette pan laughing. "Lacey Belcher! You couldn't make that up." Then it struck me: Woodrow and Wilson was a very 'pair' choice of names. You might well choose them for twins, if you were American, but you would be even more likely to choose them if you were trying to convince yourself that two was all there were. I got the pan back on the stove.

"What?" asked Spike, realising that Dr Lacey Belcher was forgotten.

"The Peters boys weren't twins. They were triplets. I guess their parents thought that three was one too many. Perhaps they had only been expecting twins, so they had to get rid of one. The living Peters was adopted."

Spike grabbed the telephone and dialled Stocker's number.

The living brother was already in custody when we got down to the police station, dressed and fortified by omelette and donuts grabbed on the way down. It had been clear from the moment that Wilson Peters' corpse was identified that the remaining Peters had to have been involved in the murder.

Stocker was looking very pleased with himself, having figured out who the survivor must be before we had telephoned. It was obvious really. "You'll never believe what his name is," he announced by way of a greeting.

"Peter," I said with sudden certainty.

Stocker looked at Spike. "How did she do that?"

Spike shrugged wearily. "She's a writer. She's got a thing about names. So, it's Peter Peters?"

"Peter Hilton," Stocker said. "His adoptive parents are Hiltons. No relation to the hoteliers. When he found out he was adopted, he conceived a resentment of the brothers that were kept. He managed to track down Chip, found out that Chip was in some sort of trouble, and used it as leverage to get to Wilson. The Charlottesville police were right to treat the car crash as suspicious. Chip and Hilton had been doubling as Wilson for the last three years. Until last week, when Hilton decided that it was time to end the arrangement and take full control of the only successful brother's life."

"And Marie Peters didn't notice," I said. "I know ER doctors are rushed off their feet, but that's ridiculous."

"Poor woman." Spike was slightly more sympathetic. "She had no reason to suppose that anything was amiss. Wilson had never told her he had one loser brother, let alone two."

"Can I speak to him?" I asked Stocker.

"Why?" he demanded suspiciously.

Spike interrupted, "How did Hilton kill Chip? Did you figure that bit out?"

Stocker nodded reluctantly. "Thanks to Ms Gambetta and her windswept friend. We think that Chip and Hilton were eating in the restaurant when Chip realised he was next on the hit list and tried to make a run for it out the back."

"Didn't the restaurant owners recognise the face?"

The detective grinned evilly. "The former restaurant owners. They weren't helping the cops with their enquiries because they were trying to cover up their fencing operation. The upstairs store rooms were full of stolen goods. So they denied all knowledge of the identical men who were having an early dinner last Tuesday. The back door was locked, so Chip ran up the stairs, hoping to find a fire escape. Hilton caught up with him, grabbed a piece of burglarising equipment, and smacked him in the solar plexus with it. Then he bundled the body out of the window. Whereupon it did not squelch."

"These stolen goods," I said. "Have you seized them?"

"You're thinking that an illegally imported fur was among these goods," Stocker said. "You're thinking that Chip stumbled over it in his attempt to escape."

"I'm thinking I'd like to ask these restaurant owners."

We were interrupted by Officer Pike. "Are you finished with Peter Hilton?" he asked Stocker. "Can we bag him and tag him?"

"Sure, go ahead," Stocker told him.

Pike headed off to the cells, muttering, "Mr Hilton, welcome to the Hotel California."

Then I was really annoyed. "Where's my fur, Stocker?"

Spike gripped my arm. My fists clenched convulsively. He hooked my belt and pulled me back against him as I felt all the self-control that Taekwondo had ever instilled in me slipping from my grasp. I bit my lip to stop me screaming out swear words and cursing the detective west of his next birthday. Blood started under my tooth.

Stocker crossed his arms over his chest, an unconscious response to my aggressive posture. "Now, this is interesting," he mocked quietly. "Clayton said that if you weren't lying about your reasons for following this case, then your attachment to the polar bear fur was pathological. What does it mean to you, Ms Gambetta?"

I opened my mouth, letting blood from my swelling lip dribble down my chin. I had nothing to say.

"You do understand that, when it's found, it will be tested to make sure that the hairs on Peters' pants leg came from the same fur, and then it will be confiscated."

Spike's arm wrapped across my shoulders, preventing the lunge that was only split seconds behind. "They haven't got it yet," he whispered hotly in my ear. "Let's go." He released me and we ran.

Activity shook me out of the paralytic strop. *Why doesn't Spike ask me the same questions Stocker did?* I wondered as we jumped into the car. But I already knew the answer: he didn't want to hear that I cared more about that fur than I did about him. *He knows this, and yet he'll help me find it. There's got to be something wrong with the man.*

The car roared across the city. "Okay," said my private detective, "the fur was in the restaurant store room when Chip Peters got killed last week, but it wasn't there by the time the cops got in sometime today, I'd guess. The restaurant guys received and passed on stolen goods, so we need to find the next link in their chain. Did they sell the stuff themselves or did they have someone else to do it?"

"We can't ask them 'cos Stocker's got them. Hopefully, they won't tell him." Who did I know who dealt in stolen goods? I pulled out my phone and dialled John Paul. Sidney answered, even though it was now the middle of the night. Sidney left my brother's side less often than his wife. I didn't bother apologising for the lateness of the hour. "Sid, who have we got on stolen goods? We're looking for a polar bear fur."

"What d'yer want one'a them for?" Sidney mumbled sleepily.

"It's been stolen from me."

"Hang on." Sidney dropped the phone and a minute later, picked it up again, sounding rather more vertical. "You've have a polar bear fur stolen from you? When?"

"Three weeks ago."

"Why didn't you tell me?"

Without answering his question, because I didn't have an answer, I gave him the address of the restaurant. "You know them?"

"Yeah. Low business. Nothing to do with us."

"Where does the stuff go from there?"

"Don't know off the top of my head. Have to ask the boys."

"So, go ask!"

"What, now?"

"Yes, bloody now." I was trying not to shout as even an American car is not big enough for that level of noise. "If we don't beat the cops on this, I'll ship you off to the Arctic to get me a new one with your bare hands."

"Okay, okay. I'll call you." He rang off. There was always some activity at John Paul's outfit, no matter the time of day or night. He would find someone to ask.

"Any luck?" Spike enquired.

"Not yet. He's going to ask."

"Can you call someone for me?" He gave me the number and I dialled.

"Yeah?" said a gravely voice.

"Hey. My name's Hex. I'm calling on behalf of Spike Delphiki," I said.

"He got a secretary that works nights?" the man chuckled through a lungful of cigarettes. "That a good job, baby?"

"Tell him I want a polar bear fur," Spike prompted.

I relayed the message.

"That so?" said the man curiously. "Don't he know I don't stock soft furnishings? It's all hardware, baby."

"He says it's all hardware, baby."

Spike smiled. "Ask him where I'd find one."

I did so. "He says to ask the dealer over at Jaywalker's. That's the guy I got Chip Peters' house from. We're going round in circles."

"Maybe not," said Spike. "We'll try."

I thanked the guy and rang off. "Who was that?"

He shrugged as best he could with both hands still on the wheel. "Can't a detective have sources?"

We cruised past Jaywalker's. This was the club's time of night and it was jumping. It was a couple of blocks further on that Spike found somewhere to park. We walked back in silence, each trying to figure out how we were going to find the man in the black Mercedes. The club queue wound back along the pavement and we walked up past it, along the section I'd paced on Sunday, waiting for the dealer to arrive.

"Evenin', Hex." The smart and beefy bouncer who had spotted me not only let in the Dangerous Visions crew, but worked out at Randy's. "Comin' in?"

"No, thanks, Irving. We're looking for a dealer."

"What for?" Irving was not impressed by this piece of intelligence. "We've got all sorts in here."

"Guy driving a black Mercedes. He cruises round here during the day, I think. Don't know what he does at night."

"I might remember," he said vaguely and turned back to the crowds pushing to get into the club.

"Oh, for Pete's sake!" I exclaimed.

Spike said, unnecessarily, "He wants money."

"He'll get a black eye," I said, shoving through the pressing people. "Irving, you fuckwit, tell me where that guy is!" I was yanked back by a handful of shirt.

"Calm down," Spike advised. "We'll find it. Between us, we could find anything in this city."

"You reckon." I was not convinced.

Spike produced some cash and waved it, the note between his hand and the bouncer's face. "The dealer."

Irving took the note. "He cruises all night too. You hang around long enough, he'll be by."

I snatched the money before he could pocket it. He protested and I said, "You want this back, meet me Sunday morning at Randy's."

"Huh. I ain't fuckin' stoopid."

Spike dragged me out of the queue. "Just stop it," he said, gripping my arm tightly. "You don't have to turn the city over with your bare hands."

"What other way is there to do it?" I pushed the money into his jacket pocket. "I want my fur back."

"I know, I know." He pulled me closer and held me until he felt me relax a little. "We just need to wait now."

"I can do waiting."

Spike moved me away from the bouncers and patrons of Jaywalker's, and we idled against the wall further down, looking like a commonplace couple loitering. And maybe, for those few minutes, we were.

Then we spotted the black Mercedes, cruising slowly passed the queue, a familiar, gold-filled face leering out of the lowered window. He waved his arm about, making sure that his watch caught the light. The sort of people that patronised Jaywalker's were not the sort to be impressed by this, but it served to advertise the man for what he was, and a couple of women, tottering on circus heels, made their way out of the line. The car slowed further and drew to the curb, the man nodding and gesturing to the women. There was another man in the car with him tonight, someone to drive and keep a look out.

The bouncer, Irving, was not seeing the car in an obvious manner, and after talking for a matter of moments, the dealer gave one of the women something and pointed her over to him. She ploughed a wiggling path towards Irving, who received what she carried in a sleight of hand that gave the lie to his earlier blunderings, and ceased to notice the Mercedes altogether.

More money changed hands at the car window, along with some other items. When the women were finished, the car cruised slowly onwards down the edge of the pavement, like an ice-cream van waiting for late children. Spike and I approached from the shadows.

The man frowned at me, recognising me at once as I was wearing almost exactly the same outfit as the last time he had seen me. "You workin' tonight?" he said.

"Sure, babe." Though why anyone would want to pick me up, I don't know. I went to the rear door of the car and opened it. Spike followed me.

"Hey! Don't want your pimp ridin' my ass," the man spoke over his shoulder to me through the back door. His driver revved the car's engine.

"You can believe I don't wanna ride your ass," Delphiki growled, "but we've got business to attend to here." He climbed in after me as I slid across the back seat, and found himself looking down the barrel of a Smith and Wesson.

"Get out, captain."

That didn't half piss me off. "Enough of the posturing, boys. I'm hunting my fur and you'd bloody well better know where it is."

"Say what?" chorused the dealer and his driver in unison.

Thick knuckles clunked on the glass of the windscreen as the passenger side window was still open. "Frankie, if you're going to shoot that guy, could you please do it away from Jaywalker's? We got the Olsen twins in tonight."

"Irving!" I yelled, swinging my torso through the space between the seats so that I was staring him straight in the shirt front, and Frankie the dealer was staring me straight in mine. The gun was squashed between my hip and the back of the seat. "Unless you can find my polar bear fur, get your dumb fucking face out of my life!"

Irving jerked back, not having noticed that it was me who had got into the car. Delphiki hauled me down into the rear seat so that if the gun went off it wouldn't take my leg with it. The driver accelerated nervously away from the curb, leaving an alarmed bouncer behind.

Frankie started laughing. "Jesus, woman! Who the hell are you?"

"Someone with no proper sense of caution," muttered Spike.

"I'm a deeply pissed off Hex Gambetta," I announced with spirit. "This is Spike Delphiki. We are looking for a polar bear fur, and if someone doesn't find it soon, someone is going to get hurt."

"Probably you," muttered Spike.

I yanked the hem of my vest out of my waistband. "This is not the gut of someone who cares."

He pressed the black cloth back down. "I know," he whispered. "I think I'm beginning to understand. Just give me a chance." His hand lingered at my waist and I clasped it with mine. This man was doing his best for both me and the fur.

Frankie twisted in his seat to see what we were up to. "Whose ride is this?" he demanded. "Are you two just out to mess up my night? Time is money, time is money."

"It is indeed," said Spike with some gravitas. "We are looking for a batch of stolen goods which were at a restaurant called 'Le Brut' last week. The restaurant was closed down by the police this morning but the goods in question were no longer on the premises. I was reliably informed that if I wanted an item like, say, a bearskin rug, you were the man to ask."

"Reliably informed?" scoffed Frankie. "There's a deal too much talking goin' on round here."

"Too much talkin' and not enough dealin'," muttered his driver sourly, turning yet another corner.

"Ah, so true," Frankie replied soulfully. "Time is money, and talk is money."

"An' shootin' the crap is money," I growled. "Stop bullshitting. If you know anything, tell us, and then we can pay you and get out of your hair." Spike squeezed my leg and I shut up.

"Okay, captain. What's yer name? Delphiki? Chip is the black market man. He calls himself a spiv. You know, real World War Two geek. I showed the crazy lady his place on Sunday."

"The skin's not there," Delphiki replied shortly.

"He don't keep his stuff there," Frankie jeered, as though that ought to be obvious.

"He keeps your stuff there," Spike said, thinking of the packet of white powder he had found in the filing cabinet. "And, oh yeah, he's dead."

"Shit! Chip Peters?" He seemed genuinely downcast.

"He was murdered in Le Brut by his brother last week. He was dumped in the side alley to drown in his own blood." Spike neglected to mention that this took a matter of moments.

"Shit! The dude owes me money." He was genuinely downcast but only because he was out of pocket.

"So, tell us where he stashes his stuff, and we might pay you for it."

"Dude," said Frankie, "I don' know. I was gonna tell you to get your rug from Chip."

Spike rolled his eyes. "You were right," he said to me, "we are going round in circles." He was literally correct because the driver swung the car back on to the road where Jaywalker's lurked. "Chip and Hilton were at the restaurant because Chip's bad business was selling on stolen goods, which included a white bear fur. They argued, Hilton killed Chip. Can you drop us off here, guys?"

Frankie nodded to the driver and we got out at the night club. To my surprise, we parted in a friendly fashion, even though no money had changed hands. We shook hands, then he made a few more deals with the queuing punters as we strolled back towards the car.

"What Frankie was saying is that Chip was operating the stolen goods line and just storing his stuff in the rooms over the restaurant?" I checked.

"Yup."

"So, how did the stuff manage to move once Chip was dead?" I knew the answer was obvious, but I was just too tired, and trying to think was like squinting at the bottom line of an optician's chart.

Spike must have been feeling the same way. "I'll tell you in the morning," he said, then glanced at his watch. "Later in the morning. Much later."

Chapter 11

A loud buzzing filled my head as my mobile phone tap danced on the bedside table. I groped for it groggily. Every muscle protested, having spent most of the night clenched in stress. I fumbled it on to the pillow beside my open mouth and managed to rub my eye clear enough to read it.

"T - 1" flashed on to the screen.

"Shit, fuck, bollocks, arse," I mumbled, too tired to swear properly. Bright sunshine flooded through the window, glaring back at me from the glass-fronted gun case. I pressed my nose back into the pillow and tried to forget that the world was happening.

A warm hand touched my shoulder gently. "What's up, love?" His thumb caressed tattooed flesh.

"Gotta go jump off somethin'," I groaned. Then I rolled over towards him. Sleep is not something that has a strong tyranny over me, and once I wake, I wake. I think sleeping in a war zone impresses that into you irreparably. I kissed him and dragged myself out of bed. "Bollocks."

Finding my shorts and t-shirt, I decided that running over to the studios would loosen me up for whatever torture our leading lady was too important to endure this morning.

"You've got time for breakfast?" Spike sat on the edge of the bed, shoving his legs into his jeans.

"I haven't got time to shower," I replied, lacing up my trainers. I pushed my clothing higgledy-piggledy into my rucksack and pulled its straps tight around my shoulders.

There was no point in showering now. I would be sweating again by the time I got to work in fifty-four minutes.

Cadaver leapt in as I threw the door open. He was having the most exciting week of his life, but today he would be staying at home. He clawed my leg by way of good morning and hopped on to the bed. Spike swept him off and caught me before I could get out of the door.

"Love you," he said, kissing me on the cheek. "Keep your head down and try not to get killed."

"Righto, boss."

I ran for it.

"Yuck," said Tom. "I am not going to be hugging you." He checked his watch and compared it to the clipboard in his hand. He took a bundle of clothes from under his arm. "You've got two minutes to get showered and changed into those." He scanned the floor around my feet. "No racoon today?"

" 'Fraid not. His owner's back in town."

He frowned, thinking he now knew why I was late this morning. Then he shook his head. "Get a wiggle on, Bobby. This is one hell of a busy day."

To oblige, I set off for the bathroom at a jog, then dropped to a walk, remembering that my Taekwondo master was expecting me this evening and I was already exhausted before I had even started work.

Diverting my route to the bathroom via the catering van seemed like the best way to make myself feel better, but the man handed me my food saying, "You look beat, Bobby."

Gee, thanks. "That Bombardier was right," I told him. "You wake up late, you wind up dead."

He was bemused but I amused myself by performing my favourite trick that I have learnt in my time as a stunt double: successfully eating a sandwich in the shower. Don't try this at home, kids.

The buzzing of my mobile phone ruined my fun, yet again. It was John Paul's number.

"Hey, babe."

"Hey, sorry it took so long," said Sidney. "The boss man was asleep and none of the boys on last night knew about the Le Brut business. But we're in business now. So, rumour has it that there was a whole bunch of stuff shipped out of Le Brut on Saturday night. Incidentally, rumour also has it that a house blew up in the Hollywood Hills on Saturday night but you wouldn't know anything about that, right?"

"That's irrelevant." It's not irrelevant, it's a hippopotamus.

"Hmm," said Sidney, sensibly disbelieving and professionally sizing up precisely how much hot water that was going to be for the Gambettas. "That's as maybe. Your problem is my third rumour of the day. Everybody's favourite corporate lawyer, Nick Jr, has been redecorating his office."

The masticated and slightly damp sandwich completed its journey down my gullet as a sickening lump. Nicholas Nicholas Jr handled John Paul's legitimate business account, and possibly his illegitimate one as well, but he was not so fond of me, regarding me as an uninsurable liability. "Please don't tell me that he's chosen an arctic theme."

"Okay, I won't," Sidney said in the quiet, neutral tones he uses when he knows John Paul is about to start throwing things.

"Could you have a little chat with him? You know, lawyer to lawyer," I pleaded hopefully, but I knew Sidney would not have rung me with this news if he could have been ringing a little later with my fur.

"Hex, you know that Nick Jr and I cannot be seen to relate professionally. Or unprofessionally," he added before I could suggest he accompany his little chat with a baseball bat.

"So, I'm on my own, then?"

"If it wasn't Nick Jr, I'd kill for you, you know that," Sidney said apologetically.

"Yeah, you'd kill for me, except that you won't. Well, I can do my own killing, thanks, Sid."

"Not Nick Jr, Hex," he said quickly. "You'd never get away with it, and old Mr Nicholas would make sure your last meal would be worms." He thought quickly. "I'm sure we could find another fur on the Internet somewhere. Gambex could import it through Alaska -"

"No, thanks, Sid. It's got to be that one. I'll think of some way of getting it off Nick Jr." I hung up before he could suggest any other second rate options. What was the point of some other bearskin?

A door squeaked, bringing me back to the fact that I was standing naked and dripping in the bathroom when Roly was supposed to be driving a car into me.

"Bobby!" Crash's voice echoed moistly around the modest right angle from the doorway. "If you're not out here and gorgeous in five seconds, I'm coming in after you."

A fit body is not supposed to sweat as much as an unfit one, but the best part of an hour later I was stinking again. Anxiety probably exacerbated what was mostly caused by being repeatedly trapped between a fake tree and a fake car bonnet, which was then set on fire. Following which, I had to throw myself down a fake mud slope.

Strapping the leather of my belt, I had my phone out of my rucksack before I'd got my vest back on. Real mud from the fake slope still clung beneath my fingernails, but I had more important things on my mind.

"Spike? Hey. Listen. I've found the bearskin."

"How? Where? Where are you? Don't do anything." There was a distant thump as though he had been lying back with his feet on the desk and, sitting bolt upright, had kicked something important to the floor.

"Chill, Winston. I'm still safely at work. John Paul's man, Sidney, finally got back to me. He thinks that one of the kids at Hatch and Nicholas has got it."

"Hatch and Nicholas is a law firm," said Spike, puzzled. "Why would they be receiving stolen goods?"

I disentangled the arm holding my phone from the inside of my vest. "They aren't. Not deliberately, at least. One of the partners has bought it as a rug."

"Great," said Spike. "I can tell you how he got it, anyway. Peter Hilton was still running free for days after Chip died, and since he had murdered him at the restaurant, it was a good idea to clear all the stolen stuff out the moment the police released the area. I spoke to Stocker again this morning and he told me that they've found the rest of the stash in a warehouse, the lease of which was among the paperwork found at Chip's house. But he also admitted that they hadn't tracked your polar bear down."

"God bless Nick Jr for that small mercy," I said.

"Nick Jr? He's the man with the fur?" Spike sounded suddenly hopeful. "You stay safely at work and I will go have a chat with Mr Nicholas Jr."

"You will? If you can get that fur off him, I will love you forever," I enthused.

"Hmm," he said, and rang off.

Oh, you bitch, I thought to myself. And headed off for another sandwich.

The day dragged on and on. I shoved food into myself at regular intervals, and eventually my abused muscles fell into some sort of rhythm, which carried me through to sometime after seven, at which juncture our hero decided that he needed to get some beauty sleep if he was going to hit the party circuit at some point that night. The director had nerve endings sticking out all over him like a hedgehog's quills, and everyone was walking on pins and needles, so Crash decided he was going to dismiss our crew as well, and blow the consequences. I caught a bus into Chinatown. It was the bus I regularly caught, so there was no danger of finding myself on the wrong street. My master put me through the wringer and sent me home with a wrenched elbow.

It was nearly ten o'clock when I let myself into Spike Delphiki's condo, over twelve hours since I had left, and I had not got into any trouble, apart from being sworn at by a director throwing an artistic tantrum. It wasn't my fault that the laws of nature prevented me falling at precisely the angle he wanted.

A waft of warm and edibly-scented air met me as I opened the door, producing a damp explosion from my taste buds, and reminding me of how much I stank. I dropped my rucksack and headed straight for the shower.

"Good evening," said Spike pointedly from the sofa.

"Evenin'. Starvin' and stinkin'," I replied. "I'll take mine in the shower, please."

"Yours is in the bedroom," he replied, trying not to smile.

This gave me pause and I realised I was being rude. I crossed the room and kissed him on the cheek, careful to keep the rest of my sweaty self off his clothes. "It smells delicious, Spike. I won't be a minute."

He stood, wrapping his arms around me, pulling me against him in a tight embrace.

I tried to struggle free. "Dude, I ming."

"I Ching?" He let me go. "There's something I want you to see before you do anything else. Even shower."

Wondering what could be so important, I allowed him to lead me into the bedroom.

And there it was, warm and white, yellowed teeth gurning in welcome.

"Fuckin' A!" I screamed. Yes, actually jumping up and punching the air. I grabbed the private eye. "Spike, you're a marvel!" I bit off my words before I gobbed out something that would offend him.

He returned my hug, then let me go to explore the fur minutely to make sure that all it was missing were the few hairs transferred onto Chip Peters' trousers. There were no blood stains, or even drops, no clod-hopping footprints from Nick Jr, nothing. I was so disgusting that I hardly dared touch it. After checking it over, I headed for the bathroom.

"How. Did. You. Do. It?" I asked between mouthfuls of a stupendously hot and delicious lasagne. Spike had no idea of the pitfalls of being an uncouth English woman eating with my Italian American family, and it was a great relief to be able to shovel at pasta that was not made to a family recipe that was imported on the Mayflower. And can you imagine eating at an Italian restaurant as a non-connoisseur member of a Mafia family? Only coffee annoys me more than traditional Italian cooking.

Spike sat and watched me eat with obvious pleasure. "Nick Jr and I have had some business in the past, so he was willing to see me. When I explained that his new bearskin rug was in fact Hex Gambetta's stolen bearskin, he was happy to hand it over."

"Nick Jr?" Gulp. Munch. Slobber. "It was never that easy."

He just smiled mysteriously and raised his eyebrows. "Told you I'd get it back."

"You did. Delphiki, you are one top bloke." I rubbed my mouth clean with the back of my hand. "What have you told Stocker?"

"We have a bearskin that was found in an office belonging to a partner of one of the biggest corporate law firms in the city of Los Angeles. I don't think the LAPD is going to have a lot to say about that."

Chapter 12

So that was that. Peters' murders were solved, my fairy bearskin had been found, and we all lived happily ever after.

Yeah, right.

A certain Mr Mack was still at large in the metropolis of angels, but at least he gave us one day off. Thursday was soup free, as far as my days go. They set me on fire a couple of times and that was about as exciting as it got. Friday, on the other hand, was the crappiest since the day the music died.

It started off fine. I got up, ran, and nothing was hurting, which is quite unusual these days. Spike made us a superb breakfast of pancakes the way only Americans can. There are certain things to be said for this country, quite apart from the men it turns out. He dropped me off at work where Crash and the director were as chilled as good lager. Roly lived up to his nickname and rolled cars when he was supposed to, for a change. Headwind set things up, Martin knocked them down, and our leading actors decided to be business-like instead of artistic.

When noon rolled around, the director declared lunch time. I rang Spike to see if he was free to join me at the diner where we had met to discuss the Peters case. He had picked up a missing persons job but was glad of a break. He came, we ate, and then it all went horribly wrong.

We left the diner hand-in-hand. The private detective had taken possession of my sticky little mitt even as he paid the check, and was wearing that contented smile of a man who has been fed and is feeling that all is right with the world. Eschewing the car, he determined to walk me back to my work before he went back to his. That was his first mistake, and you only need to make one.

The security guard had quickly learned not to argue with a Gambetta about who can be brought into the studios, so he did not quibble as a stranger accompanied me into the lot. For Hollywood, it was all looking pretty idyllic - no gophers scurrying back and forth, stained with rejected coffee, no prima donnas throwing hissy fits, just the gentle tones of a piano playing somewhere in the distance. That's what happens when the director's been smoking something and allows his minions a proper lunch break. Only the caterers were losing out, but they were enjoying a little sit down too at a bar, and weren't about to complain.

We strolled into the air conditioned shade. It looked very much as though I would have a few minutes to show Spike around my world before everybody reconvened for round two. The piano music increased in volume as I led the way through the piles of staging to our current set. There was some activity here and there. Film studios are never truly dead, but the tinkling of skilled fingers on the piano keys set a relaxed pace, and the base under-slaves who remained at work were astonished to be unhassled.

Spike and I stepped through a plywood wall into the house set. The music was quite loud now and I looked around for the piano. Even as I did so, the music abruptly ceased in the middle of a phrase.

"That's weird," said Spike.

There was a humming sound, like wind vibrating many wires. We looked up. An enormous, dark mass plummeted from above, a loose rope whipping back and forth above. Seeing Spike's movement out of the corner of my eye, I threw myself at the edge of the set. I skidded, the material of my trousers catching on gaffer taped marks. I kicked down and propelled myself over the edge.

With a multiple clangs like a collapsing belfry, the side of the object hit the top of the set wall, bouncing sideways towards us. Splinters of wood and ivory rained down ahead of the tumbling grand piano as it spun from the impact. There was a crunch and a yell, then a crumpling sound like a car going into a concrete wall.

"Spike!" A surprising quantity of dust had been lying around the set, and now all of it was spinning around me like a sandstorm, its soundtrack the fading jangle of broken piano wires. He had jumped - I had seen him.

"Spike!"

Then I heard the hacking cough of someone who had just swallowed a lot of sawdust. I bounced through the cloud and saw the familiar faded red of his t-shirt as he struggled out of his pinned jacket, caught under the crushed shoulder of the piano.

"You okay?" I grabbed him and he winced. I released him at once and he coughed again, the action making him groan. "Spike?"

"Hey!" came a cry from somewhere beyond the wrecked set, "anyone in there? Anyone hurt? What happened?"

"We're okay!" Spike yelled back. He suppressed another cough and tugged at his shoulder holster. "Help me get this off."

Stretching the elastic carefully, I twisted it round his left shoulder. He was holding his arm awkwardly. "Is it -?" I began.

He cut me off, the finger of his right hand to his lips. "Look," he whispered, jerking his chin at the splintered mess behind me.

Turning, I spotted it - a rope had been tied around the once grand piano to suspend it above the set and it now lay in loose coils across the split lid.

"Was that in the script?" he asked in a low voice, drawing his Glock from the holster in my hands.

I shook my head. Our film was no cartoonish comedy and this set was now a cartoonish tragedy. I was reminded of the fate of Eddie Valiant's brother in 'Roger Rabbit'.

"How do you get up there?" Spike pointed with his gun up into the shadows above the glare of the studio lights. High above us, in the outer darkness that was the roof of the studio, were the skeletal scaffoldings that held up the sky. It was from here that the piano had been dropped, and the perpetrator might yet lurk unnoticed, like the Phantom of the Opera.

"Over there." I shoved the holster under his trapped jacket and followed him around the shattered remains of the director's good day.

He charged up to the ladder, then paused and jerked his left arm. "Fuck it," he said to himself, shoving his gun into his belt. He grasped the rungs of the ladder strongly with his right hand and, jaws clench, commenced hauling himself upwards. I climbed after him with considerably greater ease.

"Who's up there?" rang out a voice from below. It was military man Martin.

"Bobby!" I yelled back, only just managing to use the right name.

"What the hell are you doing?" Martin bellowed.

Spike's breath was sucked raggedly through his teeth as he reached the top of the ladder. "Shit, this is high." He gripped the railing with his good hand and started forward.

I looked down. The scene below was blindingly illuminated by lights that should not have been on during the interval. People scurried like rats around the wreckage and copious swear words floated upwards on wafts of blue air. From this angle, the grand piano looked more like the Grand Canyon, cleft in two by the fall, and half of it hitched up on the back wall of the staging, it lay with legs splaying from underneath like a ballerina doing the splits. Hands grabbed at the free rope, gesturing as to its usage. This was sabotage of the most flamboyant kind.

"Here." Spike had located the fat knot that had held the piano suspended. The long end had been sawed through by a sharp knife. He didn't touch it but craned around to view it carefully.

There was no sign of anyone around. "What do you think?"

He straightened up and looked at me grimly. "I'm willing to hazard to a guess that this is the work of your friend Johnny Mack."

I nodded. I had been thinking the same thing. "Shall I call that FBI woman?"

The gantry had begun shaking under our feet as men scrambled up at both ends. Martin reached us first and I saw his trained eye note the gun at Delphiki's waist. "Bobby? What's going on?" His voice wobbled slightly as the gantry did.

"Nothin' much," I replied, with resigned gaiety. "Just another day on death row."

"Have you got Bandidas' number?" Spike asked from behind me. He had his phone out. "I left her card in my jacket."

Fetching out my own mobile, which was still unbroken, I dialled from memory and passed it over. It was better that he spoke to the fed while I calmed my colleagues down.

"Okay," said Martin, clinging to the railings on each side of him tightly enough to stop the blood flowing under his nails. "It seems that a grand piano has just fallen on the set."

"Did it fall," said Headwind jostling behind him, "or was it pushed?"

"Dude," I said, "I resent the insinuation."

Martin shoved back with an elbow, then steadied himself and nodded at Delphiki who was now engaged in a quiet but intense discussion on the phone. "Who's that guy?"

"A private investigator."

"And that weapon's licensed?"

"Of course," I asserted, although I wasn't actually certain how the law worked in cases like this.

"Is he calling the cops?"

"No, the feds."

"Ah. Okay." Martin seemed satisfied. "This is a crime scene. We should get down and leave it to the professionals." He turned in place, transferring his grip from one rail to the other.

Just then a despairing scream echoed up into the roof space.

Martin, the set designer and I exchanged significant glances.

"Get my lawyers!" howled the director.

"On second thoughts," said Headwind, "perhaps we should stay up here."

Martin and the others descended gingerly while I stayed on the gantry with Spike. Now that it was clear that the danger was over, he admitted that his arm, stuck heavily by the falling piano, was hurting badly. So much so, that he sat down and leaned back against the railing, his legs dangling. I crouched beside him and pulled the sleeve of his t-shirt up to reveal a purpling blunt force trauma that looked enough to have broken his humerus. I lifted his elbow and poked it from underneath, cursing Mack roundly under my breath.

"Cut that out," growled Spike. "I'll get a guy with a medical degree to jab his fingers in it, thank you."

Reluctantly I let his arm go, trying not to wonder if he would be able to climb down again. Then I stepped over him and sat down at his other side. My hand crept into his, and we waited for the feds.

They came, they saw, they asked stupid questions. Delphiki climbed down under his own steam, but with a burly agent assisting in case he flaked out and looked like falling off. His tanned face had paled to a delicate shade of green by this time so, having me to question, they sent him off to hospital to be patched up.

Bandidas had me carted down to the police station where they had requisitioned a space to work while they went through Stocker's file on the Peters brothers, and everything else I had been involved in. Mack's files had been copied over from England and Bandidas seemed determined to comb through every fact in them with me, even if it took us the rest of the month. Spike was pretty lucky to have been clipped by the piano.

It was all old and sticky ground, yet they made me rake it all up. Answering every question very slowly was the only way to avoid making a mistake. My time with Johnny had taught me some of the techniques of having an answer for everything but I did not have his quick wit to back it up. I majored on the things I could reveal without incriminating myself, talking about our lasting friendship and most of the things we chatted about when I visited him in jail. We finally got to the part Delphiki and I had played in the investigation of Peters' murder, and got stuck with the explanation of how I came to find the body. Outside 'The X-Files', the feds are not allowed to contemplate the para- (or just plain ab-) normal.

When they finally turned me loose, I was surprised to find that it was still light outside. The gloom of the room they had interrogated me in had led me to believe that a permanent twilight had consumed the world. But that was just the world of the feds. Outside, the sun was still shining and I headed home to Spike.

My phone rang. Extracting it from my pocket, I was confronted by a number I did not recognise, although the area code declared it to be a city landline.

"Hello?"

"Hello, Mink," said a smug and well known voice.

"Hey, Johnny." Irrationally, I was as pleased to hear from him as usual. "How's tricks?"

"Fine, fine," he said airily. "And how are you, my darling?"

"'Rather warm but not at all astonished. What are you up to?"

He chuckled pleasantly in my ear. "Well, my dear, not so long ago you wouldn't need it spelt out for you, but you've been dropped on your head a few times since then. So, in words of one syllable, if you don't leave Delphiki, I'll kill you both."

"Oh, come on," I exclaimed, "that's hardly fair."

"Was putting me in jail fair?" he demanded harshly.

"No, I should'a bloody killed you. As painfully as I know how." I was gripping the mobile so hard that it was crushing my ear.

"Why didn't you?" His voice was gentle once more, as though he was sure that the answer was good.

I ground my teeth, wishing that I had some valid excuse, like the spark of a decent police officer still living inside me. But I didn't. "I loved you."

"So it shouldn't be too difficult to leave Delphiki, then." He sounded distant now, as if he were walking away from me. "Not as difficult as attending his funeral." The line went dead.

Johnny might be bluffing, I thought wildly as I jabbed the phone back into my pocket, but can I take that chance? I remembered the bewilderment of digging my fingers into John Mark's blood-soaked jumper, trying to hold onto him, trying to figure out the right thing to say, what should be the last words a man hears on this earth. There had been something to say to John Mark, not a promise of revenge, but love, justice and heroism. I had known how to find Johnny then. But now, what could I do? I didn't have the right words for Spike.

I ran the rest of the way to the condo and arrived resolved. Spike was resting on his couch, his legs up, a book in his right hand, and a sling on the other arm.

He dropped the book and sat up as I burst in. "How were the feds?" he enquired cheerfully.

"Federal. Your arm?" I asked curtly.

"Not broken. The bone's bruised and I've torn a muscle, but it should be fine." His eyebrows pinched as he caught the expression on my face.

He got to his feet and I swept past him towards the bedroom, swinging my rucksack from my shoulder. Whirling through the room, I gathered my clothes from the drawers

Spike had assigned me and shoved them into my holdall. I lurched into the bathroom to nab my clobber from in there, then dumped the bags in the living room as I set about unplugging my laptop and packing it away.

Spike stood, leaning his hips against the kitchen counter, waiting, perhaps for some sort of explanation. When it was not forthcoming, he asked quietly, "What are you doing?"

I jammed the power pack into its pocket in the laptop case. "Leaving."

"Please. Don't."

I slid the computer into place and secured it, zipping the case around it. He left his place at the counter, and as I slipped the holdall strap over my head one way and the laptop bag's strap over my head the other, he returned. He was dragging something awkwardly in his good arm, leather and white fur spilling over and flopping around his legs.

"You forgot something," he said, his voice dry.

I looked up at him, my fairy bear cradled in his arm. "No. I didn't."

Hefting my rucksack with one hand, I opened the door with the other, and walked out into the Los Angeles night.

I caught a bus back to the dark, dusty desertion of the apartment John Paul had given me. Detective Stocker had been as good as his word and fixed the door. He hadn't even needed to change the lock. Apart from his entry, nothing else was out of place. Johnny Mack had not pursued me here.

Inside, I dropped my bags within inches of the door and stood looking around. The place had never looked so dismal.

The books were all coated in a thin layer of dust. Burns' sofa was dented where Stocker and his psychologist, Clayton, had sat. The tea things I had served them with were perched, washed and now dry on the draining board, while the tray remained on the cardboard coffee table, cup rings marring the shiny surface. The silence was heavy, unbroken by the gentle rustling of a racoon exploring.

I'm hungry, I told myself firmly, although my stomach tried to insist that it was feeling sick. The contents of the fridge had grown themselves a fur coat, so I dragged the bin over and dumped it all unceremoniously. The freezer compartment, however, did contain one lonely fish supper, so I bunged that in the microwave. Once I had finished eating, I was at a loss for something to do. Until I looked at my watch and realised that it was a Friday night. I caught the bus into Chinatown and headed for the Laughing Duck.

Part 2

Chapter 13

Guns don't kill people - I do. And right now, I was Interpol's weapon of choice.

I had wakened around noon on the Saturday and wished I hadn't. Everything that could be felt, hurt. Everything that didn't hurt appeared to have been fatally severed and sewn back on. I lay still and enjoyed overlapping waves of pain and nausea, an after-effect of the drugs they had given me. Doctors and nurses told me not to get excited, or even try to move, and demanded names of next of kin. I knew no one I wanted now. No one except the one I couldn't call. He would have come. And I couldn't allow that.

Soon enough, it was Monday and I had to give them Tom's work number so that they could call me in sick.

"Tell him I won't be in this week," I told the nurse who was helping me.

"Honey, you won't be in this month unless you work with voice recognition software," she said. Which was very encouraging.

An hour later, Tom arrived. The rest of the crew came in relays, as there wasn't much to do until the feds had cleared out of the studio and the mess was tidied up. Soon the doctor decided that I'd had enough fun for one day and turfed them all out. The next day, the Englishman came.

I was lying with my eyes closed, hoping I'd either fall asleep or that Johnny would contrive to bomb this hospital and me out of existence. The door opened and the eye that could did too, to see a greying, middle-aged man in a suit.

Beyond him was the rigid back of a military guard standing outside the door. He settled himself on the plastic chair near the head of the bed which had been Tom's throne the day before.

"So, no painkillers?" he commented, which was when I realised he was English. He arched expressive and doglike eyebrows.

The bodily pains were all that could distract me from the more serious, more internal, ones. I was going to hurt, whatever they did, but at least I could decide which pains I would feel. "I'm choosing my battles," I grunted through clenched teeth.

"Not anymore," he muttered, a grim smile curling the corners of his thin mouth. It dropped abruptly as he went on. "Let me introduce myself. My name is Bill Withers. Yours is currently Hex Gambetta. Yes?"

I grunted in the affirmative. My health insurance was on a company scheme but it was still registered under my official name. His seated proximity was making everything not wrapped in bandages itch. That is, not much.

"I'm a liaison officer for Interpol," he informed me.

"You've come for Mack?" I asked hopefully.

"I've come for you."

"I ain't going nowhere," I growled, almost incoherently.

"*Yet*. You have remarkable, animal-like, powers of recovery, Gambetta. Or perhaps I should call you Mallory." He paused significantly and his lip twitched again. "Or perhaps Mink."

Oh, shit.

"What do you want?"

"As soon as you have recovered sufficiently, you will be going straight to jail."

"I don't pass 'Go' and collect two hundred pounds?"

"You do not. You do, however, have a 'Get out of Jail Free card', should you choose to play it." His pale face blank, he settled himself back, hitching his trousers and rearranging his legs like an old gentleman, a mannerism which reminded me of Detective Stocker. "There is a narcotics cartel operating out of a private estate in Columbia which we would be delighted to close down. It is an international organisation, with strong connections in the British Isles, which is why my people are especially interested in it."

This was skipping tracks a little. I extracted my wobbly teeth from the shreds of my lip to ask, "What's it got to do with me?"

Withers made his mouth into a superior smile. "When I say 'close down', I mean wipe off the face of the planet. When official organisations, such as my own employers, find there is a need for such ... lamentable courses of action, they cannot, of course, be seen to be carrying out such actions themselves."

"Spare me the crap," I growled, my bruised windpipe seeming to swell as my blood pressure rose. "You want a wet worker. Black ops, as the Americans call it. Why me?"

"Because you're here," he replied calmly, "and because we have leverage on you."

"Do you now?" I closed my eye, suddenly feeling very tired. Jail sounded as relaxing as a spa. "Don't threaten me -"

I groped for his name, yanked my eye open and glared at him as much as you can with three-quarters of an eyebrow between both sides of your face. "... Withers. I don't respond very well to threats. If I do your dirty work, it will be because I want to." If jail appealed pleasantly at that moment, wiping narcos off the face of the planet was even more attractive.

Withers' smile revealed pointed, white teeth like a predator who knows his prey is cornered. "Think of it as a public service." He stood more suddenly than his frail frame suggested he could. "We will talk at greater length when you are stronger. And you will be stronger." He stalked out, leaving the guard behind at the door.

From that point, I had no other visitors. Anyone who may have come was turned away before they even reached my door. Withers came in every few days to make sure that I hadn't died of the biggest killer of strong people in hospitals - boredom.

It was pretty close at times. It was six weeks before I could hold a book open to read, so occasional members of the hospital staff took pity on me and would come in to read to me or just chat. But they were busy people and there are an awful lot of hours in the day when you're in pain. Whenever Withers came in, he would give me more details about the operation he had in mind for me. At first I thought he was just trying to tantalise me, to peak my interest, but later I realised that I was hearing the information as they got it. That explained why he was willing to wait for me to heal.

An advert had been placed in certain publications asking for men of the ex-military persuasion to engage as private security for a large residence in Columbia. Another man, whose identity Withers kept close to his chest, had applied for a position through this channel. I was to get in some other way, to act as a back-up. Once inside, we were to discover the organisation of the operation and convey the details of the set-up and the people involved back to our handler. When all the necessary information was collected, we would be let off our leashes. And that would be that.

It seemed simple enough to me. However, as a covert operation, this drugs bust was giving Withers a headache. He was responsible for making sure that everyone was caught in the net. If anybody escaped with information that would connect Interpol to what would necessarily end up as a massacre, then the manure would hit the air rotation device in a fashion that could not be entertained. Hence the need to nail down a woman who wasn't going anywhere.

Slowly, I was healing. Stitches came out, bandages were unwrapped and plaster came off. Physiotherapy unlocked my atrophied limbs and I threw myself as hard as I could into a training programme to recover my strength and movement. The doctor tried desperately to slow me down, but I was as thin as the actresses I had doubled for, and determined not to live that way. I don't like feeling that I might snap in a breeze.

It had occurred to me that Interpol were not the people who put together black operations but then Withers told me who he was liaising with: the Drugs Enforcement Administration. The other agent had been supplied by them. And let me just remind you that it was the Americans who coined the term I had used: Black Ops. I shoved fish and vegetables into myself, trying not to look any further ahead than giving a gang of narcos a good kicking. The best part was that I could not be getting further away from Johnny Mack if I had been on a plane to Japan. Drugs were the only illegality he had never been involved in. He saw them as a crutch for the weak and the stupid, those who could not see what was going on, or those who could and were too frightened or depressed to do anything about it. Johnny thought himself too intelligent and too daring to ever get involved with the traffic of fools.

Two and a half months trapped in one room, unless you count the en suite bathroom, was enough to drive the sanest person to the brink. I, however, had so much not to think about that avoiding it seemed to take all the time that was not required to retrain broken bones in Taekwando. I read the hospital library dry, and even watched a couple of films on television, and gradually, my strength was returning, internal and external. I was beating my body back into shape, now I had to decide on a training programme to restore the proper form of my mind.

Eventually, I determined to begin this account. An attempt at catharsis perhaps, or a fallback measure if my future took the turn it was heading for. There's nothing like a little jail time for getting another paperback novel bashed out and getting publishers interested, sadly. However, clutching a pencil in my thin and crabbed fist, I found that my handwriting, which had always been spidery, was now completely illegible. It took a little persuading to get Withers to provide me with a new laptop which he then checked every time he visited me to make sure that I was recording nothing about our 'liaison'. What I committed to paper in that fashion, you have already read. (Thank you very much.) This bit – Part 2 - is being thrashed out in a place I'm now rather fond of, but I won't tell you where because that would give some of the game away, and what sort of author wouldn't keep you in suspense when she could?

So ...

One day, Withers returned with the doctor in tow and Withers declared me fit to leave.

Chapter 14

The plane journey from LAX was a long one, and I wanted to slide down in my seat and put in some quality time with the trashy novel I'd picked up in the airport, but the old gentleman sat next to me had other ideas. His limbs seemed to object to the shape and size of the seating arrangements as much as mine did, and he provided me with a sudden vision of my future, one that had just begun. The last few years had rarely been free of aches and pains but at least I had known that they were overlapping rather than permanent. Now I was fairly sure that I would never be truly free of pain again. I waited for the knowledge to depress me, but it didn't. I had grown too used to living with injuries since I had taken the long walk across Spain, and the scar tissue that had developed on my heart was just as real, the nerves just as dead.

The DEA's agent was also on the plane. I could see the back of his buzz cut protruding above the other heads several rows further forward. It was the familiar sight of the man who had been guarding my door for the last couple of months but we had been forbidden to acknowledge one another before we made safe contact within the enemy's camp.

The old gent beside me peered through his spectacles at my book. "I wish I'd brought a story book," he said in a quavering voice. "They're much easier to concentrate on in crowded places." His eyes, made piggy by the lenses of his glasses, searched my face hopefully. His expression closed as he began to realise that the marks were neither shadows nor badly applied make-up, but scarring.

I sighed and tried to adjust my seat so that I might be a little more comfortable. I was not a dead mass of scar tissue. Try as I might to be otherwise, I needed to prove to myself, and this man, that I was still a living being. I engaged in conversation. "What are you reading?" I enquired in a friendly fashion.

He held up the front cover of a geological text. "I'm retired now, of course, but I like to keep up-to-date with my field."

"Seismology, vulcanology, mining?" I enquired, knowing a little about the wide range of geological expertise from my brushes with the workings of one of the companies John Mark had left me.

"Mining," he said, smiling with pleasure at my willingness to tackle what many would consider a dry subject. "I was a geologist with a company that sold mining equipment."

That was good. I was able to maintain a reasonably well-informed discussion with him on the latest developments in strip mining and mineral prospecting, and soon we were receiving reports of the ambient temperature in Bogota. By this time, as we were getting to know one another, the conversation had become a little more specific and personal. He told me that he had been employed by Gambex, and we were now talking about the work of that company, a topic I really did know something about.

He was puzzled by the depth of my information, and although he knew by now that I was a writer, eventually enquired, "Have you worked for Gambex?"

I hesitated for a moment, wondering if I should reveal that I owned the endeavour to which he had devoted his adult life. "No," I said, dismissively. And then the plane was touching down.

In the scramble to get off the plane, I lost track of the old man. I was more interested in keeping an eye on my partner. His name, so I had been informed, was Cain, and there was someone from the gang waiting to pick him up. I was now on my own, entrusted with the task of finding my own way into the compound.

That wasn't as difficult as Withers had been thinking. Dear old Withers had been getting his knickers in a pretty painful twist in the last week or so, trying to work out a blow-by-blow campaign to get me into 'El Mundo', the ranch/private estate out of which our target cartel seemed to be operating. Getting Cain in by straightforward means had surprised him and he was certain that his luck was not going to hold for his second agent. I had finally pointed out that he had selected me for more reasons than those he had stated initially. Yes, he had found me, and maybe he had something on me, but the real reason he had chosen me was that he knew I 'had the moves', as Johnny Mack had put it. If he could tell me where El Mundo was, it would be up to me to get myself in.

He didn't like it, but as time ran out rapidly, he had to trust me. We had tried to make sure that my recovery coincided closely enough with the progression of the case against the El Mundo cartel, so that Cain and I could be slipped in as moles to ferret out the final pieces of the puzzle to ensure we took them down, once and for all.

Cain had been recruited and drilled for his part, given a backstory and documents to support it, the works. I had been given a new set of clothes because my old set was irreparable, some Columbian money, a new hunting knife and my plane ticket. Now I was on the ground, it was up to me. In his position within the organisation, Cain would be able to report the success of my attempt to inveigle myself in, and indeed whether I made such an attempt at all instead of making a break for it into the South American jungles. Withers' paranoid brain needed to know but I was not in to double crossing him. As I had told him, I was doing this job because I wanted to. Not to do it would be to double-cross myself.

So I exercised my schoolgirl Spanish and bought a map which located the nearest town to El Mundo. Next I gave my schoolgirl Spanish a real thrashing, buying a bus ticket to said town, finding out which bus it was and where it stopped, and where and how I had to change. The worst part was trying to explain to the ticket clerk that I did know where I was going and was not simply a tourist straying off the straight and narrow. He probably feared that I was one of those irritating Westerners who think that getting off the beaten track and finding a paradise in which to smoke vast quantities of dope is both possible and exotic. If I had spoken fluent Spanish, particularly with the South American dialects, I might not have attracted suspicion, but hey …

After the first change, the bus ride was an adventure in its own right. The vehicle was held together by elastic bands and string, and every grinding effort it made reminded its brave passengers of the labour it was undertaking on their behalf. Its every effort ground through me as well. The corners of my bones, barely covered by taut skin, jarred painfully against the hard seat as my fellow passengers and I were jounced and jostled. Somehow everyone maintained their good humour. Once we got away from Bogota, children no longer rushed out to smile ingratiatingly and proffer wares. They would stop and wave as though our coming was a confusion to them and we would wave graciously back as though the battered bus was a horse-drawn coach.

By the time we reached the town, I could hardly move. I all but fell out of the bus, followed by a cloud of good wishes from those who had shared the travail of the journey. Hauling my rucksack on to my shoulder, I stumbled along the dusty street, uncertain if I would recognise the bar when I saw it. As luck would have it, a bench along its front wall supported three elderly men and their cups of a dark brown liquid I took to be coffee. A window open at their back let into a fug of smoke and body odour that called me inwards only because of the house it advertised.

I shuffled in, my boots grinding the grit on bare floorboards. At the sight of me, all activity abruptly ceased. The plump woman behind the bar was clothed in black, probably a perpetual sign of mourning but her hair had been professionally plaited into coloured braids. She glowered at me more menacingly than the men she served. Their gazes were more curious, and possibly even respectful. Picking up my weary feet, I clumped up to the bar and requested a cold beer in the best accent I could muster. After repeating my order twice, I was disconcertingly presented with a Budweiser, a beer I hoped to have escaped for the time-being. I parked myself on a stool at the bar to drink, turning sideways so that I could watch the bar's other patrons and the street outside the window.

Finishing the Bud was the work of a moment and I gestured for another one. The woman brought it over, her expression beginning to soften a little as I spent more money. So, I hauled out my protesting Spanish again to attempt a little conversation.

"Do you know where El Mundo is?" I enquired falteringly.

She creased thick brows and jabbered a reply.

I smiled, but shrugged and mumbled that I didn't understand.

"It's a bad place," she told me slowly.

I considered what intelligible sentences I was actually capable of constructing. "I know, but I work there."

"Oh, no, no." She waggled her heavy head from side to side. "No, no. Bad men work there." She added something else which went over my head.

"The men come here?" I tapped the bar with one finger.

The woman sighed gustily. "Oh, yes." Something or other. "Girls." Then she glared at me.

I smiled in a fashion that must have provoked her greatly because she sounded like she was cursing me in low tones. She was interrupted by the rumble of an approaching vehicle. She craned around me to see who was driving through the town, as cars moved infrequently. It was the first car I had heard since getting off the bus and, compared to Los Angeles, the quiet was almost eerie. The car swept past and ground to a halt. Silence fell once more, then doors slammed. Boots crunched in the dust and two men entered the bar. The senora moved at once to fix their drinks, already knowing their requirements, and I studied them as they strode across the room to a free table. Both men were wearing jeans and shirts stained by sweat and dust. The larger man had scruffy, light brown hair that had grown out somewhat, with a matching moustache in the same order. The slimmer man had an air of greater neatness about him, as though the grime on his person was only the work of one day, not the week or so that his companion was wearing. He had a blue patterned bandana tied around his neck, which I thought almost as affected as his black cowboy hat. He removed his hat and placed it carefully on the table, knocking some of the worst dust off it while they waited for their hostess to supply them with beer.

Reaching for his drink, the slimmer man said, "Gracias," in an accent so obviously horrible that I guessed at once he was English. Indeed, having taken a slurp, he proceeded to address his companion in my native tongue. "What do you make of the new guy? Do you anticipate any problems with him?"

Letting out a satisfied sigh, the other man plonked his glass back on the table, significantly lighter, and sucked some of the foam off his moustache before replying. "Yeah, I think old Cain's going to fit right in."

These two men were from El Mundo and my companion had got in there safely.

"He's a bastard, of course," the moustachioed man continued, "but the bastards are easier to keep in line. You know what they want, what motivates them."

The clean-shaven man nodded wisely, but without comment, while he drank a little more. Then he said, "What does Cain want?"

"He's a mercenary. He wants money. And he's got a bitch of a wife who's more mercenary than he is." He chuckled as he raised his glass to his mouth. I recognised Cain's cover story.

"She wants him to keep her in the style to which she's become accustomed?"

The other man snorted into his beer as though this was a great joke. He wiped his moustache with the back of one hairy paw, and said, "Yeah. She liked being an officer's wife. He says she doesn't think much of the view from civvy street."

"I think this man talks too much. I don't care about his wife. He can leave his problems in Hicksville." He toyed with his hat brim.

His companion shifted in his seat nervously, pulling himself upright. "He doesn't really talk much, I just asked him, like you said, about his, er, motivations."

"Hmmm," was the only response he got. This suspicion was all good and proper. If new men were accepted to work in narcotics production without a healthy amount of suspicion, I would have been suspicious in my turn.

I signalled for another beer. The woman delivered it heavily, accompanying my drink with a shrunken sermon that probably addressed my keen observation of the two men. I smiled, shrugged, and mumbled something that sounded placatory, to me at least. Then I decamped from my stool on to my aching pins and shuffled across to the men's table. Grasping the back of a spare chair, I leaned over further than I had meant to. "Mind if I join you?"

The men stared at me, startled. "I thought you were a native," said the cleaner of them, "the way the senora was speaking to you."

I glanced at the other man to find him leering, eyes twinkling in a friendly fashion nonetheless. I jerked the chair out and collapsed into it. My beer foamed and slopped over the lip of the bottle. This was the third day that I had been out of the hospital and I was utterly exhausted. My exercise regimen had been sufficient to restore much of my strength, but confined, there was little I could do to increase my stamina. All I wanted to do now was sleep, but instead I was about to embark on the most dangerous part of my mission.

"Hex Mallory," I introduced myself, holding out a pale, thin hand to be shaken.

The neat man to whom I had offered it, figuring him to be the senior of the two, regarded my hand blankly. I looked at my hand too. My knuckles and blood vessels seemed swollen, the white flesh, almost an after-thought between them, ingrained with travelling grime. Ordering my fingers with conscious effort, I snapped them at him. He twitched, startled, and took my hand with the tips of his fingers like an eighteenth century gentleman. "Stocker," he murmured.

Oh, for Pete's sake! Had the Catholic Church been restricting names again? I jerked my hand away and offered it to the other man, hoping for the sort of bone-grinding handshake I was used to. His fat, sweaty palm squeezed mine firmly. "James," he said. Which was all right.

"You guys work at El Mundo, right?"

They both sat back in unison.

"What have you heard?" demanded the one who called himself Stocker.

"You're recruiting mercenaries," I told him. I had no game plan but I usually find that elaborate lies are confusing and difficult to maintain over long periods under close scrutiny. The simplest plan was the one least likely to fail.

"There were a couple of jobs for English speaking security staff advertised in the States," Stocker said stiffly. "They have now been filled."

A deep lethargy that extended to the whole venture overtook me. I really couldn't be bothered with this posturing. "Look, guys," I said, "you're advertising in mercenary papers for security staff for some private estate thing in Columbia. It doesn't take a great deal of imagination to conclude that the estate's main product is white and powdery. I'm a mercenary looking for a job and I'm here. Are you gonna employ me?"

Stocker and James exchanged quizzical looks. After some moments of thought, Stocker said, "Women mercenaries are somewhat ... unusual. Where have you worked?"

I gave him a monosyllabic rundown of some of the more well-known theatres in which I had played my part.

[If you want to know about these, dear reader, go out and buy my 'Fieldwork Chronicles'. My hero is 'Jinx' Palmer, but the basic situations have been pinched wholesale from my own experiences. Subtlety is not my middle name.]

Working for narcos and other 'security' assignments were not my beer. I prefer all out warfare but this was the only thing Withers had been prepared to offer me.

He nodded at various names and dates but I doubted that he was a seasoned campaigner, rather that he had heard of those games from others. Then he asked, his eyes sweeping over my diminished form, "Do you have any ... special skills?"

It was clear what he was hinting at. There are very few women mercenaries, and although soldiers are renowned for making use of the local women, they would often rather choose someone they know. Never having found out how anyone else may handle it, I have always been free with my fists, and other weapons, not allowing myself to be pressured. So I told him my special skill. "Torture."

James grinned suggestively, stretching his moustache, but Stocker paled. He could tell that I was being serious. "Okay," he said, his voice low and grim, "there might be a place for you in our operation. The money's pretty good but if you take one step out of line ..." He left the sentence hanging, which is supposed to be threatening, but to a writer it simply indicates lack of imagination.

More beers were drunk and we chatted. Well, James chatted, my new Stocker, the narco, mostly grunted, and I tried not to yawn. They had come down to the town to buy some stores and were now indulging in a short break before returning to the estate. Yet it was not long before baddy Stocker remembered that the narcotics business didn't run itself and ordered James and me to the van.

The drive into El Mundo was almost as uncomfortable as the bus ride. The van turned out to be an old Ford pick-up with two seats in the cab. Chucking my bag into the back, I vaulted neatly after it, despite everything my limbs wanted, and settled down between the boxes of provisions they had been buying. The vehicle was old and full of grit but it got us there safely. I was hoping that narco Stocker would show me to a bed and let me sleep my journey off, but he was anxious to find a place for this unexpected addition to his work force.

The van bounced down the driveway and passed on to a dirt track just short of a huge, white and crumbling mansion. We surged to a halt before a massive, shining fence, topped with razor wire. "The boss is coming down in two days," Stocker was muttering as they climbed out of the cab. I stood automatically to gauge the fence's height. On the far side of it stood a low white building. More had been spent on its upkeep than that of the mansion. If what I had just overheard was correct, then in two days Cain and I would have the opportunity to glean the last of the information Withers needed. In two short days it might all be over. I resisted the temptation to turn a somersault as I leaped from the back of the van. It would have provoked questions. And hurt.

Stocker waved a careless hand at the low building behind the fencing. "Raw plant matter goes in, white powder comes out," he said. "No people, though."

"Take the hint," added James, perhaps indicating that he had not got it himself when expressed this way.

Stocker glared at him. "Security works outside the compound, keeping trespassers off the estate and labourers on it." He waved his hand in the opposite direction, encompassing a great tree-edged slope, up which fields of verdant green glimmered in the sunlit breeze. Between the fields and the compound was a yard along the length of which were three sheds, end on. "Barracks for security teams," he pointed. "Three shifts. Labourers are mostly natives. They don't speak English but that's okay if you speak Spanish. They're in that barn. Day shift only. That one's mine." A single, more tightly built hut stood a little apart at the end of the row. "Now, if you're going to work security ..."

James, the foreman, climbed back into the van and departed in a cloud of dust in the direction of the fields. Stocker and I continued to walk along the track behind him, and as we cleared the yard, the track divided, a dust haze hanging over it in one direction, marking the fork the van had taken. We took the other one into a belt of trees. The track ended abruptly in another yard. The wooden buildings that made an L-shape of the corner opposite us were stables. The smell and shuffling sounds indicated that they were well used. "Our security is mounted," Evil Stocker informed me. "You can ride, I suppose?"

Being able to sit a horse is one of the qualifications for becoming a rich man's wife.

"Well, then. I will leave you in the capable hands of Rico. Rico!"

A slim young man, wearing tight jeans and a pony tail, emerged from the darkness within the stables. His boots clicked on the hard packed ground. He looked me up and down with eyes that shone like black marbles and thrust his hips forward as he chose a position to stand.

"A new guard," Stocker told him in halting Spanish. "Show her what to do." He turned away at once, perhaps to avoid any further conversation in the foreign tongue and clumped away through the dust.

Instead of responding promptly to his boss' request, Rico continued to stand and stare at me in a provocative fashion. I shoved my hand out at him. "Hex Mallory."

His thick brows knitted in some confusion.

"Ola, Rico. My name is Hex Mallory." When he still didn't respond, I swapped to English. "Stuff it. Where's the horsies?"

I marched passed him into the coolness of the stable he had exited. It was even more dusty than the yard and particles of hay spiralled in the drafts caused by the animals' movements. The smell of sweat, both human and equine, was ripe. I paused to allow my eyes to become accustomed to the poor light. Three men, wearing battered cowboy hats, hunched against the rail of a loose box, chewing on wads of something with gaping jaws. "Ola," I said, cheerily.

One of them might have grunted. Rico's poncey boots clacked into the stable behind me, accompanied by a flood of Spanish that might have been excusing my presence. One of the men may have grunted again. Then Rico said something else that seemed to refer to me and horses, and which elicited a laugh from all three of them. The light of malice illuminated every expression.

"Come," said Rico. "We have a horse for you."

I wasn't surprised when the tall, dark steed that they led out into the yard reared wildly, nearly throwing the man at his head to the ground. The men laughed and converged on the creature to saddle it, shove a shotgun into the holster, and drag it to the mounting block. Now I knew I was being hazed. I was on familiar territory. Soldiers haze viciously.

I skipped onto the mounting block and threw myself into the saddle with more speed than grace, but I was glad I had as the beast shied sideways as soon as I touched it. I held on with both hands as well as my knees as the horse jarred me six ways at once. Every time I thought I had finally left the saddle, we lurched back to earth with a bone-rattling impact. Then I was sure I had it, and the next thing I knew, the ground hit me in the face.

I rolled with the impact and came to my feet, knocking the dirt off my eyelashes as I spun round, got my bearings and snatched at the horse's bridle as it snapped near my face like a whip. The men were laughing uproariously but I was gratified to hear the laughter falter as I hauled the horse's head down, grabbed at the pommel of the saddle and vaulted back up on to my steed's back.

Less than two minutes later, I was eating dust again. Again, I rolled to my feet, caught the horse and started over again. I forget how many times I came off but I didn't care. It felt good to be stretching and exerting all those muscles again. The last of the hospital restraint was kicked off, and as I was too, I ceased to wonder about pain and whether I would still cope with it. Even hitting the ground felt good.

"Stop! Stop!" shouted Rico as I grabbed the reigns yet again.

I paused, uncertain of where he was and who he might be shouting to. Turning unsteadily, I found him approaching me, his heels clipping away like an Essex girl's.

"You stop now," he told me. "You'll be killed."

"No," I replied heartily. My Taekwando and stunt training had taught me how to fall at any angle and speed without smashing my skull or any other important bones. Getting an impersonal pasting was reminding me of who I was, if that doesn't sound too melodramatic, but I had been kept so still for so long that I had forgotten the simple pleasure of physical exertion. I might be a writer but the fact was that I just wasn't built to sit still.

"No," said Rico, trying to wrest the reigns from my hand, "Eric is very strong. You have another horse. You are Stocker's new woman. We get you killed, we will not be very popular."

What was that supposed to mean? My Spanish wasn't up to fully comprehending his remarks. "We must work," I stumbled, aware that we had been having our fun for some while.

He took the horse away from me and another, smaller, whiter one was brought out. She was more placid too and soon Rico, two of the other men and I were saddled up and riding out for a turn around the estate. Our basic job was to ride around and make sure that nothing untoward was going on. If it was, our orders were to shoot first. What happened after that would be up to Evil Stocker.

Chapter 15

It was James who solved my sleeping dilemma. Having shared sleeping space with soldiers in many situations in the past, the idea of doing it again hadn't concerned me. I had assumed I would be assigned a cot in the barracks like all the others. The men, however, objected to this. They would find my presence both invasive and distracting. Stocker had decided that I would not be safe if I attempted to sleep in one of the huts. After much head scratching, James finally decided that I might find six feet of board in the shed.

The shed was a small wooden building, not unlike all the others, except in size and cleanliness. It was a storage building set a little way back from the other huts around the yard. As rodents found some of its contents edible, the shed was raised on wooden legs and a few rickety steps led up to the door. Its current occupants were a few insects, which didn't worry me as much as James hoped they might. Having shown me to my accommodation, and dropped some dark hints about what I might be attacked by, and the location of his cot should I need him (fat chance), James left me in peace. Stacking the boxes back against one side, I made enough room to unroll the blankets he had supplied me with and I folded them in half to cushion the floor a little. This would make a perfectly adequate bed and I could use my trousers as a pillow once I had removed them, which would serve the dual purpose of keeping the contents of my pockets safe while I slept. The horses had thrown me past tiredness to the kind of numb exhaustion that allows polar explorers to keep on walking. My muscles ached as though I had fought with the Chuckling Ducklings that very day, not two months or so before. The grazes on my shoulders and elbows made by the stable yard were beginning to throb dully, and my bones creaked like the old man's on the aeroplane. I should start taking cod liver oil, I decided.

As I folded my trousers, there was a knock at the door. I grappled with the worm-eaten latch and hauled the door back to find James standing on the steps, hat in hand.

"Settling in all right?" he asked. His gaze travelled down to my bare legs. The moonlight had turned my riding bruises into marbled shadows but the stitching scars were too stark to be disguised. The purpose in his features faltered a little.

"Yeah," I said, "but the room service is lousy."

He turned the brim of his hat, ten to two, round in his hands. "I thought you might be lonely."

So predictable and not even very flattering. I was the only woman on the estate who wasn't shut up in the house. Sighing inwardly, I said, "Me and all the spiders? It's a regular party in here."

His head craned, trying to see past me to whatever arrangements I may have made inside. "Well, I ..." He didn't bother to finish his sentence but took a step up. My uppercut took him hard under his unsuspecting jaw. With a croak he fell backwards off the steps, arms flailing for balance, and tumbled to a heap on the packed earth.

I leaped down beside him. "Message to your fellow chauvinists." I drove my foot, with all the weight I had built up behind it, into his gut. His breath wheezed out like a punctured airbed.

A bullet cracked into the splintering wood above us. Jumping back from James into a crouch, I squinted up in the direction of the report. The moonlight absorbed by a black hat identified Stocker, the overseer, striding towards my shed, a rifle cradled in his arms.

"James and Mallory!" I called out, naming us so that he wouldn't shoot indiscriminately.

"You okay, Mallory?"

"Uh, yeah. Maybe you could take James to his own bed."

He had reached us now as James groaned and rolled over, trying to get to his feet so that his boss wouldn't see him bested by a woman. Stocker poked him with his boot. "Get lost."

James staggered up, hat still in hand, and stumbled towards the huts, gasping for his wind.

"I'm sorry," Stocker said gently, letting go of the rifle with one hand to touch my arm reassuringly. "It's this whole South American machismo thing. It makes even rational men behave like adolescents."

"I don't think some people need much excuse." I turned away from his touch and put one bare foot on the step. "Night, Stocker."

"Call me John," he said, smiling gently.

Even I draw the line somewhere. I said hastily, "I've had some very bad experiences with people called John. Please don't take it personally if I keep on calling you Stocker." I hopped up two steps and into my shed. I really needed a few solid hours of peaceful sleep.

The next morning I was so stiff that it was all I could do to get my trousers on and not plummet down the steps in a re-enactment of James' downfall. Even a gentle jog around the yard was out of the question, so I put some time in with stretches and a couple of very light Taekwando katas, until I was able to walk like a person under ninety again.

By that time some of the men were up and moving about. One of them approached me. He was tall and slim, with buzz cut blond hair and a flattened nose. He walked like a boxer entering the ring, and muscles like steel hawsers writhed in his arms and neck as he walked. His t-shirt and jeans were caked in filth as though he had been here for six months but I knew that he had been here for only a couple of days.

"You're new here, right?" His accent was from the Deep South.

"You ain't from around here, are you, boy?" I muttered under my breath, then said quickly aloud, "Hex Mallory." I offered him my hand.

He gripped it mercilessly and I squeezed back to stop my knuckles crunching together. "Cain," he said.

Looking past him, I could see no one in earshot. "Right then, let's see if I've got this. All we have to do is find out who's in charge, then kill everybody. Right?"

"Right." His lip curled and I could see right away why James had described him with such confidence as a bastard. "I've got lines of communication rigged up. We'll plan for the endgame now, and the moment control give us the go-ahead, we can swing into action. I'll get guard patterns, shift changes and so on. You get names."

"Okay." Some people, even mercenaries, objected to treating violence in terms of a game. Out in the theatre of war (get that for a term), soldiers had taken as insulting questions like, 'Who are you playing for?' It didn't bother me. John Mark's first question as he emerged from the gun haze of the desert was, 'Which way is your team shooting?'. And because I could answer him, we knew we were both playing from the same manual. Yes, using words like 'endgame' classified Cain as an unfeeling bastard, but it also demonstrated his fixity of purpose. He wasn't disturbed by what was to come, and in terms of getting it done, that was a good thing. Fuck his immortal soul.

"And get a wriggle on," he said, "so we can drown these puppies."

The clacking of heels announced Rico's approach. "Morning, Miss Mallory," he said.

I dragged out my irascible Spanish. "Morning, Rico. I ride Eric today?"

Cain blanked Rico as though he was my imaginary friend. He turned and strolled away.

"Breakfast?" I asked Rico.

He waved an arm and started after Cain, a torrent of Spanish pouring from his lips, probably in praise of the South American breakfast which most likely consisted of ninety per cent coffee. Well, coffee's better than a kick in the teeth. So

I've heard.

After breakfast, Rico got me up on the white horse, Mirabel, and we set off to patrol the estate. James had been there at the table, shooting dark glances at me. So I engaged him in normal conversation to demonstrate no hard feeling and soon the atmosphere between us was back to normal. As long as he stayed away from the shed, we didn't have a problem. The jungles of the estate soon shook all the politics of the work environment away. I quickly realised that Rico was more about having fun than serious patrolling. He was a local lad, hoping to raise money and respect for his strapped family by working for the narcos. His real love was riding, and as the patrol split into pairs, I rode with him and he taught me a thing or two about handling horses.

Unaccustomed riding makes you ache in places you never knew you had. Even when John Mark had first taken me out to the posh Surrey stables on the outskirts of Richmond, I had never come home feeling so incapacitated. I went to bed aching and exhausted, and soon fell asleep.

The step creaked and I jerked upright. A shaft of moonlight cut across the shed floor as the door soundlessly opened. Grasping into the folds of my trousers, my hand closed around the butt of my new, solid hunting knife. Silhouetted in the doorway was a tall, lean figure. Moonlight glimmered on naked shoulders, and as he shifted, it gleamed around his leg as well. For a second I thought that Spike had found me, but then I recognised the slope of the man's shoulders, and the way he lifted his leg as he climbed the last step into the shed. He stood in the door frame, leaning one shoulder confidently against it, anticipating his invitation.

I said, "I have a throwing knife in my hand and your crotch is at eye level."

Cain turned his buttock towards me at once but he rested his chin appraisingly on his shoulder. After a moment he said quietly, "Ah'm a modern man, ah know women have needs too. As soon as you feel the urge, ah'll be waiting." He sauntered casually down the steps.

If that was the attitude of modern man, most women would be happy to stick with Neanderthals. I leapt up to shut the door behind him and saw that he really was walking about the compound entirely naked. Cain had quite a lot of something but it probably wasn't brains. I found a chunk of wood to wedge under the door and curled up on my bedroll once more, swallowing the memories that the intrusion had briefly conjured. My breathing seemed constricted by a chunk of ice resting on my diaphragm and I ended up propped, half upright, against the rack of shelves behind me. The moonlight was losing its luminous quality before I fell asleep once more.

Chapter 16

The next morning dawned bright and hot again. Evil Stocker did not appear but James ordered the men to their shifts and detailed the jobs for that day. Yesterday Rico had assigned me to the afternoon shift and I was not due to report to the stables until lunch time, so I found Cain mooching along the line of the compound fence. He didn't seem to remember the interruption he had made to my sleep, so I put it from my mind also.

"The inside guard changes more regularly than your security teams," he said by way of good morning. "And the keys are kept by the man near the gate there." He jerked his head without turning his eyes in that direction. "So ah guess ah'll have to get some bolt cutters from the shop. That'll stretch the endgame out, but it's unavoidable. If ah try to steal them beforehand, they'll be missed."

I eyed the fence professionally. "We don't need bolt cutters. I'll jump it."

"Jump it?" His shoulders twitched as he suppressed the reflex to turn and look at it again. "You can't."

"Sure I can. Get me a boost of, say, three feet - like a barrel - and I could do it." I waved my hand vaguely towards a group of rusting barrels that had been abandoned by the side of the nearest barrack hut.

Cain walked over to the barrels and looked them over meditatively. He shoved one of them off-balance, then glanced back over his shoulder, lining up the place where I waited below the looming chain link. Liquid inside the barrel slopped hollowly and he began to roll it along its rim towards the place where I was standing. The muscles in his neck and arms stood out in cords as he manhandled it over to me.

"Hi!" came a yell. "What are you doing?" James had appeared out of the shadows on the far side of the yard. He shaded his eyes and glared across at us, loitering by the fence.

"I'm standing. Cain's doing something with a barrel," I yelled back.

"What are you doing with that barrel?" James' yell was directed at Cain.

He let the barrel fall back onto its base and its contents plunged back and forth, the echo giving him a moment's breathing space. He drew breath. "Jus' movin' it, boss."

"Yeah? Well don't!" James was striding towards us now.

Cain rounded the barrel and went to tip it the other way, raising one eyebrow sceptically at me.

"Leave it alone, man!" James hollered. "Stop messing around and go and do something useful."

Cain raised his hands, then dropped them as he strolled away across the yard without a backwards glance, surreptitiously rubbing the flakes of rust off his palms.

The heavy foreman came over to me, removed his hat and swiped at the sweat that was running down his face with his grimy shirt sleeve. "What's he doing? Showing off?"

"He's a proper nuisance," I agreed. "Guess you'd better give me something to do. Keep me out of trouble."

James smiled. "The boss has come in today to have a meeting with some of his backers. He's requested your presence up at the house for extra security."

The big boss was indeed here, as Stocker had suggested when I first arrived. I had been beginning to think that if he didn't come as the overseer had mumbled, then Cain and I were never going to have an opportunity to find out who he was. It's not a question you can just ask when you're involved in a business like this. Now soon we would have the narco boss at our mercy. Or perhaps vice-versa. Why would the man request my presence? "What does that entail?"

"You're dressed in black. Imagine you're wearing a suit and an ear piece. You stand around menacingly at the edge of the scene and keep an eye on everything. If anyone tries to shoot the boss, you throw yourself heroically in the path of the bullet."

"Funny, there doesn't seem to be a word for heroinically."

"What?"

"How do I recognise the boss?" I asked. "I don't know who he is."

James shook his head like I was stupid. "Come on. I'll take you up to the house and Stocker can introduce you." He pulled a Glock out of the back of his waistband and handed it gingerly to me, a placating smile on his face. "You'll want this."

I took the weapon, turned it away from him so that he knew I was not bearing a grudge, and checked it over. The gun was clean and in good order, and the clip James had supplied me with was full. I applied the safety catch and shoved it into my own waistband, flipping the edge of my vest over the butt. Black on black, the bulge wasn't obvious.

So that was where Stocker had been all morning, sucking up to the big boss. We trudged up to the house and walked around the back to a pool area that could have been flown straight from the playboy mansions of Florida. Girls in skimpy bikinis besported in the pool, and around them, lounging in various states of holiday undress, were a few fat and ugly men, and a couple of slim, bronzed ones. Bad Stocker was standing, dressed in his cleanest jeans and shirt, hat and bandana on, with his back to us, nodding sagely while his companion talked. That man was clothed in khaki shorts that revealed a shapely pair of legs and the open-necked, rolled-sleeved, checked shirt of the rich at play. He was even wearing boat shoes without socks. As we approached, James cleared his throat deliberately and the discourse stopped. The big boss turned, the gold watch on his muscled forearm catching the sunlight like Frankie the dealer's. Like Frankie, he was also decorated with a signet ring and a chain at his shirt's open neck. He was really going for the whole drug baron aesthetic.

His brown hair was darker around the fringe than I remembered it, but the South American sunlight was beginning to bleach the top. His forehead was prison pale but his cheeks glowed with good health and humour.

"Hello, Johnny."

"Mink! Stocker told me that he'd made an irregular hiring. Luckily for him, it's my favourite mercenary."

"Didn't think you were into drugs," I said dryly. If I was making up this story, I would chuck out this plot twist as too bloody contrived. I mean, of all the drug barons in all Columbia, I had to be working for Johnny bloody Mack.

"Ah," said Johnny, raising a finger for emphasis. "I'm not doing this for fun, you know." As I wondered what other reason he'd ever had for doing anything, he took my arm, leading me away from a bemused Evil Stocker and his plain confused foreman. "This," continued my irritating arch-nemesis, "is how everybody is funding the work these days."

We took a turn about the pool, strolling onto the grass out of earshot of his backers who affected disinterest while glimmers at the corners of their eyes betrayed them. "What are you up to, Johnny?" I enquired.

"Terrorism," he said simply. "Everybody's doing it but I think I've found a gap in the market."

So, blowing up Delphiki's house and attempting a drive-by shooting could be construed as practice, and knowing Johnny as I did, it actually made a little sense. More than usual, anyway. "What gap?" I asked wearily.

"Well, it's all about Islamic suicide bombers attacking the West at the moment, so I thought, how about turning it around? So I'm forming an anti-Muslim group."

"How terribly PC," I murmured.

"Oh, you'll like this," Johnny replied gleefully, actually rubbing his hands together. "Guess what I'm calling it."

I shook my head, eyes closing in anticipation.

"Matamori," said Johnny.

I did like it. Years ago I had walked across Spain to the tomb of Santiago Peregrino. Santiago Matamoros, St James the Moor Killer, was the other identity of my favourite saint. Spanish legend held that St James had appeared on the battle field and helped the Christian knights to drive the North African Muslims out of Spain. It wasn't that Johnny was racist, I knew, just that it would be a popular gap in the terror market. He made me laugh.

"And now I've got you here," he went on, "there's a little something you could do for me. There's a fat Italian banker smoking a cigar on the bench over there."

I didn't look, but nodded.

The jovial tone left his voice. "I think he's mishandling my money. I want details and disposal. Okay?"

"Okay."

"Good. Now come and have a drink, and I bet you're dying to have a swim."

I followed him back to the men and their secretaries, mistresses, or whoever. The South American illegal drugs industry is not yet an equal opportunities workplace and it was quite clear from the very way they were sitting that it was the men who had the power at this pool side. The women were merely accessories and it sounded as though Johnny thought I would slip very nicely into that role for him. His attitude played into the hands of Interpol and so I was prepared go with it without a fuss. Peeling off my sweaty vest and trousers, I piled them so that the Glock was innocently covered, and dived into the pool in my ubiquitous sports underwear. I started doing lengths, carefully trying not to remember that the last time I had swum, I had been accompanied by a racoon.

The beach babes gave me looks. I was muscled, scabby, pale from confinement, and tattooed, and sports kit was not their idea of a bikini. They must have been wondering who the big boss had been speaking to as an equal. Once I had worked the aches out of my limbs, I hauled myself out of the pool and joined Johnny, a puddle forming around our feet as he handed me an orange juice and carried on talking. Tiring quickly of his accounts, I stood long enough to fix the features of the Italian banker in my mind so that I would recognise him without the cigar, then wandered across to Stocker.

"I see you and the boss know each other," he observed.

"I've worked for him in the past."

"Lucky for me. Why did he call you 'Mink'?"

"Because I'm a feral, hybrid, psychotic little bunny mugger." Standing there in soaked black sports kit, looking like the bride of Frankenstein, it wasn't a difficult image to conjure up.

He nodded. "I like it. Looks like you've got internal security for the house covered, so I'll get back down to the grunt work."

Chapter 17

"Right, well, that's all for tonight, gentlemen. Mink."

Johnny rose and I obediently followed. As we entered the corridor, he put his arm around my shoulders.

I pushed it off. "If you want me to work on the banker, I can't go with you now."

"Good point. See you later?"

"Maybe." Handing him the Glock, I patted the pocket containing the kit he had given me and strolled back into the sitting room. The men looked up, surprised to see me return. I parked myself in a corner armchair and watched as people moved and chatted lazily. The men had been hard at work all day and could no longer be bothered to pursue conversation in foreign languages, but the women were now coming into their element and were anxious to show off their command of tongues. I couldn't follow any of the discourse, but none of it was of any consequence, apart from the fact that the banker got up to leave alone. I followed him.

Reaching the door to his room, he turned and saw me standing there. He spoke in Italian.

"English," I said.

He sighed. "What do you want?"

"What do you think?"

He looked me up and down lingeringly. "I think you go with Mr Mack."

"No," I said. "You."

Why he could think that given the choice between him and Johnny, anyone would choose the fat smelly one, I don't know, but he was confident in his own virility. He pushed the door open and held it for me to enter.

"No," I said again. "I don't want Johnny to know. Where can we go so that no one will hear us?"

He thought for a moment, a small smile of mischief lightening his heavy features. "The pool house."

We tiptoed out of the mansion and across the terrace. Fairy lights blazed around the pool but no one was swimming. I tried the pool house door. It was open. Inside was a set of cane furniture and a tiny bar, behind which was a curtained changing area. In the room beyond was a set of weights and an exercise machine.

"In here," I said, closing the door firmly behind the man.

He curled his meaty arm around me and I squashed down the impulse to lash out, taking a grip of his shirt and tugging playfully. He followed compliantly and I pushed him down on to the seat of the exercise machine. He pulled me down to straddle his lap and kissed me with a mouth that seemed all cigar.

"Take your clothes off," he said.

I stepped back off him and gripped the hem of my vest. "Take yours off." I pulled the vest off over my head and twirled it casually into the corner.

He responded by unbuttoning his shirt with clumsy fingers.

"Here, let me." Sitting on his knee once more, I lingered over the unbuttoning, stroking his matted chest hair as I did so. Then I pressed him back against the seat with my body. He started work with his mouth again and I leaned over him to twist his hands behind his back. "This will be fun," I whispered breathily in his ear. He chuckled cigar smoke over me as I fastened his hands to the metal strut of the exercise machine. I kissed his mouth, stroked his round shoulders and attacked his belt. He wriggled helpfully as I pulled his trousers off and used the legs to tie his ankles to the seat struts.

Then I pulled out the hunting knife.

He exclaimed in Italian but I shushed him. I used the knife carefully to slit the sides of his pants which I then pulled off and tossed away, touching them as little as possible. Leaving the banker trussed up, naked and still grinning like a loon, I went back into the first room of the pool house and fetched a small cane side table which I set up in front of the man. Behind the bar I found a basin which I put underneath the seat.

Then I pulled out the kit Johnny had supplied me with. I untied the tapes around it and unrolled it on the small table, in his full view. I was smiling because I could almost smell the blood already.

"Okay," I said. "We are going to work in English. I'm going to hurt you now. How much I hurt you is up to you. You have not been wholly honest in your dealings with Johnny Mack, and that is going to change now. I don't know anything about these dealings, so you are going to have to tell me absolutely everything. Do you understand?"

He nodded so hard that I thought that the blood had left not just his face but his whole head, and that his head would now drop off.

"Say it," I commanded.

"Yes, yes. I understand. I will tell you. Everything. Please don't hurt me."

"Your English is very good, which will make this easier. But I will hurt you." I slid the box of razor blades out of its pocket and extracted one. Holding it flat along the side of my thumb, I lunged forwards and swept my arm across his chest.

He screamed but it took a few moments before the blood began to well in the thin and shallow slice. I reached out with my other hand, and ran my finger along the wound, collecting the blood. I put my finger in my mouth and was surprised to find that his blood lacked the tang of nicotine.

I licked my finger clean. "What's your name?"

"Giovanni Stephano Magozzi," he yelled out so fast that I had to make him repeat it.

I put the razor blade down and selected a needle. A long, thick, shiny acupuncture needle. "How old are you?" Before he could respond, I grabbed him by the long hair and jerked his head back, then I plunged the needle into the depths of his navel.

He squealed. I released his head and he panted, staring down at the needle protruding, quivering, from his gut.

"I asked you a question," I reminded him quietly.

"Forty-eight," he replied at once. He wasn't getting this. I was going to keep on hurting him however quickly he answered.

"What bank do you work for?" I drew the thin-bladed scalpel out of its place in the kit and dropped to one knee beside him.

He talked, he hollered. He begged and screamed. I reminded him that he himself had chosen a place where we wouldn't be heard, and carried on bleeding him. He sang like a choirboy but none of it meant anything to me. Holding accounts, credit, offshore investments, interest and all his other information were all the reasons that Nathan Bedford was managing G-Corp UK. I worked for the blood.

Now, the way I work is not like anything you might have seen on film. That's all too crude, too dull. The way I work isn't even called torture by those who consider themselves experts. What I do is called 'Bending', and it is somewhere between an art and a science. The idea being that you don't break the subject. He breaks himself. The victim of a bending will be able to walk away from it. In two weeks there will not be a mark to prove that he has been tortured, yet at the time he will bleed copiously, he will cry, he will wet himself. He will spill his metaphorical guts only. Bending is about pain, and the feeling of pain is a product of the mind. For the duration of the bending, I will control the subject's body until he can no longer control his tongue. And afterwards ...

"Thank you, Mr Magozzi," I said, licking my lips and straightening up. "I think that really is everything."

He hung forward against the restraint of his tied clothing. His head sagged forward, his jaw hanging open to admit hopeless, raw gasps. Blood and sweat smeared his mottled skin and fluid dripped from the seat leather into the basin below. Replacing the instruments in the kit, I knelt and untied his ankles. He didn't try to kick. I untied his wrists and put his clothes into his hands. "Get dressed."

He stood shakily and I rolled up the instruments, tied the tapes around the pack, found my vest, and left him to it. I waited outside the pool house, watching the movement of the light on water stirred by a warm breeze. It took the Italian banker a while to recover himself enough to get his clothes on. When he emerged, his belt was undone and his buttons askew. I pointed towards the house and he walked ahead of me, his head down, too defeated to argue.

As he drew close to the edge of the pool, I stepped close behind him, pulling out the hunting knife once more. I closed against his back and sliced into his throat, pulling the blade back smoothly through the soft flesh into his windpipe. He gasped and I pushed forward with my body. As I disengaged the knife and stepped back, he deflated into the water like a burst rubber ring, and sank. I knelt to soak the blood off my hands and returned to the house.

I did not go to Johnny, but located the kitchen so that I could wash all my instruments in hot water and disinfectant until nothing remained of Mr Magozzi. Then I took a hot shower, found a washing machine to put my clothes in and curled up on the sofa. There a few things that will make you sleep like satisfying bloodshed.

Chapter 18

A lot of incoherent screaming heralded the finding of the body. I was eating breakfast with Johnny. We English had persuaded the cook to produce fried eggs, beans, bacon, sausage and tomato, along with bread to mop up with. A steaming cup of coffee rested at Johnny's right hand but I had managed to convince the maid that I was only going to drink orange juice.

Johnny looked at me. The gun James had supplied me with the day before lay on the table between us. The bending kit was wedged with comfortable pain in my pocket. "Fifty pee says that's Magozzi."

"Your fifty pee is safe," I replied.

He put down his fork and patted my head. "You're a good little worker, Mink."

I batted his hand away.

"Isn't this more fun than Disneyland?"

A maid ran into the breakfast room, gibbering and wringing her hands. Johnny stood, took her gently by the shoulders and spoke in quiet, measured tones. Johnny's Spanish was, of course, perfect. It seemed that he had spent his time inside profitably. In more ways than one. She hadn't noticed the Glock, so I picked it up and slid it under my belt. He soon had her calmed down and sent her off into the house.

"It is Magozzi. Nice job." He flipped a sterling fifty pence piece out of his pocket onto the table beside my plate. "You earned it."

I looked at the money, trying to decide what message I would be sending if I took it. There were many things of more use in Columbia than a British coin. "Give me a gun, Johnny. I'd rather have a gun."

He tutted and shook his head sarcastically. "And that's what living in the States does to you, Mink. Guns aren't the last word, you know."

"Guns don't kill people," I responded, "I do. And you had mine last night, so you know I'm not dependant."

"True." He sat down again and smeared the last of his egg around the plate with a crust of fresh white bread. "Okay, you shall have your gun. Did you have anything specific in mind?"

"Hmm. How about a Thomson sub?" Delphiki kept a Thomson submachine gun in his closet.

"I'll put an order in for you this afternoon."

"An order?"

"Yes. My financial backers will be leaving this morning, once I have made certain that they understand the message you delivered last night. This afternoon I will be receiving representatives from an arms dealership to discuss a contract to supply my little operation. I'd like you to check in with Stocker once the money have left, then get your alarmingly skinny arse back to the house to cover the negotiations. Once those have been successfully concluded, I shall be leaving too."

"So soon? Where are you going?"

He sighed deeply. "Mink, I'm making drugs, not taking them. I'm not yet stupid enough to show you my whole hand at once."

"Aw, damn it. And there was me thinking I could report to the DEA tonight."

He eyed me suspiciously. "If you fuck me over again, Mink, I'll ..." His clenched fist waved impotently.

He knew me so well. Well enough to know that I wasn't imaginative enough to have made up a threat like that. "Which reminds me," I said, realising that only a really big bone would distract him, "do you remember offering to shoot me in the head?"

"Yes?" he responded sharply.

"You said you wanted to know what it felt like but no one who had ever been shot in the head had been in a condition to describe it afterwards. Then you put the gun to my stomach instead."

"Yes, yes. I remember." Johnny's excitement disrupted his usual calm.

"Well, you didn't shoot me then. But when the police came ..."

"And how much did it hurt?" he asked impatiently.

I thought back carefully, knowing how much this information meant to him. "Not much. It's like being stabbed with a red hot stiletto. No, having it kicked into you. You're not quite sure what's happened because a shot goes so fast that you get all the sensory indications in the wrong order. I mean, the bullet hits you before you even know the gun's gone off. That's what's weird about fire fights - if you can see and hear shooting, you can't be hit. No, it all hurts more later, after the operation. After they let you out of hospital even."

"They took the bullet out, then? You're not carrying my lead around inside you?" He sounded disappointed.

"The bullet wasn't the only thing they took out." I stood and showed him the scars, as I had shown them to Delphiki.

"You lost a kidney? Oh, well, like you always said, the human body's full of built-in redundancies." He was unrepentant.

"Not a kidney, Johnny. My uterus." I stood, not wanting to know how he felt about that. Not even sure how I felt about it. "I'll see you when the arms dealers come."

He watched me leave without comment, and I remained prowling around the mansion and its immediate grounds like an ear-pieced goon in a black suit, until Magozzi's body had been fished out of the swimming pool and sent away in a hearse to bypass the police station, and the rest of Matamori's financial backers had departed in more conventional transport. Once my handiwork had been disposed of, I jogged slowly down the track to the yard, feeling better than I had since my last night in Chinatown. I was hoping to locate Cain to report my findings before I came across Stocker.

Happily, Cain rode in with some of Rico's boys as I was approaching Evil Stocker's hut. One of the natives yelled something at me but I couldn't catch it. Cain laughed.

"He says you did a bad job up at the house," he translated, dismounting as he did so. "We heard someone died. He says no one is secure around you."

"It's true," I admitted. "But the boss thought I handled the killing well."

Cain frowned. "Are you saying you killed the guy?"

"Yup."

"And there was me worrying that your feminine nurturing instincts might take over when it came to the crunch." He threw his head back and laughed like a braying donkey. The other men dismounted and demanded to know what was so funny. Cain dashed something back at him in Spanish and they joined in the laughter.

"Did you just tell them I killed him?" I asked under cover of the sound.

"No. Just a pun. Did you get names?"

I nodded slowly. *Here we go again, Johnny.* "The big boss is one Johnny Mack. Real name, Jonathan Callander. He's on the lam from about sixteen life sentences in England. The drugs cartel is merely a money-making scheme to fund a terrorist organisation he's calling 'Matamori'."

The other security men had stopped laughing and were watching me whisper to Cain with dark, suspicious eyes.

He saw them. "My, my, you have been a busy girl," he announced aloud in English. He made a long arm and swept me towards him to plant a wet kiss full on my mouth.

I kicked him on the shin and swung a right hook at him as he released me. It didn't connect with much force, just enough to knock his head sideways. "Bastardo." I spat in the dust at his feet and stormed off, hearing the convinced chuckles of the men behind me.

Evil Stocker, narco overseer, was sitting in his hut struggling to translate the headlines of a Columbian newspaper. I told him the official version of the death of Magozzi, being simply that he had died a violent death, and no one was going to be using the swimming pool today. If Johnny wanted his overseer to know that the murder had been ordered, then it was up to him to tell him. It was business as usual on the production end of things. Some stupid US mercenary, a militia man, had finally decided to protest against the hopeless situation he found himself in with regards to the job, and had been shot. And some of the workers had been lazy and consequently whipped.

"You get back up to the house and make sure that the Iscariot boys don't get nasty," Stocker advised.

Iscariot. The familiar name jangled in my head as I walked briskly back up the track, a rough tortilla folded in my hand, thin tomato sauce dripping from my elbow. Iscariot were arms dealers to the mercenaries, to the elite Swooning Shadows. On my chest was the black dog tattoo, the same one Nicholson, Nick Jr. wore. Spike knew what that tattoo meant. Spike had had something on Nick Jr. to persuade him to give my bearskin back. Spike owned an awful lot of guns. Spike Delphiki had worked for Iscariot! No wonder he kept such a low profile in the high profile world of Los Angeles.

I gulped the last shreds of tortilla and broke into a jog. Then I stopped. Wait, I'd missed something. I'd missed too much already, not realising, as I should have, the connection between the private investigator and the sub-radar arms dealership. I stood, licking tomato sauce off my arm, flicking back through my memories. My conversation with the old man on the aeroplane had been strange because I hadn't known the company we were discussing, I owned it. Why hadn't I just told him? He had been lost to me only moments later anyway.

Delphiki. Why hadn't Delphiki just told me about the arms dealers? Why had he dropped odd hints at MacHone's Military Machines, as though he personally … sold them … their guns? *Now stop right there, Gambetta! You aren't stupid, so stop behaving like you are.* Enzo Watts' house rules stated of first importance that one must never ask questions about Delphiki. That Delphiki had been Spike's father and Spike's father was called Jude. Jude. Judas. Iscariot.

Oh, holy shit. I'd just dumped an arms dealer.

Oh, mother of fuck! His boys were about to make a contract with a man whose operation we would be shooting down in flames by the end of the week. If Johnny went down, Spike would be dragged down with him. Unless … unless I did something very uncharacteristic, and thought quickly.

I broke into a run.

Chapter 19

When the military green van pulled into the driveway of the El Mundo mansion, I was standing on top of the low wall to the side of the turning circle. The van drew to a halt and two men climbed out. Both were wearing light suits, with ties loosened, their jackets folded across the back seat. As the older of the two men opened the rear door and reached in for his jacket, the younger one finally spotted the woman covering them with a rifle.

"Hey, Greigson," he hissed audibly, "I, ah, think -"

"Of course they've got a guard on us," growled Greigson irritably as he reluctantly pulled on his jacket. "You didn't expect these sort of people to open their doors to just anyone. Be cool and you won't get shot."

Sound advice, I thought, hopping off the wall. What was less sound was bringing a newbie to a tricky negotiation. Drug dealers aren't the most stable of people, but then I suppose he had to start somewhere. The men spoke with cultured American accents, adding a minor point of confirmation to my deductions about Iscariot. I walked over while the younger man donned his jacket also. Then I waved the rifle barrel at him.

"What's your name?"

He swallowed nervously and I saw that he hadn't realised that I would speak English. He looked at Greigson for reassurance. Greigson nodded. "Mills," he said. Then he coughed to clear his throat.

"Hands on the vehicle, please." I made a turning motion with my hand. "Both of you. Spread 'em."

While I patted them both down thoroughly, Greigson said, "I assure you we aren't carrying anything."

"No samples?"

"In the truck."

He was right. Neither of them was carrying anything more offensive than a biro. But in these days of technological warfare, I had to check for bugs, hidden cameras, tracking devices and a horde of other gimmicks that might be employed against drug traffickers. My time in the film industry had taught me quite a lot about miniature electronic gadgets, which made me the best person Johnny could have chosen for the task. The only thing you couldn't screen out were people.

Right now, I had given myself a few moments alone with these men. If I was going to do anything to save Iscariot, now was the time. "Okay, guys," I said quietly, as I tapped the heel of Mills' shoe before returning it to him. "You're good to go. But there's something you should know. I'm an agent working for the DEA. We will be destroying the operation in a day or two, and if Iscariot has any presence here, things will not go well with you. Do you understand?" The DEA would mean more to them in this situation than Interpol.

"What?" gasped Mills, his face turning white and clammy.

Greigson fixed me with a look. "Why would you warn us?"

Good question. I had to come up with a convincing answer. Stretching the neck of my vest, I yanked it and the sports bra underneath downwards, enough to the reveal the head of the black dog. "Know what I mean?"

Mills' face was caricatured confusion, but Greigson nodded.

"Okay, Mink?" came Johnny's voice from the door of the house behind me.

I let go of my clothes and blessed manmade fibres as they sprung back into shape. "They're cool, boss."

The two men from Iscariot introduced themselves to Johnny Mack and they entered the house. Johnny stopped me at the conference room door. "Wait here unless I yell," he directed.

So I waited, listening to the rise and fall of voices within the room. After a couple of hours, the inflections of Johnny's voice indicated his growing frustration. Having discussed the merchandise and gone through the appropriate sales patter, most of it delivered by Mills, Greigson was attempting to extricate them from signing any kind of contract.

"Mink!" hollered Johnny.

I burst into the room, rifle at the ready, prepared to shoot both of them if it would keep Iscariot out of Johnny's impending doom. The narco boss was still seated, both his fists resting on the table.

"I'm taking a tea break," he said, with ponderous calm. "Take this pair of jokers onto the terrace."

"This way." I gestured with the rifle. Outside, I ventured to observe, "Annoying the boss, then?"

Mills allowed himself a daring chuckle.

They sat at tables beside the drained swimming pool, sipping at long cold drinks that a maid had brought them. Both men spoke fluent Spanish as Iscariot's agents in the Middle East had spoken fluent Arabic. I paced around them, swinging the rifle carelessly, hoping these two were good enough negotiators to talk their way out of trouble.

They were. They drove their van away as the evening light was beginning to fade, having left Johnny with a few samples, including my Thomson, and a promise to return having discussed the matter with their superiors. They would not be back.

Johnny knew he was being fobbed off. "They can't really think this thing is just about drugs," he growled.

I patted him on the shoulder. "Couldn't they tell that you weren't talking about equipment for guarding a narcotics venture. I mean, what does a narco need with that much plastic explosive?"

"Little minks have very big ears," he observed.

"Like I was going to pass up an opportunity to find stuff out. If I'm in this, I want to know what's going on."

He took my hand from his shoulder and held it in his. "So you're either in this up to your ears or your planning to shop me big time." He flashed his white teeth at me. "Who are you planning to shoot with that submachine gun?"

"Shoot with it? My dear Johnny, that gun is a thing of beauty and a joy forever. I'm going to hang it up and admire it. Bring it out for parties, perhaps. I am not going to sully it with gunshot residue and gore." I found myself quoting the reasons Delphiki kept his Thomson in the closet.

My work there was done, so Johnny sent me back down to the yard to collect new orders from Stocker. I had hoped to remain near Johnny, to find out more and possibly even glean information about where he was hiding. Johnny, however, wasn't stupid. Once I had served my purpose for him, he was better off if I was out of the way. He would be leaving by the end of the day.

Hoof beats arrested me as I strolled down the track, the Thomson wrapped in a sack under my arm, going over the information gathered in my mind. I was trying to make sure that I had it all catalogued properly so that I remembered what I could discuss with Cain to be passed on to Withers, and what was to be kept entirely to myself. The fact that representatives from Iscariot had even been here was something Cain didn't need to know, let alone the other things I knew about that company. Now I turned to find Cain bearing down on me, astride a black horse, which at first sight appeared to be the fearsome Eric. When he pulled up, I saw lighter patches on the horse's coat and realised that Cain was not that great a rider.

He reigned in with careless ease and pulled the horse up to amble beside me. He leaned down to speak. "I've called in," he said.

"And?"

"And the word is Go."

"We're on for tonight?"

He grinned. "The end is nigh," he said, kicked in his heels and flew on past me down the track.

There came a yell, a more articulated shout, and the sound of running feet. I unwedged the shed door and saw the first shreds of moonlight as the moon rose sluggishly above the trees. Reluctantly, I left the Thomson under the bedroll and made do with the Glock which James had forgotten to remove from my possession. Johnny had, in his usual thorough fashion, taken the bending kit off me. I checked the handgun over again, jammed it under my vest, and hopped down the steps.

An impulse pulled me into a run but I paused in the shadows at the edge of the yard. Someone was coming, and his feet beat gently on the earth as I recognised the urge which had called me to the yard. It wasn't just curiosity to investigate the unusual sounds but the sense of carnage. The man glared unseeing in my direction as he hurried towards Evil Stocker's hut, but even as he reached it the door opened.

"¿Que pasa?" Stocker stood in t-shirt and boxers, disturbed by the noises as I had been.

The man jabbered something. I moved closer to make it out, but Stocker turned back into the dark interior and seconds later was bouncing out again in jeans and boots, his hat forgotten. He and the other man ran past where I was standing towards the gate of the factory compound. I followed.

Two horses were mooching untethered between the huts and the fence, and beyond them I saw three men standing, holding a fourth down on his knees. James' voice floated out to me on the night breeze as Stocker reached him. A few words were audible. *Rico ... Killed ... Him.*

I sprinted silently up to the side of the nearest horse, which turned out to be the white bulk of Mirabel. She recognised me as I pressed against her flank and nickered gently. I patted her shoulder absently and leaned forward. Rico was not in the group. The shadows of James, Stocker, and the man sent to fetch him were cast over the kneeling man, so as much as he struggled, I could not see who he was.

Evil Stocker swung his fist and smashed it down into the face of the man on the ground who grunted and heeled sideways. The three holding him joined in, kicking with the pointed toes of their riding boots. But something else was calling my attention. The moonlight surged, illuminating what appeared to be a rubbish sack hunched against the bottom of the fence. My wild talent identified it for me - a corpse. It must be Rico. The man they were holding had killed him.

The group hauled the man to his feet and the moonlight struck the spiked hairs of his buzz cut. Cain. His endgame was over almost before it had begun. Stocker was ordering the rest of the guard to bring him to overseer's hut. "I'll get the truth if I have to beat it out of him myself," he growled hoarsely. The way he was clutching at the hand he had already punched with suggested that if that were so, he would be at it all night. I broke cover and ran towards them.

"What's up? What's going on?"

Stocker glowered but James answered, "The bastard killed Rico."

Cain was hanging between two burly men, dragging his feet. His face was bloody down the left side where Stocker had hit him, splitting his eyebrow, and his t-shirt bore the imprints of many toes. But his neck and shoulders were tense, the muscles hard, his weariness a bluff. He caught me looking and winked his good eye at me.

They dragged him roughly into the hut and threw him onto the chair.

"Right, Cain, who are you working for?"

"Ah ain't workin' for no one," Cain drawled calmly. "Rico cheated me at cards."

"So you just thought you'd kill him while he was assigned to watch the factory gate, did you?" Stocker's gaze swept his small living space, dismissing the trestle covered in papers and the small cot beside it. Failing a better weapon, he unbuckled his belt. Everyone squeezed back against the walls. With eight people in there, there was hardly room to swing a hamster, let alone a leather belt.

"Wait," I said.

Stocker glared.

"You're forgetting my special skill," I told him.

He smiled and Cain's chin lifted to shoot me a questioning look. Recalling what he had said as he stood in my shed's doorway, I winked at him. This was going to be fun.

"Get these guys out. I need space to work."

Stocker gave the word and they clumped reluctantly out of the hut. He and James remained. Stocker brought out a revolver from underneath his cot's pillow and covered the prisoner.

"Strip him and tie him to the chair," I said.

Stocker gestured with his gun. "Take your clothes off, Cain."

The man smiled, showing white teeth. "All yer had to do was ask, Mallory."

"Come on, Cain," I said, "let's see everything you've got."

"And move slowly," Stocker advised as the prisoner stood towering over us in that tiny space.

Cain pulled off his t-shirt and dropped his trousers.

"All of it. I want you naked."

He sighed and stooped to untie his laces. Once he was completely bare, he sat back calmly in the chair and crossed his arms over his chest. "Like what you see?"

I ignored him. "Tie him to the chair," I instructed. James began to do so and struggled against Cain's trained strength. I turned to Stocker. "I'll need a basin, some sharp knives, some needles, whatever you can find."

He studied my face curiously for a moment, running through his Spanish vocabulary before opening the door and leaning outside to relay my requests. Footsteps set off in different directions to locate what was needed.

By the time James had got Cain firmly strapped down, the kit was arriving, piece by piece. Rico's outraged patrol were showing some imagination in their choice of implements for torture. The bolt cutters were handed in, along with various other rusty tools from the shop. When a basin was shoved through the doorway, I put it underneath the chair and spread the sharp things out on the trestle. Someone had brought a cut-throat razor. I tested the blade's edge meditatively with my thumb.

Motioning to the men to step back, I stood in front of Cain. His eyes fixed steadily on mine. He honestly thought I had some other plan.

"Okay, Cain, this is how it works. I'm going to hurt you now. How much I hurt you is up to you." I reached out and picked up the razor. Holding it so that Cain could see what I was doing, I snapped the blade into place. Then I swept it across his chest.

He cried out, more in surprise than pain, as a long, thin line of blood welled up. I ran my finger down it, feeling the muscles tremble under my touch. His blood was thick and dark, and tasted just like everyone else's.

"Eeugh!" exclaimed James as I drew my clean finger out of my mouth.

I regarded him coldly. "If you can't be quiet, I'll have to ask you to leave."

Cain, realising now that the cut was little more than a scratch, chuckled.

I went to the trestle, laid the razor down, and opened a small, army-issue sewing kit that some diehard had brought with him. Inside a paper was a selection of needles. I picked out the largest, grabbed Cain by the long hair and jerked his head back. Then I jammed the needle into his navel and shoved his head back down, so that his chin hit his chest. He squealed like the Italian banker.

"That didn't hurt," said Stocker scornfully. "You're supposed to be hurting him. He won't tell us anything if you just poke him."

"Stocker," I said, "I'm a professional. Let me do my job or I will ask you to leave."

"Well, don't just play with him. Hurt him."

"You're missing the point," I explained. "We want him to talk, and this method is the most effective ever devised. Bending is the most advanced method of torture known to man."

"Bending?" snorted James derisively.

They were ruining the moment. I was going to bleed Cain dry and they were chatting. "If you guys are too crude to appreciate an artist at work, then wait outside."

"All right," said Stocker, "don't have a hissy fit. Shut up now, James. Let the woman work."

They were quiet, so I picked up the thinnest bladed knife I had been supplied with and set to work. After five minutes of careful cutting, Cain was breathing through clenched teeth.

I stepped back from him. "What's your name?"

"Cain," he gasped at once.

"What's your wife's name?"

"Not married."

James gasped. "But he said -"

"Outside!" I commanded.

"Shut up," Stocker told his foreman. James subsided.

"Why did you leave the Marines?" I continued.

"Dishonourable discharge. Fightin'."

I moved forward again and leaned over him. "Yell," I hissed in his ear.

He yelled. I sliced through the rope. Then I jabbed the point of the blade into a spot on his back. He bellowed.

I turned the blade in my fist and swung round, driving it into James' chest. He gasped and sprawled back against the wooden wall as Cain lurched out of the chair and slammed into Stocker, knocking the gun from his hand. Pulling the hunting knife from my belt, I slit James' throat, then slipped out of the hut, leaving Stocker to Cain.

I stood outside, leaning forward, my hands on my knees. It had required all my discipline to break off the bending and let Cain go free with the rest of his blood. I shook myself and went back to normal. The men I had expelled from proceedings were standing in a huddle, smoking and muttering. There was a thump inside the hut, then a shot. The men turned and saw me.

"¿Que pasa?"

"Nada," I said, waving a calming hand. "Cain ..." I drew an expressive finger across my throat.

They nodded, passing comment among themselves. They hardly noticed when Cain, fully clothed once more, stepped out of the hut.

"That hurt, bitch," he growled, panting. Blood was beginning to soak through all over his shirt from a thousand tiny cuts that bit like lemon juice in paper cuts.

"I know," I said. A deep and abiding interest in pain is required to bend successfully, and there is only one way to learn exactly what effects various pains have on the human body and mind.

Chapter 20

All we could do now was get on with it. There was no more time for messing about. If we got caught again, we probably wouldn't get off so lightly. Cain and I broke into a run, sliding into the shadows, away from the men and heading back across the yard for the fence. The barrel remained where Cain had left it the other day, a few feet short of the fence, but it would have to do. I took a sprint up, hopped onto it and hurled myself upwards.

There is a split second between the infliction of pain and the moment you feel it. Then it flows over you like a wave, either the pain or the cushioning ignorance of shock. Instead of being engulfed by the wave, you can learn how to catch it, how to ride it like a surfer. I knew what damage I had done to myself in that leap, but I rode it, rolling fluidly on the far side of the fence as though my muscles weren't hanging in shreds.

The guard inside the fence was running towards the ringing sound of my launch from the barrel and I landed beside him, rolling sideways into his legs. He tumbled over, trying desperately to turn his rifle on me. The knife in my belt was slick with James' blood and slipped easily free into my hand. I drove it up into his ribcage. He fell back, groaning. I hauled the knife out, crawling up over him to jam it through his throat.

I disengaged the rifle from his stiffening fingers, and checking it over briefly, slung it across my back. The keys were in his pocket. I extracted them and threw the bunch over the fence to Cain. I ran on to the long low building. A plain white door was closed at the corner nearest the fence. The track went on around the corner of the building to a wider door at the other side where raw materials went in. I hurried to the near door and tried it. It was locked, but as I jerked it fiercely, it clanked in the frame. Behind it, footsteps responded, and a moment later a hand pushed the door outwards. I pulled it wide, shoved the startled man inside backwards, yanked out the Glock and tapped him once in the chest.

I hurtled down the corridor as other factory workers looked out to locate the source of the shot. Each face I saw, I shot. Cain caught up with me as I reached the end, his t-shirt more red than white.

"We'll sweep this place and work on out."

I nodded, kicked the door, and swung the rifle to bear on those inside. Four men in white coats stood in a laboratory that could have been in UCLA. Johnny had not stinted in his set up. I let a bullet into the glassware and it shattered, spraying the room with dubious liquid. The technicians ducked automatically and I popped a bullet into the nearest one.

From the far side of the room came a low rumble as a heavy drawer slid open. One of the three remaining techs was going for his weapon. I wondered vaguely if labs at UCLA were equipped with the same hardware and caught myself making a mental note to ask Dr Clayton. Then the man's tousled head rose into my field of vision, peering over the bench to size up his shot. I cocked the rifle to my eye and let him have it in the top of the head. I heard his gun clatter to the floor as the body slid beside it.

Striding across the room, I grabbed up the gun and threw it to Cain. The tech to my left started screaming, a high-pitched wail that cut right through my skull. As Cain checked the gun, I shot the screamer, then he killed the last one and we moved on.

The Glock now had more ammunition than the rifle, so I slung the rifle over my shoulder once more and greeted each new arrival with the handgun. Cain yanked a fire axe from its place on the wall of the corridor and moved from room to room behind me, smashing equipment and rendering the place unusable.

There were three men at the corner and two bullets left in the Glock's magazine. It was a good thing I'd been counting, otherwise I might have been caught with my trousers down. Instead, motioning Cain onwards, I ran straight at them. The closest man raised his pistol and earned himself a bullet in the chest. I covered both of the others, closing the gap between us rapidly. The man who had been standing in the middle, jerked to grab out his own gun. I popped him in the head with my final bullet, striding over the last few feet and swung into a spin kick that felled the third. I kicked his nose back into his skull, then, taking possession of all three guns, I hurled myself after my companion.

The factory was cleared of life and trashed beyond repair. We dashed out through the main door and round the building towards the gate which Cain had left closed but unlocked. So far, the work had only taken a few minutes, the sound muffled by careful construction, and those waiting for Stocker to confirm the vengeance taken for the murder of Rico were still standing around patiently. By this time, Cain had a rifle slung over each shoulder and another ready in his hands. "I'll clear the outside," he whispered, nodding at the men outside dead Stocker's hut, "you start workin' on up through the barracks. Don't let anyone escape."

"Yeah, yeah." I grunted, and split off to the door of the nearest barrack hut.

Behind me, Cain was approaching the idling security patrol. I heard him growl in Spanish over the click and crunch as he chambered a round. "Hey, boys, ah killed your friend Rico. What you gonna do 'bout it?" They cried out in angry surprise and seconds later died in a spray of lead.

Inside the hut, bare feet hit floorboards. Voices called questions and grunted responses. Some very tired men were trying to figure out what was going on without going outside. My fist smashed into the splintery wood of the hut door. "Help!" I yelled in good old English. "Help, guys! Someone's shooting!" I thumped harder.

A bleary man shoved the door ajar and poked his head out, scrubbing his knuckles desultorily across his eyes. I grasped his bare shoulder and hauled him out into the moonlight. He stumbled, sleep befuddled, across the yard, away from his hut. "Scream!" I instructed as I pulled my knife and stabbed him in the stomach. He crumpled to the ground, confused by his bleeding. "Scream, damn it!" I stabbed him again in the kidney, and he howled.

Shouts of alarm were raising the huts. The doors were flung open and I stood, a gun in each hand like a movie gangster, and knocked the men down as they stepped out. Cain joined in with his rifles, but in a matter of moments, they had stopped wandering out like lemmings. We ran to each hut and cut the few remaining men down as they crouched inside, half-naked and helpless. That's not so much fun but it's the job. The native workers hadn't stirred at all. Together we kicked the door to their barn open and walked down between the beds, shooting each man as he shivered, wide-eyed between his dampening sheets.

The last reports cracked and echoed through the woodland as we ran out into the moonlight.

Cain was panting. He straightened and gasped. "Up to the house!"

"What for?" I asked, smugly pleased that I was in better cardiovascular condition than my partner.

"Wa for? Big boss Mack, ya dipshit."

"He ain't there."

He glared at me. "Where is he?"

I shrugged. "Search me. He wouldn't tell me."

"What are you saying?" He forgot that he was out of breath. "The man's left the ranch?"

"Left today."

"And you didn't think of tellin' me that we were going to lose our biggest prize if we struck tonight?"

It might sound stupid but it honestly hadn't occurred to me. Johnny Mack came and went. That's what gangster bosses did. Outfits rose and fell and their bosses disconnected and went on. Informing on him to Interpol was one thing; pinning him down in the house and blowing his brains out just wasn't something one did to one's friends. And, yes, dear reader, I did still consider Johnny my friend.

"You stoopid bitch!" For a moment, Cain was considering hitting me.

He wasn't about to wallop someone carrying twenty kilos of weaponry. I shrugged under it. "It's not like he's in a position to get Interpol into trouble, is he? He can't inform without getting himself re-arrested."

"So that's it then? We done here?"

"Guess so." It was an anti-climax. We had belted onto the track, convinced that the big game was yet to come, and in fact it had already gone. Well, that's the way it goes. We turned back to the barn and the remaining vehicles.

As the Jeep pulled away into the dust, I turned and blinked back in the direction of the carnage. It was in that moment that I realised why I bothered flying back to England for Christmas. The Mallorys, much as I might despise them in other ways, still lived in a world where killing another human being was unthinkable. I couldn't remember what that felt like, if I had ever known, but once a year I could go and be with it.

"So," said Cain, pulling me back from my gritty-eyed contemplation of destruction, "what happened to you?"

"When?" I asked, wriggling round hopelessly for a comfortable position in the hard seat.

He glanced sideways at me, just for a second, otherwise we would have bounced off the road. "They call it a childhood trauma. The bad thing that happened to you to make you want to kill people."

I thought back, move by move. All the really bad things that had happened to me had happened after my first kill. As though talk of fleas had made me want to scratch, my fingers stretched unconsciously over my shoulder to rub the polar bear tattoo beneath the shoulder of my vest. "Nothing happened to me. I was just born this way."

"So? A genuwine psychopath? You're a good deal rarer than the movies would have you believe." Cain sounded awed.

I didn't like it, so directed the line of questioning back at him. "So what are you then? A sociopath?"

"A man who has been turned out of good conscience by his upbringing or environment. Yup, that's me." His drawl was so calm that I could barely hear it above the grinding of engine over gravel.

"What's your childhood trauma?" I pursued.

"I was interfered with by my paw," he reported emotionlessly. "Ah killed him and spent the rest of my childhood in a juvenile correction facility."

"You're lying," I told him. "They wouldn't let you into the marines with that record."

"Ah was lyin' about bein' in the marines."

But he wasn't. He couldn't have lied about the marines under torture. If I had asked him, trussed up in Stocker's cabin, if he'd ever fancied a man, he would have laid his heart bare. Now, however, he was lying about lying about being in the marines. And frankly, my dear, I didn't give a damn. I just wanted to forget about Cain and go home. Home meant Delphiki.

But first, we had to meet up with Bill Withers.

Chapter 21

Withers waited at the airport terminal as arranged the following afternoon. He greeted us warmly, shaking our hands, showing concern for our long journey, but ignoring the stains it had left on us. Cain had changed his t-shirt for one which didn't bear the evidence of his torture and I was pretty sure that he was never going to report that part of his 'endgame' to Withers. A man in a suit had found and reserved a table for us at the airport café by sheer force of personality. There was so much chat and clatter going on all around us that it provided an ideal spot for a debriefing before they flew us, and the evidence of their misdemeanours, out of the country.

"All went according to plan?" Withers enquired eagerly, once his suit had been despatched to join the enormous curling queue with a complicated list of the things Cain and I wanted to eat and drink. My wants were simple: meat, no coffee. Cain was demanding this, and if not this, that, or t'other. Taken off the ranch, he sounded like a New York socialite on a diet.

But he still glared at me like a hired killer. "Mallory forgot to tell me that the boss left before close of business," he growled between clenched teeth. My inefficiency reflected badly on him.

"What?" Withers turned to me. "You didn't kill Callander?"

"Mack. Johnny Mack. No. We didn't even hurt him slightly."

"Christ," Withers hissed, his expression turning inwards as he began to calculate rapidly. "Interpol have got a file as thick as the Oxford Dictionary on that man. He escaped from Belmarsh only a couple of months ago where he was serving sixteen consecutive life sentences for fraud, assault, intimidation, possession of firearms, theft, murder - the list goes on. If we'd got him …"

Cain leaned over the table towards me. Boy, did he smell ripe. "How's come you know the guy's proper name?"

I considered and rejected several possible answers. Cain had been working outside all the time. He had had no dealings with the boss and had not followed mine. I wasn't about to reveal my connections with Johnny in case he seized upon them as my reason for letting the boss escape. "I was the chief witness at his trial," sounded suitably adversarial.

Withers watched us closely, sizing up my response, realising that Cain had no idea about my relationship with Johnny. "Remarkable that we put you on the very problem he was causing," he remarked.

"Bloody annoying," I agreed. "I just forgot that he ought to get bumped off too. I'm mean, he was an old friend, so I just didn't think about it."

"Hmmm." Withers sounded unconvinced but he couldn't blame me for the fact that I had been working for Mack this time. He had placed me there when neither of us knew that it was a little project of Johnny's. "Perhaps your old 'friendship' caused you to let him escape," he suggested.

"Mr Withers!" I exclaimed, summoning up all the high dudgeon I couldn't be bothered to really feel. "In case your file didn't include one of Mack's counts of murder, I might just remind you that the bastard shot my husband. No old friendship is going to stand something like that."

"When you put it like that," Withers retorted dryly, "I'm amazed you didn't just kill him on sight. Oh, no, I remember - you have seen him since then. You visited him in jail every time you came to England, didn't you?"

"Oh, for Pete's sake!" I groaned, suddenly put in mind of the endless suspicions of Detective Stocker. "Now isn't the time to bicker. Can't we close the ports or something? He's bound to try to skip the country."

The suit finally returned with a full tray, interrupting the interrogation. He started unloading pie and coffee and beer and chips and pastries, and I forgot the state of tension. Until I glanced up from the food and caught sight of …

Well, dear reader, would you credit it? I swear on John Mark's grave - no, he was cremated - Burns' grave, then, but it's true. There was Johnny Mack, large as life and twice as natural, sauntering across the airport concourse in the direction of the check-in desks.

I leapt up, knocking my chair to the ground and splattering hot coffee and cold beer in all directions.

"Hey!" yelled the three drenched men in unison.

Gurgling incoherently, I jabbed a finger in the direction of the dwindling figure.

Withers squinted. "Callander?" he guessed.

I nodded frantically, trying to swallow and regain control over my powers of speech.

The Interpol man turned to his other agent. "Get him!"

Then all four of us were up and running, scrambling over the low partition that marked the café's territory, and sprinting into the crowds.

Johnny allowed himself a casual glance over his shoulder and carried on walking as though the commotion had nothing to do with him. He reached the check-in desk and slid his bag onto the conveyor. Withers screamed something in Spanish at the lady on the desk, who then noticed us for the first time and paused, bewildered. Cain became entangled with a group of twelve children and about fourteen luggage trolleys. Johnny's hand moved to the papers on the desk before him as he spoke quietly. The lady smiled at him and continued to process his boarding pass. Withers bawled again and ran into a fat lady with a sharp-cornered handbag. The suit and I were within feet of the fugitive as the lady passed the boarding card over.

Johnny turned and smiled at us. In one hand he held his ticket out of the country. In the other was a gun. We scooted to a halt.

"Jonathan Callander?" the suit began bravely, but when Johnny pulled the hammer back, he faltered.

"I'll be going now," Johnny said. "Please do try and stop me, then I can shoot you with impunity." He moved slowly sideways towards the boarding gates.

I was staring at the short muzzle of the gun in his hand. The last time I had stared down the muzzle of his gun, Spike Delphiki had been there to save me but this time there was just me and Johnny. It was Johnny's fault that I was here and without Spike. It was Johnny's fault that it had been Cain at my door and not Spike. Johnny had killed John Mark, ended my career as a stunt woman, and now he had the gall to go pointing a gun at me again. And I still wasn't frightened.

"Do I look bovvered?" I demanded. I put my head down, and charged him.

I kept running, expecting at any second to be kicked to the ground, the white heat searing through my guts, but it never came. And then I crashed head-on into a shirt front of familiar scent and bundled to the ground. He thrashed beneath my onslaught. Desperately, I righted myself and recalled my Taekwondo lessons, smashing the gun from his grip and pinning his limbs. He wrestled a hand free and snatched after the gun. I nutted him in the face and his nose exploded. He subsided.

"Johnny Mack, you are under arrest for being an arsehole of the first order. You do not have to say anything unless you wish to be punched."

The suit grabbed his free hand and snapped a pair of handcuffs onto it. "Turn him over."

Johnny groaned, and rolled co-operatively as I released him, spattering nasal blood over the shiny floor. We dragged him to his feet. Withers reached us and gripped his other arm.

"Go straight to jail, Callander. Do not pass 'Go'."

"Do not collect two hundred pounds," the suit and I chorused.

"Oh, fuck off," retorted Johnny.

As they dragged him away, to sort the incident out at the local police station and organise Johnny's official extradition,

Cain stood at my side. "Let's blow this popsicle stand," he suggested quietly. He was right. We may have caught the villain of the piece but yesterday we had been on a killing spree ourselves. Now was the moment to sneak out quietly.

But I just had to say one more thing. "Hey! Guys! This time will you please nail him to the floor!"

Johnny glanced back over his shoulder and grinned. "Same to you, Mink. With knobs on!"

Chapter 22

The flight was horribly uncomfortable. The bus from the airport was worse, and by the time I reached Culver City, I was exhausted, but there was only one thing I wanted to do.

I knocked on the door and heard an answering scratch. "Hey, Cadaver," I said quietly. "I guess your master isn't in." The racoon scratched again, and taking it for a reply in the negative, I turned and walked away from the condo. He was probably at the office. I could call him and find out.

A single bench graced the parking space at the front of the condos. Here I plonked myself down, freeing my shoulder from the burden of the rucksack. Despite all the muscle and stamina I had put back on since getting myself beaten up, I was glad to drop the bag. I sprawled on the bench, not really caring when, or if, he turned up at all. I was here now and that was all I could do.

The scrunch of gravel alerted me to the advent of a blue sedan sometime later. Its driver had spotted me by the time he had parked, and he paused, watching me, before slamming the car door and walking slowly over to the bench.

"You've lost weight," he said quietly.

"I'm putting it back on," I replied defensively, still feeling too floppy too rise. Then I remembered myself. "How's it going?"

"I found the kid. Traced the damn stupid runaway but it took a while. It's kind of hard to operate when your heart's held together with Band Aids," he added bitterly. He glared down at me from his great height.

"I'm sorry."

"Yeah? Where the hell have you been? You just walk out of my life for no reason, then I hear you're in hospital, but when I try to visit, they tell me you don't want to see me." His jaw clamped, and he gazed blankly over my head, towards his home and his racoon.

They told him that? I was going to punch Withers if I ever saw him again. "Yeah, I was in hospital, but it wasn't that I didn't want to see you," I lied. If I'd just called him straightaway ... he'd be dead now. "I got caught by Interpol."

I paused, waiting for him to interject incredulously. He didn't. He just stared woodenly over my head.

I sighed, focused on his car, and went on talking. "This guy threatened me with jail if I didn't work for them. They packed me off to Columbia to shut down some drug cartel. I tell you, it was like something out of a movie. Guess who turned out to be running the show?" Again I paused. Again, he didn't respond. I supplied the answer. "Johnny Mack."

Then he spoke. "Now we get to the root of it. Johnny Mack. You went to Johnny Mack."

The root of what? I puzzled. "No. It wasn't -"

"You know, you nearly had me going there, Hex, but you got one thing wrong. It's all in the details, you see. If you'd said you'd been recruited by the DEA, or the CIA, even, I might have believed you. But Interpol? Interpol is little more than an information sharing network, set up between police forces across the world. It is not food for international conspiracy theories. Interpol doesn't have agents, just liaison officers."

"I know, but -" I stopped myself. I saw it clearly now. I didn't trust Johnny, and Spike didn't trust me. Game over.

I stood up. "Goodbye, Spike."

He just stood there, silent, still staring over my head.

I picked up my rucksack and headed for the bus stop.

I could have gone home. My apartment, John Paul's apartment, was the only thing I had right now, but I remembered the miserable welcome it had given me when I had returned from Spike's the last time.

Instead, I caught the bus in the opposite direction.

It was late in the day but the fast rhythm of faint music was issuing under the door of the Dangerous Visions office on the disgusting third floor of a crumbling office block on the seedy back streets of Hollywood. I needed something to do and I wasn't going to make the mistake of going to work for a gangster again.

Crash answered my knock. "Come in."

I pushed the door open to find him sitting there alone, his face bathed in the white light of his monitor.

"Bobby!" He jumped to his feet, legs thumping against the edge of the desk. He crashed past it, knocking the computer askew, to engulf me in a warm hug that lasted longer than I would normally have allowed. When at last he released me, he said, "You've lost weight."

"I know," I growled. "I was in hospital, remember?"

"Why wouldn't they let us see you?"

"Please, Tom, don't ask."

He sighed, pulled his chair away from the desk and sat down, trying to forget about all the things I'd never told him. Trying to forget that my surname was Gambetta.

"Listen," I said hurriedly, "I need to ask you a favour."

"Me first," he put in excitedly, happy to throw off the pall of my irregularities. "Can you ride horseback?"

Eric the black stallion had scarred me for life but perhaps it had been worth it. "Can I ever ride!"

"Great. We need a white female double for the new Western Al Tancredi is shooting. Will you do it?"

"Sure thing, boss."

"Fuckin' A!" He swung back to his computer, smiling into the electrical glow, finger clicking on the mouse key. "Oh, what favour did you need?"

"Nothin'. See you tomorrow morning."

My apartment didn't seem so bad when I had something to look forward to the next day but I was still glad to leave it in the morning. I got down to the studio bright and early, in plenty of time to get warmed up in the crew's Jump Start. They were surprised to see me. My disappearing acts had never lasted longer than a few days before now. Looking at them, line dancing this time, in a single, thin thread, I suddenly realised something that had never entirely made it into my consciousness before. Dangerous Visions was a tiny operation. Most films had a whole stunt department of their own, filled with far more resources than our entire company commanded. Dangerous Visions was a shoestring outfit. Tom needed me back because he only kept four stunt doubles on the payroll: black and white, male and female. They had been making money since I had known them, but compared to nothing, anything they made was an improvement. For me to run out on them had been a major disaster.

"So, what do you need me to do?" I demanded.

Crash and Tancredi glanced at each other. "Can you ride dressage?" Tancredi asked. "Our prima donna can ride, but obviously we can't have her doing that."

No, we can't risk her breaking a nail. "I can do it," I assured him. Whatever I might say about them, we were paid for the things actors wouldn't do.

"How long will it take you to get ready?" Tancredi asked impatiently. No wonder Tom had been so pleased to see me. The white female rider must have been slowing them down.

"Give me a few hours to get used to the horse. So, this afternoon."

"Great. That okay with you, Bill?" Tancredi called over to a thin man with white hair chatting to a gofer. The man turned and all the tassels of his worn leather jacket swung. His boots clacked like Rico's as he swaggered the few steps to our group in tight, worn jeans.

"May I introduce Wild Bill Holland, our equestrian expert." If he had been called Wild Bill Withers, I wouldn't have raised an eyebrow.

Wild Mr Holland doffed his Stetson briefly.

"H- M-," I began, swallowed and recalled my right name. "Bobby," I said, shoving a hand in his direction.

He shook it limply. "Now you hold your horses there, young Bobby," he drawled.

His voice made my fists clench instinctively and I shoved them both safely into my pockets.

"It'll take most of a week to learn trick ridin' like that," the old cowpuncher went on. Although his words were addressed to me, he was speaking to the director. "You can't be gettin' over excited with horses."

"A week?" Tancredi groaned.

"This afternoon," I said firmly, and before Holland could interrupt, I turned to him. "Let's see these horses, then."

The horses all had trailers of their own and an entourage to do their hair and make-up. The smell of El Mundo's stables came back to me momentarily, but I shook it off and trotted up the ramp to meet the mount of the female lead. She was a glorious white Lipizzan mare (the horse, not the actress). Her groom informed me that her name was Beaker. I hadn't realised how scruffy Mirabel had been until I saw the shine of this horse's coat. She glistened like fresh snow. She skittered a little as Holland and I clumped up to her, but as a trained animal actor, she was used to the idea of a thousand new faces. I rubbed her nose and spoke to her in broken Spanish, echoing the way Rico had behaved with his animals.

The groom saddled Beaker up with her everyday saddle, one of about twenty suspended on tack pegs at the rear of the trailer. Holland and I took the horse down across the back lot to the set, a boring Wild West street scene. Tancredi was about the dullest director making movies, but because he stuck with the old favourite formulae, his films made enough to keep him ticking over. That was probably why the cheapskate was using Dangerous Visions.

"You see that tree?" Holland drawled. It was the only tree on set, and what looked like an old tin hip bath was hanging on its wizened trunk. "All you gotta do, is gallop on over, swing around and get Beaker to strike the bath with her hind feet in a capriole jump, y'see, thereby soundin' the alarm. The villains, you see, are tryin' a shoot the hero. That boy'll be sittin' over here," he waved vaguely towards the raised walk along the front of one group of building frontages, "and the villains'll be ridin' into town from this road." Again he waved. "Our gal rides in before 'em and she's gotta warn the hero that they're a comin'. The actual clang'll be added in on the soundtrack."

I suppressed a strong urge to inform Wild Bill that he was an idiot. You had to do that a lot in the movie industry. "Righto." I vaulted onto Beaker's back a little more roughly than I should have and she surged forward. "How does she like the airs above the ground?" I enquired, reining her in a little too briskly.

"She's trained for 'em," Holland admitted slowly.

I kicked Beaker forward and put her through her paces. Compared to El Mundo's Eric, this was a pony ride in the park. Once I had stopped myself clinging on unnecessarily for dear life, I found that Beaker loved performing and was as anxious to show off as a human actor, possibly persuading even Holland that we could deliver on my boast.

That was until a gopher handed me the gun I would be using. It was, of course, a replica but it was also an anachronism. The film was set in the aftermath of the Civil War and the replica was a Smith and Wesson Model 3 which were not manufactured until 1870. You might say that this was a small matter, but Westerns have dedicated followings, and dedicated followings mean pedantry. I went off to find Martin.

The big explosives expert was growing his hair. I had seen it leaping about like a curtain tassel when he had pulled it back in a rubber band for the Jump Start, and something about it bothered me. "Look, Western guns aren't my thing, Bobby," he admitted. "If it's not at least semi-automatic, or prefixed by the word 'assault', I don't have a clue, but if you say it's wrong, I'll back you up."

Tancredi was not impressed when we approached him. "This is not my problem. You guys are supplying the guns, and if it's wrong, you better get me the right one." He glared at Martin. "Oliver promised me a full service when I hired you. He said his bombardier would get the guns right."

"His what?" I demanded.

"That's me," Martin explained, slightly embarrassed, "on account of doing the explosives, y'see?"

"Grand," I groaned. Then I had an idea which made me forget the things stirring in my memory for the time-being. Since Burns had blown all DV's chances as well as his face, we couldn't afford to supply the guns a film like this needed properly. But since when had I ever done things properly? All I needed was a car.

Crash insisted on accompanying me. It wasn't that he didn't trust me with his car, or his company's reputation, but he was afraid that if he let me out of his sight, I would never return. We hit the highway, and within the hour found the slip road to MacHone's Military Machines.

The place still took my breath away. Row upon row of shining weaponry, like the lock and load scene from 'The Matrix'. Tom, although an American and supposedly inured to this sort of thing, stared.

MacHone himself leaned behind the white counter as though he hadn't moved since Delphiki had gone to the airport, months before. He stared at me intently as I turned to him. Knowing now that his was the best stocked gun shop in LA because it was stocked by Iscariot, I wasn't surprised when his face lit up in a smile of recognition. He wasn't about to forget the black and tattoo style of the girlfriend of his chief supplier. Tom wandered off towards the Western section of the store but I approached the shopkeeper.

"Morning, MacHone."

"Mornin'," he said. "How's that P238?"

I wasn't even sure where the SIG Sauer was now. I just grinned knowingly and ploughed on with my reason for coming. "We're making a movie, a Western, and the guns are crap. Then I remembered you." I yanked out the revolver I had been given and slammed it down on the counter. "This is what they gave me for an 1865 setting."

MacHone straightened up. "That's not right," he agreed, "that's not right at all. What you're wanting is a Model 2." He came around the counter at once and led me over to the racks of guns that Tom was surveying. "Now, these here," he waved a hand across several racks of shotguns and revolvers, "these are your right milieu. And they're more authentic than that crappy replica."

"Nice. How many guns are we using, Tom?"

He looked at me unhappily. "A whole lot. We're supplying a good number of them from our prop box and other stuff we've found. We bought a bunch of the right sort of stuff at an auction."

"That's not good enough," I said.

"I know." He looked miserable. Dangerous Visions still couldn't afford to make investments on things like this.

I turned back to the gun shop owner. "How about a deal, MacHone?"

"Cash discount?" he suggested.

"Nope. I've got a better idea." Out of the corner of my eye, I could see Tom bracing for impact. "If MacHone's Military Machines supplies the guns, you'll get credit on the film. Dangerous Visions, that's our outfit, will make you our sole weapons supplier and you'll get a shitload of free publicity."

MacHone considered this carefully. "Wouldn't it be easier to get the guns from your boyfriend?"

"It might be, if I still had one."

"So?" MacHone was probably wondering if helping me out would alienate Delphiki. "I'll sleep on it," he said finally.

"We're shooting this afternoon."

"Five thousand dollars, cash deposit."

"Done."

"No!" squeaked Tom.

I shushed him. "You start putting this lot in the car."

"Not these ones," cut in MacHone. "We've got a whole bunch more, boxed, out back. The boys'll help you."

A bunch of muscle-bound youths in fatigues and muscle shirts materialised as MacHone led us over to the doors to the back rooms of the shop. I recognised at least three of them from the Juice Bar and Tom winked at me as he allowed himself to be led away into a cluttered darkness that smelled of gun grease.

MacHone leaned on his counter again and looked at me. "You're Hex Gambetta, right?"

"Yep."

He nodded slowly, as if that explained everything. "You got five thousand dollars, cash?"

I drew a roll out of my pocket. "That's a thousand. There's another four in the car."

He sighed and started making out the receipt.

Chapter 23

Wild Bill Holland was not pleased to see us return with a beautiful, gleaming selection of correctly provenanced weaponry, including knives, spurs and holsters, the works. Tancredi was ecstatic and congratulated old Tom on his hard work. He, poor boy, was still gibbering about the five thousand dollars. He didn't know that I'd just been paid in cash for a highly illegal operation. He definitely didn't know that there were several other rolls of five hundred dollars floating around, and would be until I could handed them over to Sidney for careful banking. All he knew was that we now had the guns we needed to fulfil our contract, and on that score he wasn't going to complain.

However, the light wasn't right for filming my scene by this time, so he let me go before I thought of anything else to scare him witless, and I headed on down to Randy's gym. Maybe it was because I didn't want to spend my time alone, or maybe I was just fed up of my flimsy state, but I threw myself in to working out as though I was a bodybuilder. Randy wasn't terribly impressed with me because I had missed the finals of the women's kickboxing, but he forgave me when he saw my scars. I couldn't have competed, even if I'd been in the right country. He fitted me out with a high protein diet and sent me off to my Taekwondo master.

You can imagine the sort of pulpy mess I set about working myself into. Every second I wasn't on set, I was pumping myself back into proper shape with the technical kit and support that just hadn't been available in the hospital. If

I had to live without Spike, then at least I could fight like a real human, and not a girl. I admit it, I worked myself into the ground, and it just isn't a good idea to get yourself strung out when you're working with someone who winds you up like Wild Bill Holland wound me up. Every single thing I wanted to do with the horses he branded as impossible. Thankfully, Tancredi was more worried about the expense of prolonged filming than he was about animal welfare, but he did have to pay some attention to his equestrian expert.

We had actually made it into the second week of my return before we had a serious incident. Crash had quickly realised that he had to involve himself in every exchange between Tancredi, Wild Bill and me to defuse the situation a little. He was mediating pretty successfully too, until Wild Bill decided to put his foot down. He actually did as well. He stamped his poncey cowboy boot and said, "Ah simply cannot allow that."

To which I sensibly replied, "Piss off, you old fool." I'm afraid Gambettas don't respond very well to being told what to do. I also have to admit that I had been carrying around with me the six shooter I was using for filming. The Dangerous Visionaries had got used to me mooching around the set with various prop weapons while we had been making previous movies, and everyone had quickly forgotten that the guns we were using to shoot this movie were real. That was until Wild Bill Holland pushed me too far and I pulled the revolver on him.

"Now, Bobby, just calm down there," Tom was saying, rubbing my aching arm. "You can't go round talking to people like that, no matter what the provocation."

"Yeah? Well, he can't go around telling me what I can and can't do. We can shoot that fu- ... cursed scene now but he's just slowing us up. Time is money," I reminded Tancredi.

"That I can agree with," Tancredi said. "Are you quite sure we can't be moving on with the chase, Bill?"

He crossed his fringed leather clad arms across his chest. "Ah am."

"You obstructive old bigot," I growled.

"Nah, don't you be sayin' things like that to me, young Bobby." He smiled slowly. "I can have you fired if ah think you're disturbin' the hosses."

"Fired?" I repeated incredulously. He wasn't employing me, Tom was. But the word set something ablaze in my mind. "This is the only kind of firing I care about." The Smith and Wesson was in my hand as though I'd conjured it. I gripped the handle tight, its weight in my hand the reality of what I had done in another time, another world, last week in Columbia.

And Wild Bill just laughed. He laughed because, standing in a movie studio, he had no idea of what was real.

My boss knew me better. He must have watched the way my face had changed once before when some dumb actor had referred to Burns as 'the Phantom of the Opera' about .1 of a second before I felled him with a flying kick from the top of a pile of scaffolding. He gasped. "Shit, Bobby, that thing's real."

The old cowpuncher's face crumpled. We were not actors. We didn't know how to play act. I was waving a real gun and he really wasn't a real cowboy. "Ppput that thing away," he stuttered.

I wasn't actually going to shoot him. I think. I mean, you just don't do it. As they say back in Portsmouth: you don't shit on your own doorstep. Slaughtering dozens of people down in Columbia is quite different to shooting a colleague in front of your employer and friends. Even in the leg.

But clutching that gun felt good and I clung on like a drowning man. There was not going to be a good way out of this situation. Then I knew what I wanted. I wanted the arms that had grabbed me back out of trouble the night we had gone on the rampage after my bearskin. If Delphiki had walked in right then, it would have been like an answer to prayer.

Instead, Martin intervened. He stepped in between the steady muzzle of the six shooter and the wavering face of Bill Holland. Bloody ex-soldiers! They always think they're so damnably hard. He said, ever so calmly and quietly, "Give me the gun, kid."

That cracked it. The muzzle of my gun was now aimed at his heart. Between the two was a layer of cloth, and beneath it, my brain was trying to tell me, was the black dog. He's not the Bombardier, I told myself. He's not my Bear. Orson is not a Swooning Shadow. He no longer wears that dog over his heart. He's dead. But I was tired, aching, and heartbroken, I knew that now. And that was all I knew. Anything else I was going to have to see with my own eyes.

I said, "Take your shirt off."

"Say what?" Martin was taken aback, entirely unprepared for such a request.

"Take your bloody shirt off," I repeated patiently, flicking my wrist slightly to add the emphasis of the motion of a gun.

"You're crazy!" Martin said with some conviction.

"She's not," Tom said loyally. "You'd better do it."

Martin yanked his shirt tails free of his trousers and shucked it smoothly over his head. He wasn't as big, or as hairy, as the Bombardier, although he was pretty fit. He still had both his arms. Best of all, he didn't show a single tattoo. His muscled chest was completely dog-free. "Happy?" he demanded.

"Yes. Thank you." Engaging the safety catch, I shoved the Smith and Wesson back into the front of my belt and, shaking myself, walked away. I was happy, ridiculously relieved that our replacement for Burns was not turning into a reincarnation of a friend who had died at my feet. Maybe I was cracking up.

He hit me in the small of the back in a flying football tackle. As we went down, I threw the weight sideways and we hit the floor side by side. He tried to pin me and grab for the gun at the same time. I took his arm, bending and twisting, trapping it back between us and the floor. Swinging myself over, I straddled Martin's naked chest as he struggled beneath me. I leaned over him, clear of his kicking legs, the gun in my belt pushing rudely towards his face. Now I was in charge of the situation again.

I slipped my knife out of my pocket and jabbed it into the soft skin below Martin's jaw. He stopped wriggling and lay beneath me, panting. "Tom."

Crash appeared nervously at the edge of my field of vision.

"Take this, and take all the bullets out." I took the gun out of my belt with my free hand and slid it across to him.

It stopped short but Tom stepped forward and picked the gun up gingerly. He opened it and pulled the bullets out one by one. He put them safely in his pocket.

"Okay," I said to Martin, "keep still, until I tell you to move." Slowly I rose to my feet, keeping the knife point close to his throat. Then I hopped clear. "Get up now. And don't ever jump me again."

He picked himself up, retrieved his shirt and pulled it back on. "You're dangerous."

"So, I'm a stunt woman. That's my job."

He watched me for a moment. "You know, you're beautiful when you're angry."

"Tom, gimme that gun back."

Martin laughed. "Forget breakdancing. Tomorrow's Jump Start, you can teach us how to throw someone like that."

Chapter 24

It was a good thing that Martin had interjected himself so recklessly. His eventual amused reaction to the scene persuaded our director and his equestrian expert that the situation had not been as hazardous as they had believed when the gun was menacing them. Tancredi took Tom aside for a quiet word, but accepted his opinion that I was sane and not dangerous. That wasn't quite true, of course. It is entirely possible to be sane and yet more dangerous than stepping on a rattlesnake.

"Now, you just listen to me, Bobby," Tom demanded as we sat in a deli that evening about an hour and a half before I was due in Chinatown for another gruelling session of martial artistry. "I don't know what's going on with you right now, but I do know that if you can't keep a grip on it, I will have to ask you to leave. I convinced Al that you were just messing around but I don't believe it myself. I know patience isn't your strong suite, and I know Holland annoys you, but that's happened before. Hell, that's what making movies is all about. It's all about pushing forward as fast as you can without upsetting anyone, and you sure upset some people today."

"What about upsetting me?" I asked, slashing steak into ribbons. "Weed Bill Holland is set on obstructing me when I'm just trying to do my job."

"You're not the only one he's doing it too," he pointed out, elegantly spearing a chip, "but you are the only one taking it personally. Maybe you should talk to someone about what's bothering you."

That was the worst idea I'd ever heard. "Are you offering?"

Tom grinned at his chip as it twisted on the end of his fork. "I'm always here for you, Bobby, but most of the time I'm thankful that you never tell me anything. I was thinking of someone more … qualified."

I put my steak knife down before my fist closed around it. "You want to get my head shrunk?" I took my right hand right off the table and stuffed it into my pocket.

He didn't seem to notice. "I know you take martial arts, and I know you were always real protective of Burns, but I've never seen you kick off like that before. It's gotta be something real serious."

There was nothing to say to that. He was right. I sat and stared at my cooling dinner, trying to figure out why I was so wound up. It wasn't like I'd never killed anyone before. It wasn't Cain; he had crawled back under his rock the moment the plane touched down. It wasn't Johnny. Detective Sergeant Strong had rung to inform me that Mack had been nailed down more firmly than Hannibal Lector. Thinking further back, the beginning of the whole mess could be pinpointed. It was the night I found Peters' body in the alley, followed by the panicked scrambling after my polar bear skin. But Delphiki had found my skin. And I had left it with him.

"Has this got anything to do with the racoon in Culver City?" Tom enquired delicately. "I haven't seen him for a while." Dear old Tom, he had no idea that my stress could have any more important cause than ...

Bugger.

"Eat up," he said cheerfully, realising that he'd hit a sore spot. "You won't keep putting the weight on if you don't finish your meat."

"Feel sick," I mumbled. Here I was, sitting in a posh Los Angeles deli with my obligatory gay best friend, eternally severed from all the men I'd ever loved. Johnny was unforgivable, John Mark was shot, Burns was in three separate pieces and Spike was lost. And Burns was the only one that wasn't my fault. Who the hell was I to kick up at Bill Holland? Sighing deeply, I started shoving bits of steak down my gullet.

Thanks to Tom's negotiatory skills, there was no need to apologise to Holland. If I didn't actually hold a conversation with Martin for a while, there was the chance he would forget to ask me why I had made him take his shirt off. It wasn't that my behaviour was completely inexplicable, particularly to a fellow soldier, it was simply that I didn't want him to understand. After all, when your life gets as coincidental as mine had recently, you wouldn't risk a thing like that either.

So I kept my head down and my mouth shut, for a change. The gears of movie making ground gradually on and my condition finally hit the peak I had been at before I let the Chuckling Ducklings beat me to within an inch of my life. Not that I was ever without some ache or pain, and usually both, but the facial scarring faded under the bleaching Californian sun. There was nothing the sun could do to melt the ice I had first felt resting on my diaphragm in the shed in Columbia. It sat there, cold and heavy, obstructing every breath I took, until I had to stop and run outside for air and warmth.

I had been standing, gasping, on the tarmac of the back lot, a safe distance from our boring street scene, the sun glaring red through the skin of my eyelids, when I heard footsteps coming up behind me. Hoping that they might stride on passed, I stood still and unseeing.

The footsteps paused behind me, waiting perhaps for some acknowledgement of his presence. Receiving none, Tom nudged my arm and handed me a card. It was white and bore only a few words:

Watts and Delphiki
Private Investigations
Spike Delphiki

I spun round and glared at him sharply. "What's this?"

"He's waiting for you. Over by the door." He jerked his head. "You okay?"

I nodded, not entirely certain of the truth, and picked my way across the set.

Spike Delphiki was standing there, dressed in jeans, t-shirt and sport coat. His hands were thrust into his jeans' pockets, his dark eyes watching me cross the space between us.

"You're putting on weight," he said as soon as I was close enough.

"Yeah. I've been working hard." I slipped my fists into the pockets of my work trousers, unconsciously mirroring his stance. "How can I help you?"

He rocked on his toes. "Can I ask you a question?"

"Sure."

"That tattoo on your thigh? The rodent. What is it?"

"A mink."

"Ah." He rocked a little more, looking down at the toes of his trainers. He glanced up briefly. "I owe you an apology."

I returned his look, frowning, puzzled. His gaze descended at once.

"Two men who work for me have just returned from a tour of South America. I read their report this morning. They were about to open negotiations with an Englishman running a drugs cartel in Columbia, when one of his security staff informed them that the authorities were closing the net on this particular cartel, and they were better off out of it. They broke off negotiations at once, and a few days later received intelligence to the effect that the cartel had been destroyed." He paused, rocking for again a moment. "They didn't supply much information about the agent who tipped them off, except that she was a woman. And the boss called her Mink."

I bit my lip and said nothing.

He sighed. "So, I'm sorry."

I nodded, no longer catching his eye.

He took a deep breath and pulled his hands out of his pockets. "Okay. Well, bye." He turned slowly, and started walking towards the gate.

I stood there, watching him walk away. "Spike."

He stopped. Then he turned. He stood, looking at me.

I groped desperately for something to say. Saying something meaningful to Burns had been easy. I always called him by his surname, so when I needed something more, I just used his given name. Somewhere in my writer's vocabulary had to be the right word for this occasion. Somewhere in all the books I had written had to be the things I wanted to tell him. But my publisher had always told me that my characters were wooden men with no emotion. That was a lack that didn't matter in pulp fiction, but in real life missing something other people have is a handicap. I pleaded with him silently to understand the words I didn't have.

Suddenly, the space between us zoomed in like a close-up shot and I found myself staring at his faded, old red t-shirt. And my face was pressed against it, my arms sliding under his jacket, around his shoulder holster, as his arms came around me and held me tight.

"I love you, I love you," I mumbled into his t-shirt, his breath warm in my hair.

He pushed me back. "What did you say?"

I forced myself to meet the abyssal depths of his eyes. "I love you."

"Do you?"

"Yes. I'm just a little slow on the uptake, that's all."

And I found myself crushed back against him before his mouth found mine.

A little later, he asked, "What time do you get off work tonight?"

"Dunno. Shall I come over to the office when I'm done?"

"No. Call me and I'll pick you up. Then we can swoop by your place and get your things. Cadaver misses you."

Much later that evening, we were lying side-by-side on my fairy bear skin in Delphiki's bedroom. Our bedroom.

Spike said, "Can I ask you a question?"

"Sure."

"Who killed this bear?"

"I did. With my own bear hands."

Acknowledgements

I have to thank my technical expert, my brother, Steve Chambers, without whom the second half of Fairy Bear would have disappeared into the ether when my computer broke.

Also, for moral support, my test audience, Efe Avan-Nomayo and Malva Eklund.

I wrote this book with almost no research whatsoever (does it show?), so this is a fairly short list. Everything I know about Los Angeles, a city to which I have never been, I owe to Robert Crais, an author who is unaware of my existence.

Thanks also to God, who's not.

Printed in Great Britain
by Amazon.co.uk, Ltd.,
Marston Gate.